ELIZABETH HARDWICK

was born in Lexington, Kentucky in 1916, and graduated from the University of Kentucky in 1939. She did post-graduate work at Columbia from 1939 to 1941 and was Adjunct Professor of Barnard College. She was awarded a Guggenheim Fellowship in 1947, the George Nathan Award for Dramatic Criticism in 1966 and is a member of the American Academy and Institute of Arts and Letters. Her works include three novels, *The Ghostly Lover* (1945), *The Simple Truth* (1955), *Sleepless Nights* (1979) and three collections of essays, *A View of My Own* (1962), *Seduction and Betrayal* (1974), *Bartleby in Manhattan* (1983). She is also the editor of *The Selected Letters of William James* (1960). A founder and Advisory Editor of the *New York Review of Books*, she lives in New York.

Virago also publishes *Sleepless Nights* and will publish *The Simple Truth* in 1987.

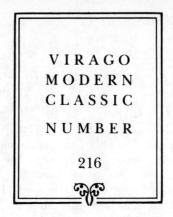

VIRAGO
MODERN
CLASSIC

NUMBER

216

Elizabeth Hardwick

THE GHOSTLY LOVER

WITH A NEW AFTERWORD BY
THE AUTHOR

Published by VIRAGO PRESS Limited 1986
41 William IV Street, London WC2N 4DB

Copyright 1945 by Elizabeth Hardwick
Copyright renewed 1973 by Elizabeth Hardwick

Published by arrangement with Harcourt Brace Jovanovich Inc

Afterword Copyright © Elizabeth Hardwick 1986

British Library Cataloguing in Publication Data

Hardwick, Elizabeth
    The ghostly lover.—(Virago modern classic)
    I. Title
    813'.54[F]   PS3515.A56/

    ISBN 0-86068-534-9

        Printed in Great Britain by
    Anchor Brendon, Tiptree, Essex.

FOR JOHN WOODBURN

PART ONE

CHAPTER ONE

$\mathcal{M}$ARIAN COLEMAN was aware that someone was watching her from the side porch of the house beyond the garden. She had seen the man's blond head and his body swaying in the swing. She saw him turn the pages of the book which he held in his hand and she thought, he isn't reading now. He's looking over here. In a spot partially concealed by a short row of bushes, she stretched out and faced the summer sun. With her eyes closed she was able to forget, somewhat, the man in the house beyond and to concentrate upon the visit of her parents.

It had been two years since Marian had seen her mother and father. Now that they were returning, they had no reality. They were like remote ancestors, those raw-boned ghosts whose sins fill you with mystery and dread and whose virtues are an obscure challenge. If there were anything wrong with the parents, if they had shamefully altered in any way, she and the rest of the family would be made to feel the blight. Like the primitive's fear of the anger of a revered bat, she was apprehensive about the elusive parents.

A door slammed in the house beyond and she opened her eyes, being careful not to turn too quickly at the sound. The man was still in the swing. He had put the book aside and was lighting a cigarette. Someone inside the house spoke to him and she could hear him answer. Before she turned away, she was certain that he had seen her look at him and that he was smiling.

Scissors snapped in the yard immediately east of Marian's.

3

"Well, when are you expecting them?" a woman's voice said.

The young girl sat up on the grass. "Tomorrow," she said. She watched the large old woman push her steel-frame spectacles closer to her face. The lower part of the woman's body was concealed by the shrubbery, but her face, always covered with a light pink rash, was thrust over the hedge.

"Wonder why they've been living away so long?" the woman continued. "What's bringing them back? Just a visit?" She put the scissors in her pocket. Her hands were black with garden dirt and she brushed them on her dress.

Marian did not know why her parents were coming now, nor why they hadn't always been here. She knew only that her grandmother had received a letter saying that Ted Coleman, Marian's father, was giving up the position in Montana. Montana was already very far in the past, like Florida, Illinois, Texas, and the other places her father had worked. These states, these jobs were merely tiny moments in the parents' lives. They left no marks. This new change meant only that, after the visit, there would be a new number on the mother's letters and that gradually the family here would grow accustomed to the way she wrote the new address across the envelope.

"I wonder why they never took you and Albert with them?" the woman asked. "I couldn't stand to be away from my daughter." She pointed abruptly to her quiet, shuttered brick house.

"They wanted us," Marian said quickly. "But . . ." She was interrupted by the girl within the house calling to the old woman.

"You say you got a letter saying they were coming? No, it was your grandmother told me that." The woman started toward the house and then suddenly halted, as if waiting for an answer.

"Yes," Marian called to her. "She wrote us a letter and said they were coming home. Tomorrow, maybe."

4

The woman stood at the steps now and hesitated to expend the effort to climb them. She was a soft sand-bag of a woman, mountainous and shapeless in her loose garden dress. "My daughter's calling me. I'll hear about the letter later," she answered in her hoarse voice.

Does she think I am hiding something from her? Marian wondered. Certainly there was nothing in her mother's letters she could have told the neighbors, even though to Marian the letters were always strangely daring. The mother wrote, on the surface at least, of the weather, of books she had read and of the food she cooked. Sometimes the envelopes contained indistinct snapshots, strangely isolated pictures of the mother and father standing beside a big rock or sitting on the steps of their home. Occasionally there were pictures of the parents with some unidentified people, but these were infrequent. The trivia of the mother's life were painstakingly recorded, but beyond that there was nothing except suggestion. In every letter there were a few discordant lines of mysterious personal import. Slipped in between the news of flowers and meals, there would be a sharp and abortive cry. She would say, "Last night I was lonely," and then, as if some censor were working, the theme would break off and the calendarlike résumé of her days went on and on. In this way, Marian, her grandmother and her brother, had a more or less implicit knowledge of the mother's sadness. Yet, they knew it only abstractly and never quite gave up the hope that one day a letter would come which would fully supplement the brief moans. They began to feel relieved when the parents would announce a change of plans, and this was frequent since the father did not seem content to stay in one place very long. With each change, Marian would imagine that a lasting equilibrium had been established.

The man from the house beyond had got up from the swing. He put his hand on the door knob, but when the door was opened he suddenly closed it again without entering the house. He did not look in Marian's direction. He looked up at the sky, as if waiting for something to happen.

"Marian!" a voice called out.

"Hello, Nell," she said. The woman's daughter was standing beside the hedge. Her large, fat face was smiling into the sun.

"I know you're excited about the visit," she said, in a voice unbearably like her mother's. "You know, this time I think they'll stay for good," she continued, her face sweetly blank as if she were thinking of something very remote.

"Oh, I don't think so," Marian said quickly. "They didn't say anything about that." At once she felt quite uncomfortable. Was she saying the proper thing? What did these people think about her parents?

"You know, Lucy is not much older than I am," Nell said abruptly. "I'm forty."

"Oh, no," Marian said rather shocked. Nell was so much the *daughter* that it was impossible to think of her as anything except young.

When Nell did not answer, Marian looked at her sharply and saw that she had gone into one of those sudden retreats. Her face was deep in a retiring, painful vacancy.

Marian folded her arms across her lap. She felt very sorry for Nell because of her fatness and always spoke to her in a special voice, one that tried to imply that she and Nell had nothing to separate them. But she could not think of the right thing to say now and so she focused her eyes on the row of tiger lilies beside the fence.

"I can't quite remember what they looked like," Nell said, her voice vague and nostalgic like one coming out of a dream. "I will see them out here in the yard and then I'll remember."

Marian could feel her parents all about her. She saw the face of her mother, that sharp, eager-featured face paradoxically overcast with a kind of tranquil anguish, and she could feel again the decorous, unused strength of her father. He was a man of powerful build and there was always about him the impression of a harnessed masculinity, such as one sees in athletes turned businessmen.

"They must have had an interesting life," Nell said.

"Why do you say that, and what do you mean?" Marian said rapidly.

"Why?" Nell repeated, drawing back. She was startled by this question, because she was one of those persons to whom questions are rarely addressed. She began to laugh in her flustered way. "I don't know," she said lamely.

"I didn't mean anything. I just thought maybe you had heard something about them, maybe you remembered something." For a moment, Nell seemed to feel some of Marian's own panic about the arrival of the parents. Anxiety spread over her simple face.

"I don't know anything about them. I don't even remember my own father," she said. "Mother does, though. She has everything of his, his clothes and just little things too."

Marian felt a secret union with the old woman in the dark house. She herself spent time in communion with inanimate objects. In her house she too found tangible objects which were substitutes for the evasive parents. In her room there was an old box, shaped like a pirate's chest, in which she kept pictures, bits of ribbon, and the napkin ring her mother had used as a child. Sometimes she was shocked by the passionate avidity of her feeling for any remnant of her parents' lives, for the piece of stationery from a strange hotel, souvenirs of dusty days of sight-seeing and timid photographs of the mother in winter clothing taken in the darkened rooms while the snow blew outside on the streets. There were symbols of every phase of the mother's life, as if these stages contained within themselves a relentless finality which the young girl would recapitulate in her own life. Like a curious spinster, her appetite for these mysteries was insatiable. In the fragments of her mother's life the future was before her: marriage and motherhood, the intermediate laziness and the early shadow of the precarious tight-rope walk of old age.

The man in the other house had settled down in the swing again. He had taken up the book and Marian could see that the sun was shining in his eyes. He is bored, she thought. He wants this afternoon to be done with. In the way the man lay there and waited impatiently for the passage of time, he reminded her of her father on those faraway Sunday afternoons. She felt there was something frighteningly private in this forced indolence, something that excluded women. She wondered what the man was thinking, just as she had always wondered what her father thought when he was silent. Though she had no particularly definite feelings about her father, the mother, due perhaps to some isolated, youthful circumstance, always seemed to indicate that Marian held some preference for her father. An imaginary, almost secret, bond was supposed to exist between them. Gradually this had worked to prevent any display of the real affection she felt for her mother. She could never say, as she wished, those intimate words of partisanship; she could not, with her mother, master that female, tender way of speech, or accomplish the sudden and skillful warmth which would draw them into alliance.

"Papa would be heartbroken if he knew what had happened to this neighborhood. That terrible section over there," Nell said, looking beyond Marian. Suddenly her mother's harsh voice came through the air. "I must go," she said softly and began to make her way toward the house with the contented stride of a grazing animal.

From her lawn Marian could see many houses in the distance. Her eyes passed over the homes immediately next to her own and then met what seemed to be a sharp incline, a sudden drop as irrevocable as the first dip of a roller-coaster. In this incline were the houses of poverty. The sullen dirt and endless noise were always there, like a warning to the clean, damp quiet of her own home. Now the wild yelp of the dogs of the poor came through the sun-filled yards. It was a yelp heavy with danger. These dogs that lapped up the dry dirt in the front of the shacks were as much a part of the neighborhood as the people. There were big dogs and little, sparse, slick-haired ones; all of them dead things covered with scabs and fleas. It disturbed Marian to remember their wretched bodies, their anesthetized movements, the greedy flapping of their tongues, as if they were engaged in a conscious parody of the folklore of dog lovers. They were wild scavengers, sucking all the nourishment from the ground and seemingly the blood from the sick people in the houses, and yet were pitifully unable to keep themselves alive. The sound of the dogs died away and in the distance she saw a thin, sun-browned arm lifting the week's washing up to the clothesline. There was in this distant, working woman a sort of strenuous grace, and the rhythmic up-and-down movement of the back, the instinctual, solitary repetition darkened the afternoon. There was in this body which she saw in the sunlight, something of the stony stillness of an alligator lying on the ground and looking out at the world with slow, half-opened eyes.

Marian brushed back her hair and let the sun beat down on her face. The gluttonous summer insects flew about her, but she did not lift her arms to brush them away. The swing on the porch of the house beyond squeaked and when she looked in that direction she saw that the book had been dropped and that the man was staring at her. He knows already what he is going to say to me, she thought. He has decided upon the first words. We both know that he is coming over here and it is only while he is on the way, while he is pretending that it has only suddenly occurred to him, that he will be self-conscious.

It was necessary now for her to think more definitely about him and about his family. His father is dead, she remembered. He was the tiny, thin man with a Kentucky mountain accent. This is the son who is about ten years older than I am and who has been married and divorced.

She heard him leave the porch swing and descend the few steps into the yard. He paused, rocking back and forth on his heels, and absent-mindedly stared at the sun falling on the dark green tree leaves. Marian watched the way he moved. He was slightly swivel-hipped, big-framed and graceful. He picked up a little gray stone and threw it into the air. Then he turned toward her and she knew he was looking at the tips of her shoes and the top of her hair, the parts of her body not concealed by the bush. Walking slowly, and with a half-smile already on his face, he crossed from his yard into hers. As she had known he would, he stopped before her and looked down into her startled eyes. His skin was fair and she noticed that his eyes looked reddish-yellow in the sunlight. His lips were parted, but he did not speak. Every muscle in her body felt wooden and mute and she thought, with those lightning calculations one makes in front of a possible foe, I will be childish and quiet. Feeling that she could not move quickly enough, she retreated fiercely into childhood and her face met his with a frightened, protective embarrassment. She could feel a strain in her back from the position in which she was sitting, and yet she could not move.

He had on white trousers and a shirt striped with blue. It was open at the collar. At the base of his throat she could see the dry, blond hairs. Because she was looking up at him, his eyes seemed rather gaily out of focus.

"Sun bathing?" he said.

She nodded and he sat down beside her on the ground.

She reached out for a weed and drew the stem through her fingers. The sun was as clear and white as ice now, and the faint perfume of lilacs blew steadily through the air. In the distance the church bells rang out the time. The illuminated quiet of early afternoon lay over the street. Sometimes the steamy sound of a truck moving over the smooth road could be heard. A bird suddenly stepped in the shadows of the trees.

"You look a little bit like your mother, if I remember her," Bruce said. "Maybe it's the eyes with the nice smooth eyebrows. And a little bit like your father. The mouth, I think."

"Your name is Bruce," she said. He nodded and closed his eyes against the sun. She looked squarely at his face. It was relaxed and had fallen into its purest shape. The face was like that of a baby who had grown into full manhood with a beard and lines, but still retained the child's lack of pain and indecision. It was a face of the present, a startling face that seemed to have reached some ultimate static stage. It was remotely arrogant and cruel. She looked at her dress and saw that it was wrinkled, unfit to meet his close-eyed gaze which was as engrossed, quick and discerning as the face of a buyer inspecting a warehouse of goods.

He opened his eyes and laughed. She smiled back to him, without knowing why he had laughed. She thought, rather uneasily, that the laughter of adults was always very different from the laughter of children. The former indicated a recognition of the familiar, but in children it came from the shock of the new. She had the feeling that he had been through this moment before.

"Ted isn't in town?" he asked.

"My father?" she whispered.

He paused and stretched out his arms. His face was hot and red, and his cheek bones stood out like parched ridges in a rock. He started to speak again and his voice was loud, a market place voice, assured and casual. "I met him several times. Fishing I think it was. Not that he was doing much fishing. . . . I don't know what he was doing at the lake, unless . . ."

Marian threw away the bruised weed she had picked up. "That must have been a long time ago," she said coldly. He looked at her amazed, and almost pleased, she thought.

11

Did he know that she had stopped him because she wanted so much to hear about her father that the actuality frightened her? There was too much objectivity in his voice and she wondered if he too knew her parents were grotesque in the way they remained warring lovers. The last time she had been with them she had felt this strangely youthful tension. They had never relaxed, never accepted the triumph or defeat, which it was she did not know, of marriage. They were still sparring in that sensuous valley of courtship.

"At the lake," she said. "You say it was the lake?" Her eyes were fast upon his face, because she hoped that he might, without saying anything upsetting, give her some clue to her parents. She was only sixteen and she feared her inexperience might make her judge them wrongly. She was looking at him as she had often looked at the parents of her friends. Every "dear" and "darling," every automatic evening kiss made her start, because it was important that she know exactly what older people felt and meant. She observed every flickering eye, every hand placement, and listened for sudden lowerings of the voice. And then she compared them with the glances, sighs, and weighted exchanges she had seen in her own parents. Sometimes she was filled with envy for her friends with the solid, chattering families; but at other times she hated them and their faces seemed greedy. She felt that they were paltry in their ravenously explored familiarity.

When Bruce did not answer she said, "I suppose it will be much hotter later on," as if she had been thinking about the weather for a long time.

"You don't really want to talk about your father," he said gaily. "That's rather admirable and shows an amazing intelligence. Most of us spend too damned much time talking and thinking about our families."

He turned on his side now and looked at her. She could see in his eyes that the time had come for the final and complete examination of every feature, the weighing of every fault, like turning a naked body on a slave block. He seemed to say, This is what it means for me to be male and you female. This and no more. She lifted her face to him and it was as servile as a eunuch's, until he turned away from her and seemed to settle down within himself because he had found her satisfactory.

Bruce's hand lay palm flat on the grass and she noticed the wide, flexible fingers and the reddish skin pulled tightly over the knuckles. She felt that whatever he had seen in her in that one glance was the beginning and end of all he would ever see. It was as if some hardening mold had fallen over her. There would be no room for alteration.

"How old are you?" he said suddenly.

His voice frightened her, and she did not answer. Her thinking and reacting seemed to come from a tight, airless space between the skin and bone of her forehead. He threw her into heavy half-consciousness, like the minutes before sleep. After a moment, she merely said, "Oh?" questioningly, as if she had not understood.

He chuckled indifferently. "Well, anyway, you're damned young. Damned young."

What will they think when they see that I know him? she wondered. They would scold her and advise her because he was older than she. She could imagine her mother and father gently reprimanding her. The thought pleased her. They had never offered suggestions in the past.

Bruce went on in his firm, adjusted way. "That's nice, being young. You're rich."

Remembering words that might have come from a drilled lesson, she said, "But so are you young. You are not old."

"Yes, perhaps. But I have never been a young girl which is something different."

"Is it?"

He sighed. For a moment he seemed to forget her

"Why did you come over?" she said, drawing him back.

He only laughed and looked away from her.

"I thought you might come when I saw you sitting on the porch. You looked bored." She was frightened because of the diffidence in her voice. Would he perhaps misunderstand and think that she spoke without warmth?

There was a sudden change in the man. This change brought a surprising intimacy. He spoke to her freely and with the urgency of a born gossip.

"I suppose you know I've been divorced . . . just recently." His round, dry eyes met hers and she noticed a brief trembling of his lower lip. "It wasn't entirely my fault. Though she didn't look it, she really was colder than a nigger's heel." He was not thinking of her at all now, except that he was conscious she was listening. He could recall in one moment each intimacy, annoyance, exploration and clash of his married life. This myriad, instantaneous recollection clearly gave him a sensuous thrill, at once greedy and childish. His large-featured handsome face looked at her pleadingly, as if he would devour in one bite the full usefulness of her innocence. And if he did not look for approval or understanding, he expected a lack of criticism. By his casual manner, he acknowledged that he knew he had struck upon a piece of good fortune in having her to talk with on this hot, endless afternoon.

"God," he said expansively, "she was an Eastern woman. Not from around here. Nice family, rich, everything. But I thought I had known bitches and every kind of piece, and I had another think coming!" He looked into the distance and laughed. "As someone said, every love affair is an unique experience. You never make any progress. You've always got to start back at the beginning."

A fly buzzed around his ankle and he kicked at it lazily. Marian was silent. She was thinking of a room with new, pastel furniture and of the slow way the backs of the chairs became darkly stained from married heads dozing after dinner. Bruce ran his hand over his eyes and seemed to experi-

14

ence a deflation which, when she noticed it, made her feel unworthy of him. Looking at him now, his surface scratched a little by her silence, she felt deeply moved. She was anxious that he should go on talking in the manner easiest for him, the style of the prodigal confessor. It irritated her that he should think her annoyed when he spoke of another woman, and yet she could not tell him this because she sensed that her lack of annoyance would not quite please him either. She was grateful to him for having talked to her at all. There was a verbal generosity about him which flattered her.

The sun was very hot. They were both frowning deeply. A voice called through the air and she looked to her house to see if it might be her grandmother. There was no face at the window.

"Do you want to move into the shade?" she asked shyly. His face looked vacant and weary from the sun.

"No. I suppose you are sleepy, though. Your eyes are almost closed." He put his hands under his head.

"Oh, no, no," she said eagerly, feeling that she rushed too quickly at him, but unable to restrain herself. Now that he had broken the silence she felt an ease and assurance, as if they had been strangers until one had fallen and the other had grasped the falling arm.

"What do you do?" he said abruptly, drawing himself up on his elbow and looking directly into her face. She did not turn away. It seemed to her that he knew too much about her for concealment to be effective. She looked back into his eyes and then slowly her glance fell to his mouth. "I mean what do you do besides go to school. There must be something," he added.

"I play the piano," she said and experienced a real shock when she heard the words come out of her mouth. She had very quickly learned one lesson; she had answered him the way he wanted to be answered. He had wanted her to give him something interesting about herself, something to supplement the mere self, the appreciation of which would require more effort than he wished to put into it. She wanted to unsay the words, because she saw immediately in the way pleasure spread over his face that it would always be, "Marian plays the piano" or "Marian used to play the piano." She thought of rooms filled with cigar smoke, and saw the round prints of glasses on the ridge next to the keyboard, and heard the safe sound of her own playing flowing through the house. For a moment she rocked back and forth and said to herself, Do I play the piano? Do I? It seemed a vain exaggeration, as if a person who wrote a weekly letter or made a laundry list called himself a writer.

Bruce came closer to her. He took a cigarette from his pocket and offered her one. Suddenly both of them smiled, and when he lit the cigarettes they felt that the day was really beginning. The grass beneath them was damp and green and they sank into it happily. The breeze blew a strand of hair into her eyes and when she lifted her hand to brush it away she could see him observing her brown fingers.

"I knew it," Bruce said, his voice trembling a little. "Of course, I didn't exactly know that it was the piano. But something, yes. A girl like you . . . you aren't vain enough to do nothing." He was thinking that she was one of those rare women who didn't know what she looked like, didn't know how she compared with other women. For a moment he thought it might be amusing to tell her the way in which her somber and mature eyes negated the expression of her rather childish mouth. And her long legs. . . . But he didn't speak of these things; instead he let his wide hand fall on her arm.

When Bruce's hand touched her arm, Marian felt that it was some monstrously heavy entity without any relation to the rest of his body. She remembered that winter morning when she was about ten years old and how she had walked to school clasping the hand of a girl in the neighborhood.

Suddenly a flame had spread through her body and she had dropped that hand. It was like the breaking of a shell; a sudden, complete and violent shattering. Shivering there in the middle of the street, she had realized for the first time that flesh was not inanimate. The contact of flesh with flesh had, in that moment and forever after, become something conscious and dangerous. She had passed from that to the abrupt drama one experienced when an acquaintance touched your elbow as you crossed streets, and she had learned that while talking and laughing you managed somehow to break the touch and to draw away from each other without indicating that anything difficult had passed.

"I can always tell," he went on, an unaccountable excitement in his voice. "If you do anything, your type, I mean, you do it well. It's impossible to imagine you playing rippling pieces. You're too melancholy for that. Perhaps when you grow into a real beauty . . ."

"But, I . . ." she said hesitantly. "Really, I don't . . ."

A frown came over his eyes which she could not understand. She felt there was a resentment there of her modesty, but she did not and could not know what he was thinking. He was thinking: *How much can I tell her and how soon?* He was impatient with her because her straight arms and legs, tanned to the color of light maple, had reminded him of something. He wanted to touch her, and with a lowering of his voice, tell her about his experience with a Negro girl whose legs were straight like hers and whose dusty face had the same bafflement. He wanted to tell about the smell in the girl's room, like dry tea leaves, and the cold, bare floor and the slim, iron bed: all of those bare and stripped and solitary furnishings he remembered. He would say how he had gone in there when he was just a boy and she, not long from the country, had taken him speechless into the cold, iron bed. He remembered the eyes swimming in their dust-colored pools and those brown-gray lips which he left unkissed, though no one had ever clearly told him that you

17

did not kiss Negro lips, but he had known. He could imagine Marian's stern, but eager, surprise and how her hand would begin to sweat a little as he talked. But she would not find the words to stop him, because he knew well that white women had an inexhaustible curiosity about black women. They asked if the skin was as they thought it was, pebbly like gooseflesh on children, and if they closed their eyes, and how they looked when you, later, sitting before the white supper table called to them for water or something.

Marian had turned her face from him, and he felt that he had for the moment lost her interest. There was not yet the proper intimacy for his revelations, so he continued with her as if his thoughts had not been interrupted.

She could not remember all the things he said. He talked on and on, as if he had read her mind from birth. With a widely comprehensive cunning he drew out all her resources. He might have played the piano and not she. Every practice hour, every personal use to which she had put her limited knowledge of the piano, every consolation and boredom with it, had become his. In this short time, Bruce had taken most of her life from her, and not only the facts, but the feelings, the motives, the hoped-for and doubted future. He was a pirate reduced to these paltry and ridiculous acts of brigandage, a swaggering and flourishing rogue taking toys from a child's buggy. At times Marian withdrew from him in disgust. As he talked, she could not help but notice that he knew very little about music.

Looking up at the sky, she said to him briefly, but with what seemed to her a crushing force, "I'm afraid you don't understand!" It was an insuperable task for her to throw this shutter over herself while he sat beside her with his eyes shining and absorbed.

"What?"

She could see his profile, his straight, large nose. His

18

hands were folded across his chest. "I don't feel exactly
. . ." she said, her voice downcast and empty.

Bruce's face reddened a bit, and his eyes fluttered briefly.
"Perhaps not," he answered. Again his hand fell on her
arm. Then a blinding warmth shot through her and she was
ashamed of her former coolness. Her mind was whirling
with excuses for him, excuses strong enough to make what
he felt noble and fearless. She was unaccustomed to these
changes in herself. The world had become thick, intricate
and yet soft as a mass of dew-wet grass.

"I'm not a good pianist. Not really," she said at last, forc-
ing her voice beyond its normal pitch so that he would hear.
This much she demanded of herself, this she must say so
that it would not be on her conscience when the bright
afternoon was over. With relief she saw him nod, and then
draw her fingers into his.

"I'm a natural impresario," he said in a remote voice.
"Yes, it's a gift and a curse with some people. An impresario
about everything."

The sun disappeared and they were left in one of those
sudden summer afternoon darknesses. Marian thought of
her parents driving down the golden-brown toasted roads,
and she felt that this retreat of the sun which had turned
the world into a thin color like gray gauze must have
settled upon them too and that, perhaps, they stopped
for a minute and closed their eyes to think of the shadows
on the porch of the grandmother's house. She had grown
accustomed to the man sitting beside her, though she was
not yet entirely free of embarrassment, not rid of her desire
to be with him and away from him at the same time. She
could not yet trust him and if he sighed or if a frown came
over his face, she felt utterly disowned. And also, like a
greedy worm gnawing at her, she could not forget that he
held her hand because she had told him she played the
piano. There was only this web-thin tie between them.

The purr of lawn mower came through the air and she

looked into the yard next door and saw a Negro man walking back and forth with the mower. Blades of grass flew around his ankles. Now the back door of her own house opened and she saw her brother's head appear around the screen for a moment and then disappear.

A little startled by this, she waved to him jerkily. "Albert," she said to the man beside her.

"Oh, yes, your brother," he said indifferently and did not turn around.

Sitting up on his side, so that his body shielded her from the view of the house, his hand touched her bare leg. "Never wear stockings. Never," he whispered tensely.

She pulled away mechanically. Bruce stood up and she was surprised to find him much larger, much older, than she had thought. She turned away from him and looked up at her house. The curtains in her grandmother's room blew back and forth in the breeze and she knew from the line at which the shade was drawn that the old woman was still resting. Marian did not want to go into the house, but she saw that Bruce was leaving. The getting away, saying good-by, the tentative dropping of the eyelids had no reality for her. Something was said, something, perhaps only a tone in his voice, that did not end their meeting. He seemed to be saying that he would see her again, but that now he had other things to do. It was Saturday afternoon, and Saturday afternoon was followed by Saturday night, and out of the dark houses the people would run, entranced, toward the light and noise downtown. She could already see in Bruce a preparation for this. His face seemed to her vaguely shadowed with the red glaze of bar lights, and she could see his face looking into another face bright with the same red glow and could feel his nostrils pierced by the sharpness of an adult woman's perfume.

"Well," he said abruptly. As he walked away from her he caught a side view of her face. There was something puzzling to him in young girls. Those expressions that were

20

already bitter and disenchanted. He saw the way her skirt lightly touched her knee cap and for a moment he felt sightless. He could feel her behind him, looking at him as she might have looked at a closed door which was beginning slowly to open.

When he reached his own house, he turned around and saw Marian moving away from the spot where they had been sitting. She looked very frail and young and the sight of her hair blowing around her shoulders filled him with gloom. "Oh, God!" he said half-aloud, and he was a little terrified.

CHAPTER TWO

*W*HEN the ashen light came through the window of the house, it passed imperceptibly over the young and old alike. Sister, brother and grandmother slept on, for the dawn had no meaning for them. Not far away, only a block or two, a lean white foot strikes the floor and seems to make a noise as loud and urgent as the ringing of a bell. There is no privacy in this family box, just as there is a surfeit of privacy in the houses beyond. Here the mouth on the baby's gray face opens and waits for the mother. The woman's heavy eyes look toward the ceiling and she concentrates upon the brown water spots there. In the alley behind her house, the slick, black bodies of Negro women turn in the rough folds of a sheet pieced together from flour sacks. Before their agate eyes are half-opened these tired bodies have already imagined their day's flight across rotten meadows, and they have felt the first sunlight on their necks as they cross the intersection of the city streets, running, until at last there is a dramatic pause, like a racer facing the tape, before they take a breath and push the keys into the nation's back doors. Far, far away on islands somber and hidden, a widow's body lies over the painted flanks of her dead husband and when she reaches up to touch the fiber-filled nostrils she finds they have become cold as iron during the night. In the city women awaken in the worn, female-furnished rooms and while slowly breaking their embrace with the pillow, they face the cold electric plate concealed behind the desk.

Sunday had passed. Monday morning the soft thud of the newspapers falling on the porch of each house in the block and the sound of the newsboy's sleepy whistling awakened Marian. The house was very still and through her window she could see a flawless sky. There was no reason to get up and so she lay there looking up at the ceiling of her room. She had been asleep when Albert came in and she wondered what he had done last night. Did he slip happily into the dark house and rush to sleep or had he lain restlessly in his bed and listened to the ticking of the clock on the table? She thought of her grandmother as she had looked under last night's lamplight: wrinkled pieces of flesh that might have been drawn together by some cruel needle and her false teeth which rarely ever showed because she never opened her mouth fully. At night the teeth lay hidden under the bed table in a bowl as shallow as a cat's drinking vessel. Marian had only seen them once like this and they looked beautiful and fragile like her grandmother and very female.

"Do you suppose they realize I am out of high school?" she had asked the old woman as they were going to bed.

"They?" she said vaguely, staring at the pattern in the wallpaper.

"Mother, I mean."

"Oh, tell them when they come. They must have meant to come Monday, because this is Sunday and they are not here."

"Yes, I must tell them. What will I do now?" Marian said, but her grandmother had turned into her room. There was no answer and she knew that the old woman was looking at her own reflection in the mirror above her dresser.

Marian wondered how it was in other houses. The same sun and the same sky were every place, but here it was so terribly quiet always. All over town girls like herself were awakening in their rooms, but when they turned over they touched another body in the bed, perhaps one on each side because there were not beds enough to go around. In these houses it was impossible to imagine the whispered, elliptical conversations Marian, Albert, and the grandmother had.

"Where are you going, Albert?"

"Out."

"Who with?"

"Some people."

"Yes."

"If I could . . ."

"If there is a call . . ."

"Oh, yes."

Staccato blasts of a horn sounded on the street: one, two, three. Then a pause and it sounded again with a long blast. Now Marian knew that the drunken old man who lived up the street was stumbling into the car that took him to work. She could hear the old man's cough and then a loud cackle of curses before the starting motor drowned out his rebellious voice.

Albert's bed squeaked faintly and then everything was quiet again. Only a few streets away, in the very poor section, the morning was greeted quite differently. Since dawn they had been talking and making the noise of working people: arguments over money, the beginning of a day's drudgery, the cry of babies, and perhaps the sound of the filled washing machine. These people could not be more impoverished than she who had never had a penny in her pocket, who could never make plans of the simplest sort. Was it silence, the refusal to change that made her different? Was it never talking about it, never letting the worry become the open threat, never taking on the harsh tones, and the table manners of the poor? Did these attitudes actually create money? For some time now Marian had been passionately wishing for argument. It seemed to her that one big fight, one talk and wrangle over money, one shout of the bitterness and confusion all of them felt, would restore the family to the world of human beings. But this luxuri-

24

ous, well-mannered silence would not be broken; it clung to them like some half-erotic symbol of power. Storms threatened, but did not appear. They were cowards, miserable, water-color cowards. And then she would realize that admission of defeat would be more unbearable than secrecy. If the static gentility were ever shattered, it would be more brutal than the slaps and screams which filled the poor houses. They wouldn't battle and then, refreshed, fall on the bed and go snoring into sleep. Instead she and her family would crumble into sniveling complainers, neat and threadbare beggars, melancholy, tender-faced derelicts.

Marian's window faced the back garden and she could look onto the street beyond. Very quietly she got up from her bed and sat by the window. There was no sound in Bruce's house. The windows were raised and the house was calm and secure. She felt an odd sense of triumph because she was up early. Bruce's awakening would be regretful. The night before would arise with him and, until he had shaved and eaten, he would be a tired, confused adult who had to pay the price for being older than she, for knowing liquor and women. But when he was awake, he would gather up the scattered faggots of his ego and he would be a man, strong and immediate, a man who could start each hour as if it were his first. Somehow Marian knew how he spent every moment of his time. She could imagine him in every pose: his eyes small and light when filled with the smoke from the cigarette between his lips; the palms of his hands slapping together as he sat in the law office, the nodding of his head when the lulls in interest came and, later in the afternoon, she saw him falling into a split-second manly sleep. At noon he would emerge from the office building and fall into a loose circle of men on the street for those rapid, business conversations. When the end of the day approached, he would begin to plan those finely interlocking nights of his life.

The sun touched the tips of the six crosses that dotted the

roof of the hospital in the center of town. Well, she thought, so this is love. The grasping of the color of another person's life is the substance. She had not expected this ambiguity and felt a little deflated. She had imagined that the man would be a bare and pure symbol, as clear and certain as the pious, sparkling emblem on top of the hospital. She knew that Bruce would think of her because she was new to him. He would feel an annoying impatience that would goad him into seeing her once, a second time and, perhaps, for a long period. Would he be surprised that she could sit at her window and look at the house in which he lived and think of him in and out of it with an inquisitiveness as impersonal as a camera's? She was bewildered and a little afraid of this curiosity and felt that she had been betrayed by her own mind as well as by him. She could not help but mourn the loss of warmth, the security and completeness which the childish ideas of romance had promised. There could be no doubt that this was not the hard, demanding surrender she had imagined. The messiah had seemed, even upon first meeting, a little tattered; the hope of salvation was still problematic. She moved away from the window because she feared he might be awake now and might see her. She soon began to wonder if her face would give away her thoughts, if he would be able to discover her secrets. Already she knew the value of concealment.

A key turned in the back door of the house. The thin scraping in the lock and the creaking of the wooden door shook the house. It was as if thousands of tiny lights had suddenly been released. The sparse colored girl had now opened up the day. Her light footsteps in the quiet house transformed it into a warm and splendid home. For a few minutes Marian stood very still and listened. Now she heard the opening of the front door and the lifting of the shades in the hall and living room. The joy of the opening of a day raced through her and she wanted to embrace the articles of furniture in her room. She could not wait to touch the damp wood of the breakfast table on the side porch or for her grandmother to appear in the long, gray dress and to see her brother's intent and handsome face staring out at a tree or waiting for the telephone to ring.

When she heard the oven door open and shut, Marian went down the steps. In the kitchen, now becoming warm from the oven, a young, very lean Negro girl bent over the sink and let water run over the glasses which were left from the night before. She wore brown and white oxfords and white socks, out of which her thin, black, bowed legs jutted like curved lead pipes.

"Hello, Hattie," Marian said. For no reason she giggled vaguely.

Hattie had alert, trigger-set, dry and scorched eyes. She moved with a rapid jerkiness and her body had the jagged tautness of a vaudeville tumbler. She was a very ugly girl and the clothing and conventions of a domestic servant were as ridiculous on her as they would have been on a caged animal. "Where's the old pee hag?" she said, coming close to Marian and her soft, amazed laugh rocking the kitchen. Marian stepped back a little, as she always did when the first shock of Hattie's exquisite venom struck her. There was in her mind the awareness that she was expected to stop Hattie, to halt the wild, whispered obscenities; but she could not. A love of the unknown, of the brilliantly, violently expressive held her. The girl was an accomplished mimic, and she could twist her shaggy-helmeted skull in a way suggestive of the most elusive gestures of the family. For her the people of the world were perpetually in a state of indecent exposure, and she could, with a mere glance, size up the most intimately erotic secrets of everyone she met. Of these things she would give Marian only a suggestion, and then she would break off as if she held these secrets in reserve, like live explosives under temporary lock.

"Grandmother's still asleep," Marian said, picking up the

27

dish towel to dry the glasses. She was ashamed for having left the dishes overnight. The way Hattie slapped them in the water and pulled them out showed that she was angry. When Marian picked up the towel, Hattie left the sink abruptly. She put strips of bacon in the oven and began to stir the pancake batter.

They did not talk. Occasionally a giggle, a gesture or a sigh passed between them, but that was all. While Hattie was busy at the stove, Marian looked at her profile. On her fierce features there was never a suggestion of fatigue. Perhaps her ugliness concealed it. Hattie, though not yet twenty, looked ageless. There was hardly a sign of youth about her and she might have come from the womb, warped and fast as lightning, wild and worn. They heard water running in the bathroom upstairs. They too, Marian thought, feel a sense of joy when the little girl arrives. When they smell the bacon and remember Hattie's feet running over the floor, they feel bright and purposeful and glad to be alive. There is a God then and nothing bad can happen because the house is shuttered from ugliness and worry by the services of this eighteen year old girl. They have the comfort and well-being that comes only from waking up in a house already active. Marian wondered if Hattie might be aware of this, but she could not find the answer on that face too mobile to fathom. She was disgusted with her own joy and with that secret return of strength which had surged through her when she had listened sensuously to Hattie opening the door. How do we pay her? she thought vaguely. She dared not ask her grandmother, because they didn't talk of such things. She did not ask Hattie either, because she was afraid of the answer.

The wind caught up puffs of dust and sent them flying through the air. Looking down the street across a grassless, vacant lot, Marian saw a file of smoke coming out of a chimney. She pointed to it and Hattie said, jerking her curved shoulders, "Niggers cooking. Using coal in this heat!" They stood still for a moment and in the silence Marian could hear Hattie brushing her wide thumb over the knuckles of her hand. When she turned to look at her, the girl's face was stony and ancient. The silence was broken by the noise of a wagonload of chickens and above the cackle the unintelligible, tobacco-filled howl of the huckster spread mournfully over the sunswept street. Marian did not go to the door to see him. She knew what he was like, he and the other country people whose heart-breaking placidity was out of place in town. She had seen them standing before Woolworth's at night imprisoned in the sad cell of their flesh. They seemed to be the inhabitants of a faraway land who had no needs beyond their own solid, monolithic personalities.

"I ain't cooking for them if they come," Hattie said suddenly. Her voice was harsh.

Marian turned away from her without comment. Hattie was thinking of the hot smoke in the Negro hut and her remark brought Marian back to her parents and to the realization that this was to be the day of their arrival. "They will come," she said to herself.

The grandmother had come downstairs and was sitting at the head of the breakfast table. "Mail?" she said to Marian.

"Not yet."

"Miz Gorman," Hattie said, her head coming through the kitchen door.

Mrs. Gorman turned around slowly and her pale eyes did not seem to see anything. They might have been gazing back into the recesses of her own mind and merely pretending to look outward.

"I can't stay for tonight," Hattie said, her eyes not leaving Mrs. Gorman's face.

In the weighted silence, Marian and Hattie stared at the frozen figure of the grandmother. Mrs. Gorman never seemed to be actively considering the point at hand; she seemed, rather, to have already thought of everything of importance and to imply that conversation was merely a recollection of a former experience so similar to the present one that she had only to remember what had happened before and to repeat the pattern. She looked intently at the great oak tree beside the house. "It will be a shame to cut it down," she said abruptly. "But they undermine the house. The roots do." She stopped, as if the thought of the muscular, destructive roots gave her pleasure.

Hattie shifted her feet, and on her face there was the reflex and loose expression learned through years of drowsy waiting: the expression of generations waiting on the wall benches in the courthouse, mutely gazing at the brass spittoons, waiting like school children in the dusk outside the Family Welfare Office, waiting at the grocery stores, waiting at the back door until the knock was answered.

At last Mrs. Gorman said with a low laugh, "I'll fix dinner myself."

"All right," Hattie said and disappeared into the kitchen.

A soft breeze blew over the side porch. They sat at the table, the two faintly alike faces relaxed and still, waiting for the coffee. Mrs. Gorman's handsome profile and her vague eyes remained unaltered. It was impossible, from moment to moment, to tell upon what her mind had come to rest. She remained outside every event, as if her memory were no longer than a sigh. Mrs. Gorman wore a gray dress with long, loose sleeves. Her shrunken left arm hung limply from the sleeve or, when she was eating, the stiffened left hand would rest upon the table like a frail and lonely branch. After her excluding silences she would sometimes give a laugh, in which the muscles of her face never moved. The laugh was the beginning of each of her short conversations. After it, she would turn her damp eyes back to the world and indicate that, after long thought, she had come to a decision. But her imprecise words and actions gave few clues to its nature.

"What time do you think they will come?" Marian asked.

Her eyes were fastened tightly upon her grandmother and she tried to force her to concentrate upon the problem.

"Who?" the mysterious voice replied. And then after a long pause and a static chuckle, she repeated, "Who?"

Mrs. Gorman's narrow white nostrils quivered momentarily. Marian could feel her own face burning. She almost wanted to strike her grandmother, but the cool face baffled her so that she could never be quite certain the evasions were deliberate.

"Mother and Papa," she said dully, as if she had been cornered into some ignominious position.

"Mother and Papa," Mrs. Gorman repeated mechanically. She looked at her granddaughter briefly and then, in an expression of sweet fatigue, her eyes retreated to their old emptiness.

Marian did not expect her grandmother to answer. By now she was accustomed to this way of life in which there was never a finale, in which everything was ritualized to the pitch and intensity of a funeral. The endless, unsnipped tatters and threads of life in this house had worked themselves into a fine net and it was impossible to untangle the old omissions. Moments without consummation, days without decision, secrets kept for years had muddled everything forever.

When Albert made his dazed and petulant appearance, Mrs. Gorman said, "Yes, I think they will come." She brushed a crumb away from her lap and added, "You know more about them than anyone else."

"I?" Marian said.

"You were with them last. You know what the situation is," Albert said. He lit a cigarette and rubbed his free hand over his eyes. Albert was astonishingly handsome and therefore had no reason to be upset about anything. He could, like his grandmother, remain quiet and seem to have been very interesting, could smile and leave the impression that some preference or valued approval had been generously given. His face after sleep was perfectly smooth and bright, though as the day went on his calm would be imperceptibly threatened and faint lines of discontentment and insecurity would form around his mouth.

"Yes, yes," Mrs. Gorman said quickly. "You saw them last. What was it, my dear? What was it?"

"What?" Marian said. "Nothing." She could not remember how this had started, how it had become taken for granted that she knew the secret of her parents.

Whatever she may have felt before was now without certainty. What, when one is sitting on a shadowed porch, do elliptical glances from two years back mean? How could she now bring back that subdued fierceness in her mother's eyes or recall her defiant body sitting upright in a chair at midnight? Several years ago Marian had spent two weeks in Florida with her parents. She could not remember how she had got there, in what way she had returned or what impressions she had had. But, once—this must have been the case—when the grandmother and Albert had made some statement about the parents, Marian must have indicated some new knowledge she had brought back from her visit, bold facts to replace conjecture. They had questioned her intermittently, but she had eluded them; and now, suddenly, as though she must rush it out of herself, she took up the coffee spoon and said in a harsh voice, "It's a woman." Guilt flashed across her face, because it seemed dishonest that she had waited until the day of their arrival to present this fact, if it were a fact, to the family. It was as if she wished to meet the parents at the door with accusations to blast whatever strategy they had prepared.

"It will be nice to see the little devils again," Albert said oddly. "It will be very interesting to hear the new plans and the fine excuses and the birth of another million-dollar business." He laughed and stretched his legs and drew in his breath sharply. In the summer brightness Albert looked

32

very free, almost nakedly, wickedly free. He always spoke indifferently about his parents, as if they had no real existence for him. He was thankful for their negligence, and constantly felt blessed that he hadn't their wishes and reprimands to consider.

"Lucy never really cared for any man," Mrs. Gorman said dryly, speaking of her daughter.

Without the will to hold out from them any longer, Marian began tonelessly, "No . . . No, it's not that."

Albert turned his head and let the open, indifferent smile play about his face. From time to time he would glance away from his sister with a look of preoccupation, as though he weren't at all interested in what she had to say about the parents; but, when she paused, his eyes would draw up curiously and show that he waited eagerly, not so much for the facts themselves, but for what interpretation Marian put upon them.

With the dull, plangent monotony of a recitation, Marian told them about the Florida sun, the cracked, lazy cottage in which the parents lived, the flowers, the sound of the surf and the rapid nights filled with thundering music and dozens of browned faces set in that holiday blankness for the harassed passing of superficial time. Somehow she told of the dance, and of her father's bronzed face, his tall, careful body. She remembered the weakness around his mouth, and the way his giddy, glazed eyes looked foolishly into the full contentment and pride of the face of a heavy, white-skinned woman. That was really all she had to say; these little remembered bits of a dance in which her father's body was pressed close to the plump woman's. And after she had spoken about it, she could not be sure that it wasn't a lie; because simultaneously her mind recalled the slow, gentle way his body settled into a chair at home, the warm masculinity and tenderness of his lips dozing in sleep, his comforting answer when his name was called. She could re-

33

member his face, pitiful and forlorn, when he was worrying about money.

Albert coughed, drew himself up, and walked out of the room. Marian remained at the table. "Maybe he . . ." she started to say. Profound inattention spread over her grandmother's face and ended their conversation. The old woman said nothing about her son-in-law's infidelity, but Marian thought that her normally pale eyes suddenly brightened. Laughing abruptly, Mrs. Gorman got up from the table and proceeded upstairs. Marian heard her slide down on the bed and, fearing that she might be ill, waited for a time and then tiptoed into the bedroom. She found the tall body lost in a glorious sleep, as if the grandmother after a weary and restless night had achieved some ultimate satisfaction she had never known before.

In the quiet that always came over the house after breakfast, Marian helped Hattie with the housework. The little girl's short body and mud-colored face dominated the house and Marian followed her around foolishly, ineptly. She was embarrassed to appear so inefficient before Hattie; her hands felt clumsy and she seemed to do no more than pick things up and put them down again unchanged. She knew that Hattie was watching her in a kind of outraged amusement and she said, "I do all right by myself. You think I'm awkward and I can't do a thing."

"Don't be laying your badness on me!" Hattie said, raising a cloud of dust with her broom. She stopped the broom and said, "You reckon they really meant to come? No signs of them yet."

"Of course, they are coming. We must have misunderstood and they meant today instead of yesterday."

"They sure do take a lot of airings. One minute there isn't no talk of moving and the next thing you know they're lighting out!"

When Hattie's cracked and almost cruel voice broke

through the air, a ripe, uninhibited feeling would rise up in Marian and she wanted to talk to Hattie about the most intimate matters: about her parents, her grandmother, her brother, and Bruce. She wanted to break through the sighs, the secrecies, the niceties, break through into a coarse, shouting, foul-mouthed world. She knew there was release for her in that harsh, objective world. She envied the dark, contemptuous faces that might listen in the evening to Hattie's stories of this household. She wanted to hear their laughter and the shrill voice saying, "Tell the old bastards to go to hell!" She wanted to see the full depth of Hattie's mimicry, her quick bull's-eye interpretations, her memories of the days here, her inferences of what lay behind the conversations which her coffee cups interrupted. The world Hattie raced toward in the evening seemed to Marian to hold all the clues to her own; there she would find herself and her family. In the acrid, damp-odored houses, around the confused table, in a home where legs were spread wide and arm pits showed, she and her heritage were held up like hooked fish with the wild eye exposed. She was sure there would be nothing left of her family's public identity.

After a while the mops and dustcloths worked their way into the windowless winter breakfast room. Marian hated this room with its bare electric bulb falling straight from the ceiling and cruelly lighting up their faces and the spots on the wall as they sat there for cloistered eating. In the June warmth, the room was steamy and damp.

"It's like a laundry," she said.

"Most likely," Hattie answered flatly, stooping over to pick up a damp cracker which had fallen to the floor. "My mother used to work in the Gorman Laundry," she added, turning around to face Marian with those nervous eyes.

Why has she never told me that before? Marian thought. With something close to horror, Marian faced the fact that Hattie's mother must know bitter stories about her dead grandfather, the owner of the Gorman Laundry. The whole house was stamped with that business, and with the memory of her red-faced Irish grandfather. She remembered him sitting behind the brightly lit desk in the large building, directing the work in the steaming, barnlike rooms above. Around this red face, she saw the bulging, endless white sacks loading into the slow, rope-drawn elevator. She could not think of the dead man without remembering the rows of heavy, sagging women in carpet slippers who stood over the ironing boards. She remembered also the two odors of the laundry: that of the sour bundles unloaded at the back and the sweet, fresh-air packages in slick, brown paper which passed over the front counter or were delivered by the trucks. As a little girl she used to slip into the laundry in the free prodigality of the middle afternoon, and, as she moved past the smiling faces of the women at the front counter, she would feel a shameless joy of possession. She knew they must smile at her and call her pretty because of her grandfather. Going by the tangled pipes, she would see the sweat that rose luminously on the lead, and then softly, sensuously, she would enter her grandfather's office. Her body glowed from the greeting he gave her, the kissing and tusseling. The office was heavy with the sweet smell of tobacco juice and there were always men in there, men who smiled when the grandfather reached into his pocket to give the little girl money. The laundry was the most powerful symbol of Marian's childhood. The feelings she had had about it were of enormous magnitude and profoundness and as erotically mysterious as some nourished lust. The sight of the Gorman trucks on the street was like living day and night in the comfort of a feather bed which banked you on both sides and drew over your head the sweet peace that shut off forever the leanness and exposure outside.

"I'm glad we don't have the laundry any more," Marian said. "I felt sorry for those women working there."

"I guess they felt plenty sorry, too," Hattie said. "Since you didn't work there, I don't see why you cared." Hattie's eyes were like clamps on the other girl's face. Marian could not tell her how her pride and joy in the laundry had turned sour, how she had realized the little whimsicalities that were fed by the owned thing. The sweating machines and heavy irons had tended the fine fabric of this family. She knew now that the laundry hadn't been a mere building on Main Street. It was the rare calm of her grandmother, the indolent beauty of Albert, the hearty, private chuckling of her grandfather, the gentle and richly complicated mother, and the wandering father. If it had not been for what the grandmother still had of the laundry, even after it was sold and the grandfather had died, Marian would not have had this home as a refuge. She would have been with her mother and father.

"Hattie, Hattie," Marian whispered. The appearance of Bruce had made Marian in need of a confidant. She wanted to ask Hattie for knowledge of those things supposedly learned under torn quilts in Negro houses. She was certain Hattie knew about these things. Through black women the primeval dark waters of love were supposed to flow uninhibited.

"Hattie, do you think ten years' difference in age is too much?" she said louder.

"Too much for what?" She was down on her knees in the corner where the desk stood. Marian could see her ironlike neck bent downward.

"Too much between a boy and a girl."

When Hattie did turn around, her eyes were astonished. "Boy, I don't know," she said.

"What do you think?"

In the dark caverns of Hattie's face there was an endless questioning. "I wish I knew some of them answers myself," she said abjectly. "It don't sound just right, does it? But maybe you can't tell until it's too late." She whistled softly, like a child who has been startled.

Hattie stood up now and brushed the edge of her short

skirt. Marian, who was taller, looked down at her baffled face. "Now, for getting married . . ." Hattie said. She hesitated, because she, like Marian, was struggling to understand the old witchcraft. She too lived with a struggling instinct that had to be bent to the role of daughter, sweetheart, and wife. Marian wanted to touch Hattie's hand and to hear about her troubles, but the girl suddenly flew into the kitchen.

There were no telephone calls, no knocks at the door, until when the sun had died and rain clouds appeared and there was a chill in the air, Bruce came walking through the garden and knocked softly on the back door. Going ahead of him, as if in a trance, Marian led him into the living room. When she reached the fireplace she swung around and looked at him. He stood before her, strong and undeniable as a high wind. She heard him speak and his voice was sharp as a flute as he whispered the amenities he might have felt necessary in a room filled with people. The house was as still as a convent at midnight and the conversation he had started upon was out of place. Marian stood speechless before him and watched the way a change was coming over his face. "Yellow. That's nice for you," he said. And suddenly, in the quiet, he was filled with a profound, desolating impatience. The shadowed living room was bewildering. She saw him moving toward her with a stern expression on his face. Her own blood was suddenly chilled and she felt pity for him. She began fumbling with a button on her dress and twisting her hand in her pocket. She felt completely blank. Beneath this blankness, fear was rising up within her. Still his famished, impatient talking continued about useless things which she could not piece together. At last his voice stopped altogether.

Bruce saw that she was staring at him. He seemed to recognize the blinding shock and coldness and he put his arm around her shoulder and drew her head down on his chest. She could feel his heart beating and she thought he was screaming, as in a nightmare monologue, you want it, all women do, all young girls, even though you stand silent pretending tears and fright and anger. She wanted nothing, nothing, nothing. She did not immediately move away from him, however, because the warmth of the desire in his eyes and the echo of his body fascinated her. Here was the full depth of that wondrous and powerful abyss which separated men and women; here was a mystery more magnificent and terrifying than anything she had ever felt before. It made her feel strange and lonely and she was frightened— not of him, but of herself. The biggest disaster would be his knowledge of the peculiar emptiness inside her, for she was able to see that he, being male, was tuned to a certain imaginary pitch in women. A baker's truck stopped abruptly in front of her house and he lifted her head and drew away from her. He began to talk again with loud assurance, as if he had not touched her. She was startled at the way he was able to erase the moment before from his face and voice, and to step back to the impersonal, guarded manner he had used on their first meeting.

The house was noisy now. Hattie was talking to the baker, and upstairs the grandmother could be heard puttering about her room. Bruce looked unbelievably bored, and Marian smiled at him. There was nothing between them. She remembered the piano, and noted that it had quickly disappeared from his thoughts, to be revived again when it could be more useful. Shortly afterward, Bruce left.

No dinner was cooked this evening. Marian carried a tray of sandwiches and coffee to her grandmother who lay on the couch in her bedroom, serene and dominant. Because of her shrunken arm, she handled herself strangely, but without embarrassment. It was this, the slight deformity, which gave her her dignity, the dignity of the frail. And for the same reason she was immediately interesting to all who saw her. Faces changed and eyes brightened in her presence. She put the nervous, the active and fumbling to shame. People sat beside her, hardly breathing, as they watched the aimless turning of her head and saw the unperturbed pale eyes.

Night came over the house smoothly and they did not speak of the parents. It seemed now that they wouldn't come. Marian imagined the arrival, after a few days, of a letter which would announce, without apology, that Ted had seen a town which appealed to him and had decided to settle there. This decision would be followed by the mother's long description of the new scenery and the details of the little house they had found.

The doorbell rang sharply in the darkness past midnight. The family awakened to the half-expected signal of the parents' arrival; but it was a dull awakening and the self-consciousness of sleep lay heavily upon the house. There was no spontaneity, no eager embracing, since each one wished to retire immediately and to postpone the greetings until the next day. A single light burned in the downstairs hall, and it vaguely illuminated the self-absorption of the figures which were lost to each other in the tight shell of these solitary hours.

Lucy Coleman stepped through the door and looked quickly at each of them, as if she must prepare herself for alterations. She might have been defending herself against an unexpected threat in the darkness. She was nervous from suppressed fatigue, and her sharp, unrelenting face penetrated the room like a knife. She kissed the cheek of her mother and then, looking at Marian and Albert, held out her arms tentatively, as if they might refuse her. "My darlings," she said and they came to her. They were pressed to her sides and she, embracing them, began to laugh. This woman who was soft, gentle, and compassionate, who had a great flair with flowers, who had a fine, precise style with tradesmen and cleaning women, who gossiped about prices and the weather, held her own children very awkwardly.

Marian felt miserably let down, as one does when a passionate correspondence has ended and the object of the passion appears in person. Albert was struggling with his face. He seemed to be making an almost inhuman effort to appear younger than he was, to insure his status, and to pose his handsome head so that no glance of criticism or surprise should come from his parents. His mouth was petulantly warm and with some mysterious facility, he looked very fresh, very simple and appealing.

Ted Coleman stood beside his wife. He held the bags even after they had entered the house, until, at last, noticing this he dropped them to the floor with a guilty smile. He wore a crumpled Palm Beach suit and dust had settled on his face and hands. Though this was not really his house, he seemed more relaxed and more grateful for being at the end of something than his wife. Lucy Coleman looked around the hallway without speaking. Her eyes would light upon an old umbrella stand or upon a tall, undusted vase and she would stand there as if amazed by these items. The others, watching her, felt immediately the insufficiency of the house. Marian was overcome with guilt and longed to get her parents out of the room, to straighten and to dust more carefully and to have her mother re-enter the room with surprise. Lucy Coleman's eyes wandering about the place were like sudden flashlights now. A portrait on the wall was noticeably tilted and last week's newspaper lying on the bench beside the fireplace was inexcusably sloven. Marian saw her mother's eyes shift to her and to her grandmother almost contemptuously, and a faint smile crossed her face as if she were asking if those two female figures were really women. Removing her gloves, she walked toward a vase of mountain laurel and pulled off a few dead sprigs of leaf.

As she opened the front door to throw the dead leaves out into the yard, she said to her husband, "Well, we are here." The house had quickly become hers again, and she offered it to him jokingly, almost bitterly. When she spoke to her husband, the two of them were disguised and hidden from the others, and the grandmother and children blushed as if they had stupidly broken into an intimate and embarrassing scene. Every moment between the parents seemed intent and guarded, very much like the captivity of young lovers approaching marriage. When at last Lucy turned back to the family, when the poised smile went out to them, the woman was supreme in the room. Her thin body, and the bright, intense eyes over her sharp nose, put them all to shame. Beside her, they were pale and unambitious. They felt that their presence, their lack of force were unwarranted insults to her and they again took it for granted that she must always be dissatisfied.

The parents spoke of the trip, but without interest. It was too late to ask questions and in the lazy midnight the experiences of everyone seemed too dull to relate. The grandmother was silent, still dreaming, as if she stood effortlessly in an unbroken sleep. The family chatter started abruptly.

"Well, look how tall she is, how pretty," Ted Coleman said to Marian.

"It's too late to talk now," Lucy said, smiling. "But tomorrow we will tell each other everything."

She turned to her son and laid her cheek against his. "Are you sleepy, little boy?"

Albert's lips turned back in a half-smile.

"Such loud pajamas! Green silk!" Ted said to Albert. He slapped him lightly on the shoulder, unmindful of Albert's suddenly anxious eyes.

"Poor Mamma is sleepy," Lucy said. "Tomorrow, tomorrow we can tell each other everything," she repeated.

They filed up the stairway and went into the bedrooms. Marian's father winked at her self-consciously as she turned into her door. He did not know what else to do, since obviously this tall, brown daughter was no longer a child and he could not quite face an adult offspring.

"Good night, Mother, good night, Papa," Marian said. Then all of them laughed sleepily.

CHAPTER THREE

*T*HIS company I was with worked on the theory that it paid to put out a good article," Ted Coleman was saying.

The day had been very hot and, in the late afternoon, Lucy Coleman withdrew from the rest of the family and sat alone on the porch. The conversation of her husband and daughter came through the window.

"Doesn't it also pay to put out a bad article?" Marian asked.

"Well . . . Not in the long run . . . My experience has been . . ." Lucy heard his voice drop and she ceased to follow the talk. The porch was dusty since it was not often used and she found the one straight chair rather uncomfortable. Before her in the golden summer street the houses of her childhood were napping in the great sunlight. Out of these houses unfamiliar figures came: young wives, new and certain as fine silk, stepped out of cars and ran across the lawn. Some familiar faces remained. She watched an elderly woman stare in a ritualized way at her garden plants and Lucy remembered the face when it had not been old. Yes, she thought, everything was more or less unchanged. It was the same late afternoon street. Boxes of groceries arrived, the children had on the day's second clean dress, bunches of workingmen occasionally came around the corner and made their way onward to their poor homes, the streetcars stopped and let out the same weary workingwomen. In all of this there was nothing that called to her, nothing that she needed or was needed by and it seemed mere accident that her feet had once felt this ground or that she had been cradled in this house.

She thought sadly that memories were ridiculously planned and stilted things. Looking at her house she should, by custom at least, press her long fingers together and say, "I was a bride here." The porch beneath her was streaked and cracked from winter exposure. She tapped her toe against it and thought, I was born here, was a girl here, a fool here, a daughter, a wife, a mother and a stranger.

"Where is Albert all the time? What's he so busy doing?" she heard Ted Coleman say.

"He has lots of friends. He doesn't stay at home much. . . . He . . ."

The sound of the conversation at her back excited Lucy pleasantly. She found a certain enjoyment in being at home like that inspired by a play or a picture. She was aware of the surface dimensions of the scene before her, of the figures of her family, and she was also able to sense, as in a play, the hidden aspects of the figures. In this atmosphere her consciousness of self was greatly heightened and that consciousness brought with it an immense unfulfillment. There were moments, sometimes hours and days, when she felt able to comprehend herself, to catch something solid and of one piece, some round and firm center about which she could say, Here am I. Here *it* is. Here is a woman or all women. At such times a feeling of power rushed through her and she was the most beautiful woman in the world, the most beloved wife, the most satisfactory and satisfied lover. These feelings were never sustained very long. There was always something in her memory that caused her to doubt herself. The most vivid of these recollections was the time, on their honeymoon, when her husband had slipped away from the hotel and she had found him sitting in the drugstore with his head bent toward the waitress. There was something on his face, an abandonment and gaiety, she

45

had never seen before. She heard him talk to the girl in a voice she did not recognize, loud and boisterous. And when he laughed she was shocked by the deeply masculine and intimate quality he revealed for the unknown girl. She was not jealous; she was confused. This moment without any history or meaning which he had given the waitress was far away from the gentle, almost prudish, manner she knew. She never got any closer to him, perhaps because he loved her.

Lucy Coleman had an uncontrollable desire to know the most intimate secrets of other women, for that seemed to be the only answer to her doubts about herself. Plump, high-breasted women with the sloven curve or round buttocks, their intense abandon, women who offered a drink easily and then slipped off suddenly into the darkness with their fat, pink arms slapping against the man's thighs; that must be it. These rich, swishing animals, slick as eels, were women: women as men understood them. She was something else perhaps. Some special category: a wife. It seemed to Lucy that she would have been satisfied in Victorian England, in a society where women had duties rather than rights. In love, as in everything else, duties evolve from the lowest common denominator, from the ordinary, universal potentialities; but rights represent the challenge of the most gifted. The fat buttocks had the right to challenge her, to insist that her satisfaction be measured with their own. But it was impossible for her to know what relaxation other women were capable of, how their bodies felt in a man's arms, what lay inside them and was brought out for husbands and lovers.

"Now, if I were a young girl, do you know what I would do?" Ted was saying. He broke off and began mumbling to a cat which had found its way to the house that morning. She could imagine her husband's tan, rough hands reaching out to the kitten, punching it in the belly, rubbing behind its brittle ears. She shivered slightly and desire for her hus-

46

band overcame her, desire to be the kitten caressed by him, the unresisting flesh over which his hands moved. Her body felt paralyzed and a slow pain came over her back. The pain was like the wonderful illnesses she always longed for in times of anxiety. Her feeling for her husband was accompanied by a yearning to fall back once, just once more, to the irresponsibility of a thoughtless, warm vacuum. It was as if she had some primitive, early remembrance of an ecstatic half-death under a sonorous sea.

"What are you going to do next year?" Ted Coleman said.

Lucy listened very closely and she could almost see Marian move her chair closer to his. "I don't know," the daughter said, her voice excited and tense. "I want to go to college. Out to State." She said the last with her voice rising in a question.

Now what is he going to promise her? Lucy wondered. What is he going to say and what will she say in reply? She felt a strange happiness that her husband had been cornered by this question. He did not answer immediately and his wife could imagine him preparing an extravagant reply.

When at last he spoke, he said, "I played center at State . . ." and his voice went on and on in a story she had heard many times. Perhaps Marian already knows how she is going to school, what she will use for money, the mother thought. Her husband's voice lulled her and the flash of guilt she had felt about her daughter passed away quickly.

"There was this fellow there. Played on the team. Bull, we called him, and . . ."

"Do you think I will really go on to school?" Marian interrupted him. Her voice was suddenly different, not louder, but higher, higher. "If I could make my plans definitely . . ."

"I imagine you'll get there," the father answered. "Now this Bull, as we called him . . ."

Her husband began to laugh and Lucy thought how young his laughter was. His body still had the muscular heaviness of a football player and his voice also retained that loud, husky conviviality. It had taken a long time for Lucy to accept his surface completely. She had believed that something was hidden, something which would gradually change into the indirection of women. But he had never lost or gained anything. He remained what he had been when they married: a man beyond doubt, beyond qualification. She had never seen him really angry, only helpless occasionally. She thought, It is slight, strange boys like Albert who have the temperament.

"Why did you leave Montana?" Marian asked when he paused to light a cigar. He was standing by the mantel and Lucy could see the way he held the match for a long while until it had blown out. In the way he puffed, he managed to give the idea that smoking a cigar was the most important thing in the world.

"Ask me no questions and I'll tell you no lies," Ted Coleman said. Lucy could feel the young girl's eyes upon his face as he started to explain the true nature of the insurance business.

A short woman in a bright yellow dress appeared on the street. She stopped abruptly and Lucy heard a high-pitched exclamation. The woman ran up to the porch and they embraced each other warmly. "Lucy, little old Lucy!" she cried. She had a buffalo figure: thin arms and legs and a balloonlike frame between the thin extremities. Her enormous smile, the long, white, slightly loose teeth, made Lucy very sad. At this moment it seemed that she had known this woman, Mary, forever, and that she was the only person she had ever known. She had not known her parents, her children, her husband; but there had been a time when she had known this woman, when they had lain together at night in the wide bed in the room where the chestnut tree touched the screen of the window and had gossiped until dawn. (*Lucy, you'll be married first. I know it. You'll be married and have silver with the new initials on it. I don't think you'll live here, though. Maybe in New York, with an Eastern man. . . .*) She and Mary had always talked of men, as one could never talk to men. They had confessed what knowledge they had; they asked questions and in the darkness it had seemed that at last all blindness and doubt had vanished. (*What is it women feel? Is it like men? Have you . . . do you? Will we sometime, too, like men?*) And then shadows would appear, and even with friends, reservation and sham returned, ending these conversations in that lonely, confused corridor of the female lie.

Lucy looked into Mary's face and realized that she had been so negligent of all human relationships that she did not even know whether or not this friend was married. She looked at her hands and saw no ring. Mary's face reddened.

"Ted? How is he?" the bright, insistent voice rang out.

"He's fine," Lucy said, feeling very foolish and, at the moment, experiencing a vague distrust of her friend.

Mary had a plain, restless face, resigned beyond protest to the meaningless laughter, the eager sympathy which alone could make life active and colorful for her. There was silence between them, until Mary, her eyes looking straight into danger, said, "Will you stay now, Lucy? Stay here?"

A last ray of sunlight crossed Lucy's eyes and she frowned. She felt rather cruel, not answering immediately, because she knew her silence would be a reproach. She reached into her pocket and drew out a cigarette. When it was lighted, she said flatly, "No, I won't. I can't."

"Can't. Can't stay?" It was impossible to classify this tentative remark. Mary seemed to want Lucy to give her some explanation which would squelch criticism before it actually appeared.

There was no time to make ugliness and guilt soft and understanding. Lucy knew that her chance to speak to Mary, to tell what little of the truth she could, would pass

49

away if she didn't take it now. Clumsily, she must try to pretend that they were still young girls, proud of having no secrets, proud of the ability to say terrifying, damaging things to each other.

"I know everyone thinks it's terrible that I go away and leave the children. I know they think it's disgraceful that we can't stick to anything." Lucy paused, and she saw that Mary's face was heavy with emotion. She was like a child, gratefully partaking of some choice confidence. Lucy thought sadly that there must always be women like Mary in the world, women with faces that showed deep concern over every triviality, women who wore the drawn brow of sympathy like an emblem, who specialized in the quick, hushed, understanding reply. Now, she had nothing to say. Whatever she hoped to tell had vanished. "I simply cannot live here," she said and turned away.

"But Marian is just at the stage when she needs advice. She doesn't seem to know one person from another. You know, doesn't understand the *difference*," Mary said mysteriously. "I have seen cars full of wild-looking girls and boys out here. Not often, of course. But when that strange crowd isn't here, there's no one. It's nothing, but either she's starting out wrong or . . . well, she just isn't starting out at all!"

Mary's large, anxious face made Lucy want to laugh. "I'm sure she can take care of herself. She's quite grown, so far as I can tell. And then she has her grandmother, you know. I couldn't do anything, Mary. You know that."

Mary did not seem dissatisfied. She shook her head, as if she were solemnly swearing to keep this sacred trust between them. She drew close to Lucy and her eyes burned with a deep intensity. "Lucy," she said quickly, "I had an abortion! A long time ago. About six years . . . in April!" Lucy took her hand and found that it was trembling. She was certain that Mary had never told anyone before. Some immense relief shook the sturdy woman, as though by confession she had erased the act.

Lucy heard Marian laugh suddenly and say, "How silly! Papa, you know that isn't right!" She reminded herself to ask Marian about her friends.

"Well, I'm not so certain it's so silly," Ted said awkwardly. "If a man's in a position to do you a favor like this friend of mine then it seems only natural that I'd go to him first!"

Lucy and Mary sat quietly listening to the conversation inside the house. After a moment, Mary said, "See how nice it is to be here. Marian loves both of you. I know it. You should hear the way she talks about you, how much she wants to know about you. She worries, too. Whenever I see her on the street, I ask her what she has heard from you and she seems so happy to tell me all the good things."

Lucy did not answer. She couldn't concentrate upon Mary's words because she was listening to her husband. Since she was not looking at him, she was able to hear him with a bitter clarity. "Now, in business you've got to learn to . . ." he was saying. How stupid he sounds, she thought, how vague and uncertain. Even with his own daughter he did not have the finality, the crude, tactless certainty men like Lucy's father had had. His mind had no connection with his powerful, agile body. He sounded clumsy and it frightened her. She herself had never had an argument with him, because they never discussed anything except in terms of expectation.

She heard Marian contradict him on a point, and his voice rose in a pompous, trivial rebuttal. Lucy did not follow the conversation; she listened only to the pitch of the voices. Is this uncertainty something new? she wondered. Her body was tense and dismayed. She had not been aware until now how much she had taken from her husband, how she had made him a failure to match herself. Because he had a limited flair for business which not even his nomadic

51

life could entirely destroy, she had always imagined him brilliant and forceful. She had always been certain he would prosper. But the voice she heard now was unimportant, the voice of a man with unpaid bills, petty dishonesties, and crumbling pride. She had never allowed him to stay long enough in one place to accumulate the trappings of character and strength. It seemed that each new place crowded her out, because he settled into it so very easily. Wherever he worked he found friends. He quickly said, "The Johnsons and the Smiths are nice" and introduced her to the drunken wives of his colleagues. She was afraid of these people, because she had not had enough satisfaction to want friendship. She wanted him alone, across a silent table, or beside her in the automobile. She wanted to share sunsets with him, to feel the cold wind at midnight, to awaken with him in a quiet room at dawn without memories of the night before, without the everlasting resumption of last night's gossip, without reference to new personalities. She had dragged him on and on in her search for privacy, going toward that last edge of the world where a man and a woman are left utterly alone. It had seemed to her that if she could have this solitude, could achieve some union with this man, could gain some ultimate and final knowledge of him and herself, if she could know what distracted him when he sat in the chair by the table pretending to read the evening paper, what restlessness lay behind his eyes when he would suddenly smile weakly at her—then she would be satisfied. Hearing him speak to his daughter had made her ashamed, but she had not the power to give him back what she had taken from him. And he too had not the power to be more than he was.

Mary snapped the lock on her purse. Her large bosom heaved sadly. "Stay here, Lucy," she said. "It isn't any different from the other places, is it? Your mother's getting old, too. Remember that."

Lucy was silent. There was nothing more to be said between them. She held out her hand to Mary who was standing solemnly on the porch steps. They parted mutely, but not without sadness and feelings of loss. They had tried to share secrets again, but growing older had robbed them of the ability to share. They were more alone than ever for their effort.

As Mary walked up the street leaving Lucy alone again, the conversation inside the house moved on to a different level.

"Suppose I don't find anyone I want to marry?" Marian said.

"But that's easy," her father said, laughing. "There's always someone you want to marry, seems like. If that's the only trouble you run into, you'll . . ."

CHAPTER FOUR

A FULL moon was shining behind the barn. It shone down on the hubcaps of the cars parked around the frame building and beyond that the moonlight fell upon the dark, rolling farm land in the distance. There were about twenty cars parked on the sides of the barn and each car must have brought a load, because there were easily two hundred people inside. Albert had seen them riding on the running boards, their jackets flopping in the wind and spit dripping down on their chins. The night air was cool and clean if one kept away from the door of the barn. In the building the air was mysteriously and foully transformed into the odor of cheap whiskey, cigarettes, and sweat. The atmosphere in the barn was conglomerate and stale and yet it had some of the awkward gaiety of the simple, damaged people. In the field the rich scent of manure and weeds filled the tense night.

He stood outside the barn and listened to the voices of the people. A young couple stood behind an automobile and drank from a bottle. Their voices were low and humming, hushed and yet excited and convivial. Albert heard the deep intakes of breath and the brief gasp of resistance to the whiskey as it flowed down the raw throats; after that the red, oval-shaped glow of a cigarette appeared in the darkness. For no reason at all, he began to think of his sister, Marian, and of Bruce. The thought made him uncomfortable and he erased them from his mind.

After a while he walked through the barn door; he entered the place slowly, tentatively, because he felt foolishly alone. In the brightly lighted, haphazard and raucous atmosphere of the building, he had a disturbing awareness of the incongruity of his body in such surroundings. He was as sharp, lithe, and curious as a glistening dagger. Near the slow-eyed people, he was mysteriously alert and complex. Among these brutally overt images, his own face seemed to him a baffling mask and he wondered how he appeared to the eyes that caught his for a moment and then shifted away. At home tonight he had had somewhat the same feeling. When his mother looked at him, he felt alone and out of place. When his father forced him to perform a kind of masculine duet for the women at the table, Albert had experienced this intensity of self that was both timid and proud. Looking about him, he observed that he was stronger than many of the farmers who were skinny without proportion, stalklike. But he was alone and had never before seen a cock fight. He imagined his ignorance of the sport was displayed on his face. In the center of the barn was a pit and above the pit were several rows of bleachers filled with spectators. There was nothing going on in the pit now and most of the people were moving around on the side lines. The hot dog and soft drink stands were busy and everywhere the sound of crackling, country voices mingled with the anxious clucks of the fowls in the coops.

Albert looked over the group, hoping to recognize some of the faces. In a general way he knew everyone; knew their clothing and the inevitable turn and color of their conversation. The faces here were the same faces he saw in town on Saturday night; these bodies blocked traffic in front of the five and ten when they came in from the country; they stood on the courthouse steps and listened to the legless banjo player. They were part of the world he had always known, though he could not identify one person. If he had had a friend with him, his nervous voice would have risen above the crowd in intimate, obscure conversation that would have shamed the country people; if he were not alone, perhaps his deficiencies and sense of being different could have become exalted and cherished things. Slyly, he looked over the group and wondered what he could make of it. Already the place had the suffused and profound glow of an after-image, and he was careful to secure the substance of the evening in his mind. Already he was imagining how he would tell his friends about the barn, the incredible, slick-haired women, and the peculiarly apt obscenities the men whispered to each other. He felt as if he were an exotic traveler on some amazing journey. The home he had left just a few hours before did not seem real to him. He was not the one who had meals with his grandmother and his sister; he was not the boy who was the son of the man and woman visiting in the house. A tall man with a saddle nose and loose chin managed the negotiations in the pit. He was talking with two farmers who held birds in their arms. Since cock fighting was illegal, there was on many faces that agitated expression one finds among bookie attendants, an expression of perfunctory and rather pleasant worry.

Shined shoes, stiff, shallow hats, dresses of thin, gaudy cotton, and tinted cheeks: the deadening monotony of people in the unchartered outskirts of small towns milled about Albert. There was not even a young and unattended boy from whom he might, cautiously and intently, ask a match. He heard two men talking and sat by them so that he wouldn't appear so conspicuously alone. The men were having a friendly argument. One was a tiny man, not more than five feet, with a fat stomach that bulged out of his trousers. The stomach did not seem to belong to the little man and it made him look like a very young boy costumed and padded for a fat man's role. The other man, a medium-sized, red-faced farmer with hands like picnic hams, kept calling the little man Pony. The farmer was known as Ace and he kept clapping his big hands down on Pony's shoulders.

"I tell you I saw that rooster in the coop and it sure looked to me like it had been doing settin' up exercises . . . Strong enough to fight a drunk nigger," Pony said.

Ace looked toward Albert and laughed. "Pony, you don't know a rooster from a hen," he said. "I know that bird and he's got no more fight in him than a purring pigeon. It knows as much about cock fighting as a sow does about being Chinese Ambassador."

Pony jumped into the air, as though he were preparing to take flight. He waved his stunted arms about miserably as Ace talked on. "For a man who used to ride the horses, you sure got a blind eye about animals," Ace said.

"Listen, Ace," Pony said. "I never chew my cabbage twice. I asked you once to make a bet with me on this fight and if you don't want to just say so." Pony had a nasal voice. He spaced and clipped his words with a strained and precise deliberation, not without sadness. As he talked, his tiny pink eyes looked grimly at the listener, as though he feared he handled the language incorrectly because of his stunted body.

"I'm not taking your money," Ace said slowly and with relaxed humor. "I just can't look at your face when that rooster starts laying a speckled egg in the pit." He shook his head, and winked at Albert. "Honest, I don't believe you even know chicken shit when you see it," he added.

"I ain't asking you to worry about my money," Pony squeaked. "I'm able to look after myself in this game. If you don't want to bet, I'll just get someone else."

"Maybe this man will bet with you," Ace said, pointing to Albert.

Albert's small, blunt hand grasped the lapel of his coat. He could not speak immediately, because he was not certain what the men expected of him. Did they find him privileged and, though unlike themselves, friendly and easy?

57

Did they notice his dress, his smile? The two men beside him were rough and casual, warm and yet unpredictable as ignorance. They were strangers to complexity and wonder, but he must keep paces ahead of them, must anticipate and govern. He distrusted his own face, because he knew it was marked with the tense emblems of all minorities. It was stamped irrevocably with the minority's immense consciousness of self and immense doubt about the way it appeared to others.

Pony pressed his lips together and waited until Albert said, "Sure, I'll bet with you."

"You see that man with the hat on? The one in the ring," Pony said. "Well, I'm betting on the bird he's got in his arms. The fat gray one." Pony arched his eyebrows and his forehead was filled with tiny wrinkles.

"I'll tell you," he said generously to Albert, "you ain't got a dog's chance of beating me. I looked both of 'em over and I know that the stringy bird hasn't got the chance of a feather in the wind." He paused and then added, "But if you want to bet just for the fun of it, all right."

Ace said, "Pony used to be on the track. He was thrown off for doping himself instead of the horses. That's how smart Pony is."

"Aw, bear's ass," Pony said.

Albert noticed that Pony was wearing a tight leather jacket which was too small even for him. It wasn't much bigger than a child's sweater around the chest, and the sleeves hit the little man almost at the elbow and made him look smaller and more pitiable than he actually was. The jacket, impoverished and trifling, angered Albert.

Pony's small, dry face turned to Albert. "You know," he said, "I've got what's known as gambler's ears. Some people, like Ace here, bet with their noses. He thinks he can smell a winner, but with me it's a different thing. I've had it all my life. When I was just a kid"—he put his hand about three feet from the floor to indicate his youth—"I used to

58

hang around the track all the time. I'd look at the horses just before they come out of the paddock, and it's the damndest thing, but sometimes I come across a horse that would make my ears tingle. Feel like they was on fire, with needles punching in 'em. It'd seem like it was all I could do to keep the ears on my head. They'd begin talking and whispering to me every time I'd stand by this certain horse. Alongside the other horses, I didn't seem to have no ears at all . . . I always knew a winner just by the way my ears felt."

"I expect that was the devil talking to you, Pony. Or earwax humming, probably," Ace said.

Pony ignored Ace. His nasal speech droned on in Albert's ear.

"Tonight when I saw the gray bird in the coop, I felt the same thing. My ears commence to pester me. Seemed like a fly got inside and was buzzing around." Pony paused for a moment to reflect. "Still want to bet with me?" he continued. "I'm trying to play fair with you, because I know everyone don't have this gift of mine. I never heard of anyone else with it. Just thought I'd tell you before the fight begins." Ace pulled a bottle out of his jacket and offered Albert a drink. Not wanting it, but not knowing how to refuse, Albert took the bottle. The drink went through him like an angry quiver, but, when the first shock of the whiskey subsided, he wanted to laugh. He suddenly felt happy to be here alone and remembered with both pity and incomprehension his sister's fantastic efforts to move in the parents' orbit. He was proud of his own solitary paths.

From his seat in the bleachers, Albert had a complete view of the crowd. Out of what had been a strange and jumbled group, he found that one or two of the faces began to take prominence in his mind. The vague and panoramic became particular and local when he attached his attention, quite accidentally, to a few faces and articles of clothing.

Comforting symbols emerged—the feather of a hat, a squint eye, a peculiar walk and a certain reminiscent smile. He noticed a woman standing in the front of the pit. She was thin and had a rather large head. Her hair was parted in the middle and drawn down into two old-fashioned buns over her ears. The woman was standing directly under the light and Albert could see the extraordinarily wide part in the middle of her head. The part was a heavy white color, in contrast to her dark hair, and it looked as if someone had taken a piece of chalk and had drawn the flaky white line. Her face was long, yet it was broad at the forehead and she had heavy lids and popped, thyroidic eyes. That was all he could see of her, because the people shifted and soon she was lost in the crowd. He did not look for her, since he was not interested. It was only that her strikingly annoying appearance stayed in his memory.

The barn was rather hot, though the country air outside was cool. Most of the people wore coats and dots of perspiration stood out on their lips and foreheads. Now the saddle-nosed man was in the ring with two birds, the owners having moved out and left their candidates to their fates. Though the birds were heeled with two-and-a-half inch spurs, Albert thought they looked surprisingly mild and dumb. There was such an easy contrast between the physical appearances of the contestants that they immediately caught the enthusiasm of the audience. Pony's choice was fat, with a plump body and proud smooth feathers. The other was peaked and stringy, plucked and scalded looking, with a beak that was a sharp, shining point.

The fat bird moved around the pit, vain and patriarchal, as though he were looking for grain to slip into his throat. The other bird waited. They still might have been on exhibition at a county fair. Then the fight, or what there was to be of a fight, began. It was difficult for Albert to see what happened, because his attention was diverted by Pony's yells and predictions and by the little man telling him what he was seeing now and what he would be seeing when the fat bird got into his stride. The emotion which Pony and Ace put into the cock fight was impossible to Albert. The barn suddenly seemed almost unbearably hot to him. He would smile at the two men beside him, but when he opened his mouth for conversation with them his voice was strangely timid and he thought that he saw them smile nervously.

When the contact between the birds was established, the stringy one dug into the fat one with practiced force. The steel spurs plunged into the soft breast with an automatic rhythm, a weary aggressiveness. Albert's eyes followed the spurs. The skill with which the weapon was manipulated thrilled him. The spur itself looked like a ridiculous ornament. However, in spite of the innocent appearance, the spur was driving into the corpulent, regal bird, punching through the feathers and into the skin. The thin bird threw himself up in the air like a puppet on a string, so that he might strike more effectively. Chicken feathers were now spread over the dirt bottom of the pit and they kept falling like thin scales.

Pony was yelling, "Don't get worried! The queen takes a long time to warm up. She's slow, but she gets there." People turned around to laugh at the jockey.

Albert felt a whirling sensation inside his stomach. "It must be this heat. This goddamned, squeezing heat," he said to himself. The sensation brought about another agony: the feeling that his face was becoming distorted. He imagined that the soft curves of his body and face were being drawn into taut lines. The smoke in the barn and the heat from the whiskey seemed to be discoloring him. Heavy black shadows filled in the hollows of his cheeks and his chin felt small and stuffed.

The sensation of illness came upon him quickly. Yet, even in his discomfort, he forced himself to pretend to watch the fight. He saw the woman with her hair parted

61

in the middle standing on the right side of the pit and it seemed to him that her eyes were almost popping out of her head. They were pushing out with such intensity that the skin around them was pulled into curly wrinkles.

Pony's face, too, began to look horrible. The features, so tiny and childlike, were, under the tension of the fight, becoming heavy and bulbous. A lock of hair stood up on Pony's head and made him look like a foolish imp.

The big gray bird was going down like a whining balloon. Warm blood gushed through its feathers. The startled and defenseless bird retreated and Albert saw its red eyes, craven and wild, peering blindly through the stabbed head. A jab here and there from the ragged urchin cock and the royal purple declined, without grace, the splendor dropping bit by bit.

"That bird's sick!" Pony yelled hoarsely. "Something's happened to him. Put him back in the pit. He needs time to warm up."

Ace laughed, but he didn't seem very happy. The quick defeat of the fat bird, even though he had predicted it, rather depressed him.

"Say, I got to go outside for a minute," Albert mumbled when the fight was over. The uncomfortable eyes of the men looked deeply into his face. He reached up to smooth down the blond wing of his hair. The men looked at each other quickly, tensely.

"I haven't paid you off yet," Pony said softly.

Albert waved him aside.

"What's a matter, you sick?" the little man said. "You're as pale as an old maid's ass."

"It's just hot in here. I've got to get some air. It's just the heat, that's all . . ." Albert said. Speaking required an enormous effort. The barn and the people around the pit were losing their shape; they were merely lines and movements before his eyes and he himself was losing his identity. He was falling into an incredibly humiliating blankness. There

62

was only enough pride left in him to make him try to hide his condition from Pony and Ace.

"I think you're sick," Pony said. "I think you're going to throw up. Well, worse things can happen. When I was on the track, I stuck my finger down my throat so much I couldn't puke now if I wanted to."

"It's just hot," Albert whispered. He stepped away from them, but Pony followed after him.

"Say, you're nothing but a kid. Ace shouldn't of give you that drink."

"Maybe not," Ace said.

Albert wanted to strike out at Pony, but he could not. The little man pulled him, drooling and dripping, to the door of the barn. When they finally got into the field, Albert gave full vent to the convulsive and urgent sensation inside him. With that over, he forgot the two men and began to feel a feeble, beautiful happiness. For a time it seemed that he was quite alone in the world, that the fields, the sky and the breeze belonged to him alone because he needed them so greatly. In the loneliness of the night, the image of the woman with the scaly, chalky part in her hair came back to him. She stood over him and snow began to fall from her, snow that both cooled and smothered him at the same time. The moon in the sky seemed to be a tiny circle cast in the middle of the field and the trees were straight, black lines, convoluting, turning and pulling themselves into queer shapes around the permanence of the circle. The circle was motionless, an anchor in the whirling bewilderment that came from his sick body. He had fallen face up on the ground, and the moon was shining through his closed eyelids.

Then Pony's voice, squeaking and whining, came brutally into his consciousness. "Come on back in," Pony said. "You got that rot gut out of you. Come on back in and see the next fight. Hell, Ace should never of give that poison to a kid like you. It even makes me belch once in a while."

Albert wanted to rise from the ground and beat Pony into a tiny heap of leather and squeals. He wanted to tell him that he was ugly and ignorant, undesirable. And he wanted to go inside and find the woman and jerk her hair out. Her horrible, flaky hair. But he was sick again and could not move. Pony and Ace left him in the field.

He lay back on the ground. The wind carried the noise from the barn out to him. The noise was loud and thrilling now, like news coming over a radio. He had the sensation of experiencing something singular and stirring, something which he dominated and made exciting and humorous. He was lying on the ground and the cool air was blowing over him and yet he was close enough to the people to be part of the cock fight. The voice of the saddle-nosed man announcing the next pair of fighters excited him and he felt a pleasant tension over the outcome, a tension which he was already beginning to verbalize as he would when he next saw his friends. The whole scene—the barn, Pony and his shrunken leather jacket, the country people with their hot dogs and kerosene liquor—became brilliantly real and interesting. Over the beer glasses, across the unknown space between him and a stranger at a bar, above the muffled giggles and admiration of his friends, the scene would live once more. Pony and Ace would be there, shadowy and partially undelineated as if Albert knew secrets about them which the listeners could not share; but they would be there, the little men, strangely potential.

Albert looked up at the pale sky. He began to like the sport of cock fighting, from his retreat in the meadow. Striking a match to look at his watch, he found that it was late. The family would be asleep when he got home and that, too, made him strangely happy.

CHAPTER FIVE

Mrs. GORMAN spent most of her time in her bedroom. The days were always the same for her. There were waiting hours, between breakfast and lunch, hours of no particular stress and in which she walked blankly from bedroom to bath, or stood silently before her mirror and ran the comb through her hair and dropped the loose strands into the wastebasket. In the morning the pale dressing gown was never removed, as if she had developed a supreme discipline which forbade the doing of any ritualized act before the appointed time. At the stroke of one, she seemed to experience a modified haste and while lunch waited on the table, she took off the dressing gown and put on a gray dress. After lunch, in the first hours of the early afternoon, she slept: a solemn, utterly accepted sleep, as if it were the dead of night. She awakened refreshed, her face blank and soft, almost poreless. From then until dusk she had countless duties to perform, none of which took her beyond her room. The corners, the shelves of her closets, were filled with boxes which were the substance of her activities, and she guarded them as sacred, untouchable things. There were boxes filled with scraps of cloth which she would sit over and peer at curiously, as if she were solving a puzzle. On the floor were stacks of magazines which, on certain appointed days, she took in her lap, and flipped through slowly, gazing over and over at marked pictures. Then the whole batch would slip down to the floor again, for she had decided that each one must be kept. For other days, there were pictures and papers in her desk. At this time in the afternoon, Hattie came into the room for her hasty cleaning. While the girl was there, Mrs. Gorman gave especial attention to her collection.

Today she had on her lap a box filled with buttons. She took each button out singly, held it up to the light, and ran her thumb over the shell. Sometimes she would stack the buttons one on top of the other to measure size and then, bringing them very close to her eyes, she looked at the thread holes to see which were alike and which different. Ted and Lucy had been in the house for several days now and the grandmother had begun to tire of them. She tired of people very quickly, because she had little interest in their problems. There was always noise in the living room now and sometimes when she sat there in the evening and acknowledged the heads turned toward her and saw the smiling faces, a certain feeling of pride was aroused. But this wore off quickly, because her vanity was not great, or at least it was not of an ordinary kind. She knew that the family made special conversation for her benefit, but her listening and response to it were mechanical. When she was silent they no doubt thought she was thinking and dreaming deeply of life. In reality she was incapable of thought, incapable of judgment and evaluation of any event of the slightest complexity. What she did have was surely unknown to the world. She had an animal interest in the clash between the sexes and in the precise animal nature of her family.

In her cloistered existence and from her sense of already having slept a lifetime in a forbidden dream, she had developed an indefatigable fascination with this one aspect of life. Though her frail beauty, the mysterious withered arm which had made her physically reticent, her quiet upbringing and marriage, made it impossible for her to give verbal expression to her interest, she had knowledge of an

66

almost frightening degree about the hidden violence of unions between the sexes.

When Hattie entered the bedroom to run the functionless carpet sweeper over the floor, Mrs. Gorman suddenly dropped the box of buttons and sat there watching the girl. When Hattie, head down, came to the carpet beneath her chair, Mrs. Gorman lifted her feet several inches from the floor, and turned her neck slightly to avoid dust. She was like a primitive woman constantly under the taboo of some critical woman-stage which forbade her to move or to participate in any domestic functions. Her serene inactivity was cherished as if it were a sacred duty. Having always been in this seemingly predestined state of privileged restriction as young bride, pregnant wife, and beloved matriarch, she had become accustomed to acceptance. While she watched the young black girl work around her inert body in the chair, she neither moved nor felt guilt for not moving. As a Fijian woman in the first hundred days of pregnancy may not go fishing lest the nets break, so Mrs. Gorman could not in any way alter her position for fear she might lose it entirely.

Hattie's eyes avoided those of the old woman. They seldom spoke to each other. In one way the grandmother and the girl were equal: in disinterest. Hattie was a part of the house and yet she was not subject to its disappointments, hopes, and terrors. When the doorbell rang, there could be no news, however good or disastrous, in which the girl was implicated. Her footprints, her desires, her preferences could be seen everywhere in the house, but if they had been erased she would not have cared. She did not share in the stings of possession. When she left them at night, she was lost to them. When she closed the door, murder, burglary, or fire might in the darkness engulf them, but she who had tended and arranged the house, fed the residents, would not be the principal mourner.

As Mrs. Gorman watched the girl, she wondered if she

had a lover, a young man, or perhaps a very old one. She imagined Hattie's life in terms of the pictures in the detective magazines which were hidden in her room. Poor houses to Mrs. Gorman were always like the houses in these pictures: a frame building stuffed with rotting paper. And the poor world outside her house was divided into victim and killer. The victim with sagging breasts and an old, unraveling sweater around her shoulders; the killer, a grisly, vague-eyed man, always wearing overalls. In her vivid imagination for transgressions, Mrs. Gorman endowed Negroes with a particularly active capacity for immense sinfulness.

The girl went out of the room and Mrs. Gorman pinned back her curtains so that she might see what went on in the garden. At first, her daughter Lucy appeared and the grandmother heard the humming of her thin soprano voice. Lucy's shoulders were a bit stooped and she walked slowly around the garden. She took careful steps as if she feared haste might interfere with the pleasure she found in sights and sounds. She would stop suddenly and look at a cloud formation in the sky or, without warning, stoop to the ground to uproot a weed or two. Despite the factual data of her wandering life, she was not a woman made for restlessness. There was no disorder about her, no flagging of interest in the known and familiar. It was the familiar she most loved. Her hands were strong and possessive and she drew objects of love to her with a finality and faith which fatigued others. Her possessiveness did not extend very far; she did not care much for clothing or jewelry nor for any kind of munificence. But, on the other hand, she would cherish a particular set of china or a little trinket with an insatiable fury. It was this type of desire, the need for the minute and specified article that gave her face its peculiar, bitter loneliness. She might have had big things, houses and friends and money, but apparently she could not have the solitary ownership of the little familiarities.

Watching her, Mrs. Gorman thought absently, Lucy has such long, thin feet. The kind that seem to be stuck like a shoe tree into the shoe. The kind with the long, rigid bone. Men don't like such feet. Men don't.

She saw Lucy stop abruptly when her husband came into sight. He was smoking a cigar and the back of his shirt was damp with perspiration. The hot afternoon made him impatient. Feeling impotent against it, he had a sort of simple-minded, outraged expression on his face, as if he had to keep smiling stupidly while being struck. His mouth was open slightly and when he grasped the cigar end between his teeth and tried to talk through them, he seemed to be harshly scolding someone. His back was to Mrs. Gorman and she noticed again how tall and strong he was. All the members of his family had been tall, rather grim people of pious honesty and thrift. They were literal and dominating. When the marriage between Ted and Lucy was being planned, the Colemans came several times to the house and Ted's mother was driven almost to distraction by the evasive conversation of Mrs. Gorman, the weakness and lack of specificity in all plans evolved by this family. She was restless and angry and she could not sit around the house waiting for breakfast, staring placidly at the confusion of the crowded, drowsy rooms. The second day she was in the house, she got out the mops and with the shocked help of an old colored woman cleaned the place thoroughly. With her face set in a resolute expression, she threw away everything on the tops of undusted shelves and emptied musty closets. Soon after, she left. One of Ted's brothers hanged himself after bankruptcy, though in Ted himself the blazing fear of damnation and failure was unknown. But he had the body of his family, the tall, firm, faintly middle-aged masculinity. Beside him the thin, stooped wife rubbing a blade of grass through her fingers looked like a country woman or, perhaps, a spinster. There was something of the dizziness of a see-saw when the two figures were seen in juxtaposition, as though the ground beneath lay patiently waiting for the loud, defeated thump of one or the other. Whenever they stood together, they seemed to enclose themselves in an airless dungeon and to stand there gasping for breath. Theirs was a compromise which had to be agreed upon and renewed daily, as if in the small interim some new condition always arose which negated the former contract.

They were standing close to the window now and Mrs. Gorman saw Ted point into the distance and she heard him say, "Niggers moving in. Niggers. Remember when the old Knox place used to be on that land?"

His wife turned her sharp face to him and her large eyes shone clear and agitated. Beneath the high profile her lips quivered slightly. "The old Knox place," she said, and her hand fell upon his arm. "The old Knox place. There were violets there in the spring and Mary and I used to put cookies in our pockets and steal in through the back gate to pick the violets. Then we would lie on the grass or swing on the rope tied to the tree beside the well . . ."

"Niggers moving in," he repeated, his voice soft and thoughtful. "It's a goddamned shame."

"In the fall, the trees . . ." she said. He turned away from her for he had seen a loose piece of paper on the grass. She watched him pick it up and take it to the garbage can beside the door. The smile remained on her face, but her eyes were cold and silent now.

She is not like me, Mrs. Gorman thought, as she watched her daughter. No, she hadn't been moody and changeable in that way. The old woman laughed softly and stared at her daughter. What does she want? What does she want? Mrs. Gorman kept saying to herself. She had been surprised from the first that Lucy had been able to get the lusty and handsome man. She had seen danger from the first. On the day of the wedding, she had watched them carefully and had noted the ferocious tenacity in her daughter's eyes, and on the face of the groom an unforgettable confusion and wonder. He had gone to the altar utterly amazed at himself. Mrs. Gorman did not for a moment imagine that his amazement came from a conscious rejection of his wife or from any particular leaning toward another woman. He had never been that deeply involved in anything. The old woman could not have verbalized her emotion regarding these two people; she would have been incapable of sustained analysis of the situation. The knowledge that she had came to her through her extraordinarily acute sense of struggle, and from her love of the intimate vulgarities. It seemed that she had inside her a powerful instrument which recorded the selected shocks.

She thought of her own husband, the chubby, good-humored Irishman, the indefatigable, joke-telling, pink-faced laundry owner. The good host, the patient listener, and the pink-blue eye which teared in distress. For a moment Mrs. Gorman forgot about the people in the garden. A satisfied smile came over her face. She was the only one who had known her husband; the only one who had seen him weep, who had watched the pink cheeks turn white with fear and astonishment when he looked at her rigid, undemonstrative face across the table. She had lived with him for the whole period of her adult life and she knew that she herself was more a man than he. Though she had come to him inhibited and ignorant, her dignified body was capable of a desire way beyond his reach. Before her marriage, no one had ever spoken to her of the nature of marriage; yet she had known from their first days together that she had been cheated. She knew also that he had married her because she was reserved, silent, and physically deformed. In his desire to protect his laughing, open joviality and to conceal his frightened, stunted instinct, he had imagined that he was playing safe. There would be no reprimand from the well-bred girl in the pale dresses; the undemonstrative face promised security. There had been no reprimand, but when she became cooler and cooler to his embraces, he began to love her fiercely. He could not bear for her to have a headache. If a frown came over her face, he abjectly prayed that the worry might be transferred to himself. Every masochistic desire in his nature was satisfied by her; he began to love her for her withered arm and to cherish the stiff, slightly off-balance way she held herself when she walked across the room. He loved to caress the undeveloped left hand and to kiss passionately each child-like, useless finger. He allowed her to do almost nothing for herself and she became more and more quiet, more and more relaxed. When he was downtown in the laundry filling his nostrils with the clean, damp steam, he liked to think of her at home in a rocking chair or on a couch, motionless, cool, dry, and smelling of talcum, her eyes resting blankly on some object in the room.

And then, to her surprise, she was pregnant. She felt somehow defeated that his passion should bear the same fruit as any other, but her senses were excited by this new circumstance. It was, perhaps, the only irony and humor she had ever found in life. When she began to grow fatter, she would often sit with her husband at night and laugh softly to herself. At last he began to laugh with her, as if they shared some secret from the world. The coming of the child aroused in him a new aggressiveness. He began to concentrate furiously upon making money and, as he became more tender at home, his public arrogance increased. During the pregnancy she sat alone all day among silk pillows and observed, with unbelieving concentration, the bodily changes she was undergoing. She built a glorious prison around herself and felt she was undergoing a blessed, unique martyrdom. Her indolence was so great, her preoccupation with herself of such magnitude that she was like an enormously powerful and privileged goddess. Never having been very active, she now ceased to move altogether. There was no indication that she understood fully the end and purpose of her confinement. Perhaps she really did not know, since words never meant anything much to her and she had knowledge only from experience. Perhaps she thought her cherished state was endless and that she would grow and grow in this soft lassitude toward no end. In any case, she was utterly stunned and bewildered when the shock of childbirth actually arrived. Adoring husband, home, and beauty were scraped from her consciousness with one stroke. She was alone in the way that one can only be when pain is involved. She was wretchedly reduced to the body that she had a few hours ago found so interesting. She never got over the pain. She felt that some horrible and unexpected grief had drained her of all her blood and warmth.

Mrs. Gorman saw that Marian had now joined her parents in the garden. They sat under the tree and talked. Mrs. Gorman had no idea what was to become of the girl. If she had been asked, she would probably have said that she expected her to marry. The old woman was aware that Marian was reluctant to ask her directly for money and she was rather confused about this. The grandmother would have been pleased if the girl had come crying to her for money to be spent foolishly. She would have given it gladly, even though her income was disappearing, because she had profound convictions about a woman's right to be spoiled. When it occurred to her, Mrs. Gorman told Marian to go downtown and charge a dress or a pair of shoes. The money for the music lessons came from the parents and when no money arrived, the lessons were not taken. In every way the grandmother found Albert a more normal person than Marian; he was constantly asking her for money, he lied and schemed and made his secret way. Mrs. Gorman had overheard Marian telling all her young friends to stay away from the house during the parents' visit. She said openly that she wished to be at home every minute because she saw her mother so very infrequently. Albert was more natural. The visit did not alter him in any way. And yet

Mrs. Gorman had recognized the possibility that the grand-daughter was teeming with plans and that she might, some day, shock them all.

The first appearance of Bruce astounded the grand-mother. She found herself embroiled in a completely un-foreseen drama. The young, snub-nosed boys Marian knew were boring, but Bruce was different. She grew more im-patient daily and could hardly wait for the crisis of the new relationship. In the afternoons she was reluctant to take her nap, because she liked to spy on Marian. At first she had thought that the seduction—she was certain of that much—would take place immediately, because Marian had not the vanity to prevent it. She watched for signs of it in her granddaughter, in a fresh solitude or worry, or perhaps a sudden gregariousness or interest in clothes, whatever form the change might take. So far, she could detect noth-ing.

Late in the afternoon, Bruce came into the garden. Mrs. Gorman pulled her curtain back a little more. The four of them stood in a circle, and she could hear the laughter of the two men, and could see Marian's body turning away from the other three as if in shame. All the excitement in the situation was confined to the girl. It was she who felt an agony that Bruce, the mysterious and personal new friend, should be there with her parents. She imagined that all of them detected the enormous emotion she felt. The grandmother saw the girl's body tremble slightly, and her teeth move up and down over her lower lip. The parents and Bruce were talking; they were quite oblivious to the tenseness of the fourth person.

Bruce was telling a story. There was a certain weariness and insinuation in his voice, a polite injection of impolite matters. He could not lift his voice or laugh or reflect, with-out in some way shrewdly indicating that he had dipped himself into every cesspool of the world and had come out interesting, enviable, filled with the most coveted knowledge. Somehow the reminiscent laziness of his voice, the almost brutal clarity of his personality, the surfeit marked on his face reminded Mrs. Gorman of the people around the old summer home they had once had. As she listened to Bruce, she could hear Virgil Pike's banjo strumming again in the morning air, and she remembered the smell of slop jars in the Pikes' house. She lost interest in the people in the garden and began to relive that old summer.

Mrs. Gorman and the colored woman were carrying provisions up the hill to the summer house when she had first seen the Pikes' place. It was a square, boxy, gray-white house built at the curve of the road. Red and green paper Christmas wreaths, browned at the edges, hung in the window the year round. The first thing she saw was the amazing color of the kimono the Pike girl was wearing. Edna Pike sat on the porch of the cottage from sunup to sundown in this outlandish, many-colored kimono. Her face was heavily painted, with even a big round spot of rouge on her chin and around the corners of her eyes.

"Godamighty!" the colored woman whispered when she saw the girl.

Mrs. Gorman put down her bundles and stared at the figure. The colored woman jerked at her sleeve, but she brushed her away coldly.

The girl, noticing the women, jumped up on the stoop of the porch and began to do a wild dance. "See anything green!" she yelled out to Mrs. Gorman. "Lick it up clean!"

Then a banjo started inside the house and a man's voice called out, "Shut up that yelling!"

Mrs. Gorman walked past the girl and went along the side of the house. Through the window she could see the young man with the banjo. His feet were propped up on a chair and he sang to the ceiling. He wore a dirty pair of overalls. Virgil Pike sang in a weary, mountaineer tenor. There was not a great deal of music in him and his singing seemed to come from a deep and shattering boredom. He sang swiftly,

75

sometimes off key, aimlessly, as men whittle away a piece of wood. There, sitting before the bug-stained window, it appeared that he could no longer remember useful movement, that he had, for some reason, given into a laziness so profound that it was like the presence of death in his hard bones. His eyes flickered only the tiniest bit when he saw Mrs. Gorman standing beside the window. He had the relaxed gaze of country people, the expressionless patience of men who had sat for generations in front of the country store, who had watched and waited so long that they had lost all reason to react. Mrs. Gorman was close enough to smell the sourness of his overalls and when she and the Negro woman proceeded on up the hill, the rich, male sourness remained in her nostrils.

The child was left in the city with a nurse and Mrs. Gorman and her companion stayed in the country place alone until, on the week-ends, Mr. Gorman and his friends joined them. The first night she was unable to sleep because of the boisterous activity in the house below the hill. She had never before heard such noises and the wild laughter, shrill and boastful as a cock's crowing, was new to her. The sister's high voice with her savage, monotonous screams came clearly to her. Mrs. Gorman could not decide whether the girl was happy or angry, because there was an absence of definite emotion in the outrageously sustained screamings. At times there was the thump of dancing. Virgil's banjo became more discordant, and she could tell that it passed from hand to hand during the revelry. From the faces she had seen around the store, she was able to imagine what people were in the house. The disturbing, senseless tranquillity of the country men was no doubt being released in the noise they made for the bored country girls.

The night was endless. She lay there waiting for the morning, as if she were to approach then some great event for which sleep could not prepare her. She had not yet grown accustomed to the summer place. She was frightened by the shadowed corners of the bedroom, the articles of furniture outlined by the moonlight. Her life at home vanished and when she tried to recall the feeling of sleep in her own bed she could not. She felt that something new was trailing her. Something sinister lay about her, without past or future. She did not feel that she moved or ate or thought or talked in the same way as she did in town. A slow, strong abandon crept over her and she felt completely stripped of personality, position, and wifehood. She sat like a phantom and breathed for the first time magnificently impersonal air. There were strangers to whom she was inscrutable for they could never know the life she had left or the peculiarities of the new situation into which she was traveling. She was very young at this time and a fierce danger and excitement invaded her naturally; the danger came upon her with the momentum of some predestined stage which the blood and flesh only half-recognized, and she did not combat it.

During the long night, Mrs. Gorman kept saying to herself, She'll kill him someday. As sure as anything, she'll kill him. In the picture she had of the wild Edna and the handsome brother there was an ultimately intolerable opposition. His indolence would betray him. He would sit in the house with the banjo on his lap, but he was unwilling, or unable, to release the force necessary to crush what Mrs. Gorman imagined to be the witchery of his sister. He let the girl sit on the porch and strike out at the world with the sullen, mock-gaiety of a prostitute, and all he could do was to yell at her with no more energy than he would use to swat a fly.

At last the noise from the Pike house subsided, and Mrs. Gorman went to sleep. She had not the courage to go to the house the next day, but she passed it on her way to the grocery store. Virgil was not in sight, but Edna Pike still sat on the porch in the bright kimono and skirmished verbally with the men across the road.

"I guess you're about the prettiest thing around here," a man with a lean face full of dull sexuality called to her.

Edna shook her untidy hair violently and yelled back in her monotonous voice, "Aw, chicken butt!" The men liked to prod her into curses and obscenity and when she talked their faces lighted up with laughter and the tobacco juice dripped down on their chins and lay congealed there like dried sap on bark.

"They got an old aunt in there so sick she can't eat," the man behind the grocery counter said to Mrs. Gorman. "That Edna won't even give her a drink of water."

The next morning Mrs. Gorman knocked at the door with a plate of food for the aunt. She looked very clean and composed and she saw a strange confusion come over Virgil when he found her standing there with the covered dish. He wore the same overalls. His face was a parched tan color and the tan went down his neck to the opening of his shirt collar.

He rubbed his hand over his mouth and smiled shyly. "Christ amighty," he said, "if Edna sees this before Auntie she'll gobble it all up."

Virgil led Mrs. Gorman to the bed of his aunt and let her look down on the shrunken, twisted, slowly dying body. "Here you are, Auntie," he said softly, pushing the plate before her. He smiled childishly and with great embarrassment. And then after a moment he looked at Mrs. Gorman as if to say, "What am I gonna do! God, what is there to do!" The old lady was incontinent and lay silently in her own filth like a monstrously malformed baby. The stench in the room was unbearable, but Mrs. Gorman stayed on a few minutes. She looked around helplessly, feeling that, being woman, she ought to be able to put the place in order with a few quick movements. But nothing constructive occurred to her, except to lay her white hand once, lightly, over the brown claw of the sick woman.

She went to the front of the house with Virgil and there

she heard Edna cursing the men across the road. "She'll kill you. Kill you, sometime," Mrs. Gorman whispered to the young man.

He looked at her curiously and laughed. "People don't understand Edna. Honest," he said. "All those men think she's after them, but Edna don't want no man. She's got a long, black skirt under that kimono, though you can't make people believe it."

An imperious fury came over Mrs. Gorman. His simple fearlessness made every bone in her body ache. "You fool! You fool!" she said hoarsely.

Outside Edna was yelling, "See anything green! Lick it up clean!"

"See there," Virgil said weakly, running his tongue over his lips. "Edna don't mean nothing."

Day after day, except on the week-ends when the guests came from town, Mrs. Gorman went to the Pikes' house. She didn't talk to them much or unbend in any way. Her visits were like those of a mailman, silent, dutiful. Everything about the people at the curve of the road had an aura of transcience which she found irresistible. Trains ran over a railing directly above their heads, as if they were a constant reminder of the fast pace of their lives. Though Mrs. Gorman could not imagine herself or any of her family dead, she could not imagine the Pikes, the men around the store, or the girls who lived beyond the fields, living very long. The country idyll had in this spot of the earth run foul. Gradually she began to see that Edna was harmless, and that the danger to Virgil lay in those drunken, weary, battling nights whose echo she heard in her house.

Quite suddenly Mrs. Gorman stopped talking to the colored woman she had brought with her from home. She wouldn't meet her eyes, wouldn't give any orders beyond what could be done by pointing. The woman was the last thing that remained of her real life, and so she refused to recognize her existence. She never went to the Pikes' house at night, but she lay awake and listened to the noise from the place. Gradually her sense of hearing became so acute that she felt she knew, down to the last detail, what went on there. Suddenly a strange voice came from the house, the voice of a woman. It was an angry country woman's voice and was usually followed by Virgil's low, apologetic laugh. She heard the woman for three nights, and at last could stand it no longer. When the colored woman had gone to sleep, she slipped out of the door and walked toward the road. A coal oil lamp was burning at the Pikes' and she could hear Virgil playing on the banjo. She crept down the hill and stood under the tree by the window. It was after midnight when she forced herself to go back to her own place. She saw Virgil and the woman alone in the room, both of them drunk. She saw the woman's hard, strong fists beating on his face. She returned to her house and went immediately to sleep. What she had seen didn't bother her; she felt neither remorse nor shame. The only impression it left upon her was that she felt differently about the man. She found him more complex and interesting than before. When he smiled or moved like a yawning dog, it was no longer laziness. Instead it was an assurance, a power, greater than she had ever seen before.

She didn't hear the woman's voice again, and so she didn't leave the house at night until the time in early August when she heard a shot and a scream, a strange, new scream, from Edna. This was different from her old moanings; it was a cry of fright. Mrs. Gorman threw on her dress and ran down the hill. She knew what had happened. In a drunken fight, Virgil had been shot. This was the end of him, and he, like the others before him, left no traces in these raw, ignorant outskirts of the land. When she got to the house, it was very quiet. Only the moans of Edna could be heard. She had slipped off some place in the darkness to cry. Virgil's dead body lay on the bed, and his face was covered with blood. Everywhere in the room there was the sweet smell of liquor. Mrs. Gorman went to him. She pulled the dirty, bloody overalls from his body. He had on long, speckled-gray underwear with a vent opening in the back. For a long time she sat there with his body in her arms and ran her cold hand over his face and through his matted hair. She was useless and inept, and did not know how to help him. She could not even wash him. Blood stained her dress. Even a few strands of her fine hair were dipped in the blood on his breast. She let the odor of liquor and the sweaty smell of his overalls cling to her, as if she were powerless to let go. The lamp burned out, and in the darkness she left him.

As she went up the hill the strange events of this misplaced summer began immediately to fade from her mind. She looked into the darkness and wondered what she was doing out at this hour.

That was the end of the Pikes, unless she counted what her memory kept of Virgil, and the day, when summer was almost over, that the man from the grocery store came up to tell her that the old aunt was dying and needed a woman's help. She turned slowly in her chair, and her pale eyes stared into his. "I don't know those people. They wouldn't want a stranger at such a time." The confused man backed off from her porch.

Mrs. Gorman's eyes had been closed and now, as if coming out of a sleep, she returned to the scene in the garden. There they were: mother, daughter, father, lover—and now the son, Albert. Albert stood away from the group. He was smoking and there was an expression of desperate casualness on his face. He was looking downward and when a word was addressed to him he would appear pleasantly startled. He would smile shyly and then slowly drop his eyes back to the ground. He had a strange effect upon the group. His silent charm made them happy and his manner, while odd, was rather exciting.

He doesn't get it from me, the old lady thought dryly,

though physically she and Albert were somewhat alike. He gets it from his grandfather, maybe. She could see, despite the physical disparity, certain likenesses between her husband and Albert which amused her. Of these things her emotions were independent. She could not know tragedy, shame or fear, but she knew something of disguise.

There was laughter in the garden, and a kind of festive pride emanated from the people. Bruce's voice with its intimate, anecdotal quality, its abundant certainty, led the chorus and was followed by the subdued aggressions of Ted Coleman and the timed and paced interjections of Albert. Marian was watching her mother and sometimes they had a low, private conversation. Once Bruce lightly brushed her arm and the young girl looked slyly at her mother's face, as if she were rejecting the touch. Mrs. Coleman in no way indicated that she had noticed either the touch or Marian's quick glance.

Mrs. Gorman drew her curtains. She was very tired. Downstairs Hattie was beginning supper. She still had time for a short nap, and she always found it pleasant to rest with the smell of cooking rising up to her bedroom.

CHAPTER SIX

*T*HE FRONT door was open and from time to time the breeze jarred the unlatched screen and the creaking of the rusty hinges could be heard in the living room. A neighbor's car swerved onto the garage path and the sounds of scraping tires, the slamming of the car door and the clicking of the lock came through the summer night. Laid out among dark trees, house after house, street after street, was guarded by the tall arc lamps under which a thousand insects swarmed in a drunken frenzy. The black gardens were still, but laughter came from the boys and girls pressed together on the cushioned porch swings. Curtains were drawn back and heads over card tables were easily visible. In this pure depth of night everything was open, windows, doors; and shades were rolled up. Yet they were also closed, this house and that house. Perhaps it was that each light came from its own plot of ground; abrupt hedges or driveways separated the houses completely. Something confined and excluded with frantic privacy, as in the dark coldness of a winter night.

The gin Bruce had brought was making all of them heated, but it had miraculously aided the conversation which had now reached a peculiarly sad and intimate point. They were talking in low, casually reflective tones, very warm and suitable to adults who feel themselves, perhaps only momentarily, struck by the enormity of life.

"A man told me this bank business might get worse. There's no telling when it will stop," Ted Coleman said.

He did not look frightened or worried; instead he seemed only to be remembering the specific plight of the nameless man.

"Banks. The one thing you could believe in. When they start to go, you're just up a creek," Bruce said. It was impossible to tell whether or not he was interested in the conversation. There was an over-responsiveness in him, a superfluity of reaction which, after a while, diminished the power of his quick sympathies. Sometimes, however, he bit the corner of his lip and seemed to betray some residue of personality, some secret fears and ideas that were never to be expressed.

"This man I was telling you about," Coleman said. "He said he's got his and he doesn't care if he has to close down his shop."

"Well, that's nice," Marian said quickly. "That's just fine."

"I don't know whether it's nice or not. I'm just telling you what this particular fellow said." The father's voice did not alter. His eyelids lowered and he stared thoughtfully at the cigar in his fingers. His daughter was looking at him angrily, and he, realizing this, was more and more tangled in his own contradictions. There was a certain orphaned quality about this man, even when he was surrounded by his wife and children. He was never quite able to command the subtleties and the emphases of the frame of reference in which he moved. In spite of the fatherhood and adult symbols which had come to him automatically, he was a god dethroned without ever ruling, an emperor speaking from an early and impotent exile.

"I don't believe in banks," Lucy Coleman said. "I never quite believed in anything I couldn't hear clinking. Once Papa gave me a bond or something and I was terribly disappointed. I'd much rather have had a quarter. The piece of paper had no reality, if you see what I mean." She was wearing a striped cotton dress and shoes of red canvas. Her

84

bare arm was bent upward and her hand lay limply on her throat. The sun had tanned her skin lightly and her sharp, alert face looked vivid and appealing. When she spoke her voice always gave evidence of some private drama that made everyone turn to her with concentration. Now she seemed to be laughing at herself. And then abruptly she turned to her husband. "Match?" she said. He came toward her with the light and she closed her eyes, as if she had suddenly gone into a reverie.

"You know there really are a hell of a lot of people in the world," Ted Coleman said after a moment. The lines in his wide forehead deepened and he repeated, "A hell of a lot. Did you ever stop to think of it? It makes you feel right foolish."

"And most of them are foreigners," Marian said, vaguely laughing.

"Huh," her father said. He took the cigar out of his mouth and laughed. For a moment everyone looked at Marian. She crossed her legs and began fumbling in her pocket for a handkerchief.

Bruce watched the cigarette burning in his hand. His eyes were streaked with faint red lines. "Jesus, you don't know what to do," he said, as if it were now his moment on the stage. "The old man had money, made money. Even he—and I won't say he wasn't ignorant as all hell—made it. There are ways."

There was silence now. Silence for the image of Bruce's father and those like him; the little, marvelous men who could never rise to true grandeur because their beginnings would not be erased from their faces and voices. But nevertheless they were worthy and honorable, like the lesser domestic gods of the household. Bruce's father had been born in the Kentucky hills and this had given him a peculiarly folk hero quality, as if he had come out of an institution which had denied him ambition; for the fruitless, desolate hills were a sort of institution in that those who came out could only be, after the leanness, a tragic or comic demon, and he, of course, chose the tragic. They all knew the history of Bruce's father; they could see him rejecting the dry earth, turning his eyes away from the hills, looking toward the towns. The towns! The towns! He was to be an émigré, one of those who believed in the City of God, one who felt God immediately perhaps when he entered the new threshold, strong from privation, silent with envy. Mountaineer jokes came from his humorless, cautious mouth, because he knew the value of occasional clowning, and the foolishness of hard work. Unlike the émigrés from Europe, he knew that hard work was the enemy of wealth and that he who opens the store at dawn and closes at midnight is curiously unfitted for American life. There must be time for joke-telling, time for conversation on the sunlit streets. From the first his dark eyes, crafty as his jokes, saw everything with a remarkable clarity. From the first there was the vision of a woman, not a strong, pioneer woman, but a soft, petulant thing: a female just right, measured, sought and found with regard to the past, the present, and the certain future. There must be a woman placidly imprisoned behind the home walls as a symbol of the first, bold step. Men like Bruce's father did not bring their wives into the store to stand behind the counter at noontime. That would have admitted struggle, and therefore the possibility of defeat.

Bruce's face, in the shadows of the dark corner in which he was sitting, was very much like his father's, except that it was less lean and more faithless, perhaps because his father had been more lean and less faithless and had therefore absolved the son from many struggles. Bruce looked up now and said, "Jesus, America is a rich country."

Ted Coleman lifted his cigar in the air and the smoke circled around his face. "Yes, a rich country. Richest in the world, I reckon."

Lucy had been only half-heartedly listening to the conversation, but the import of masculine words seemed always to be accepted by her. She might have been listening to the reiteration of simple truths. One foot was drawn up under her in the chair and her body looked very small and young in contrast to her keen, rapacious face. "You know Mamma is so funny," she said suddenly. "I can never quite make her out. She's always been so cool and calm. When I'm away, I sometimes try to picture her, but I can't. There's something too fragile, too wise and kind about her and unless she's right there before you it's hard to make her real. You know she never once struck me, not even when I was a child. Imagine that. Not once." She stopped and turned her head away from the group. "For some reason, I don't feel very much like her," she added. When she turned around again, she looked at her daughter and smiled rather sadly.

"Yes, Mrs. Gorman is an amazing woman," Ted said. "She's very reserved and dignified."

They were looking at Marian as if she were supposed to speak now and she said, "Grandmother? She's . . . I'm too used to her to know her, maybe." As she spoke, she realized that she didn't mean anything in particular, that she was only saying what had come into her mind. Bruce laughed softly and there was an amused, private expression on his face.

"Don't be so sad, Marian," Lucy Coleman said. She turned to Bruce gaily. "You know, I expect Marian to do something mad. I don't know exactly what, but something crazy like running away with a revivalist. I knew a girl once that did that. She was the soprano at the Baptist Tabernacle. She was wonderful, small and plump with fat blonde curls down to her shoulder. Her face was terrible though, but because of the curls we called her Mary Pickford. Mary Pickford Maybrier. Well, anyway, this revivalist came and she fell for him and chased him all over the country. You can't exactly blame her, because he was very dramatic. His main story was about the murderer he had converted. He had the gun the man shot his wife with, and at the right time he'd bring it out and pass it around the church."

Bruce said, "I don't think Marian would run away with the preacher. She'd set out after the murderer." He sat back in his chair and looked directly into the girl's face with an expression she had already come to recognize, the expression of an accomplice in some secret crime. There had been periods during his visit when Marian felt that she had no connection with Bruce. He belonged to her mother and father and what knowledge she had of him was somehow sinister and degrading. She felt a sort of relief in that it seemed impossible, after this family conversation, that she could when alone with him return to that tense and purposeful isolation in which they as man and woman went through the stages of an adult destiny. And then suddenly he would change and by a smile—that expression of complicity—start again their private theme.

"How do I remember her?—Mary Pickford' Maybrier—" Lucy Coleman said vaguely. "I don't remember many things from childhood. Sometimes I can't recall a single person I went to school with." She seemed a little startled at what she had said and turned her eyes sharply to the floor, as if trying to concentrate and to remember lost incidents. She drew in her breath then and said, "I have been away for a long time." She had been in too many places, had lived in too many houses, and been neighbor to too many people: now they were all the same, and the permanent home, the childhood, the relatives seemed no more to her than those transient neighbors.

It was quite late and the room was badly lighted by the three-bulb chandelier of dull brass. It seemed somehow cold and cheerless, not at all like a summer midnight. Marian turned on a lamp by the table and for a moment the light seemed to flood the room with warmth. Then it receded mysteriously, leaving the room, the empty glasses, the piled cigarette trays somber and dead. The talk seemed to die, and there was a horrible emptiness everywhere. These houses were not made for silence and fatigue; everything was too even, too orthodox and impersonal. The bottom shelves of the glassed-in bookcase were empty and on the top several history books, personal memoirs, and *The Choir Invisible* by James Lane Allen could be seen. A current *Saturday Evening Post* lay open on the sofa. Over the mantel the black leather Bible with its curled edges lay unopened and dusty, for there was no crazed, naked, God-fear or God-love here; that was the property of the tattered madwomen who gathered around the courthouse on Sunday night and flung their dirty banners at the sky, or for the oblate, tidy Salvation Army members. The room was powerfully complete, angle and flat surface enclosing imperceptibly. The white of the water-marked paper on the ceiling blended into the green and white wheat pattern on the walls, and over the mantel there hung a grimly friendly picture of a setter whose eyes seemed to look out of the facing window. There had never been a real stranger in this house: only the native. Dark ones, swarthy-skinned, strange-tongued, foreigners with thick, alien eyebrows never entered the unknown homes, the America lying cunning and anonymous in the rich earth. In every corner, in every face, there was a quiet, lawful, unchallenged exclusiveness, unplanned, unrecorded and violent. But the members of the family made strangers of themselves to elude and trick the pale faces, the soft voices, the calm acceptance. Mother, daughter, father, and friend: each behind the mask saying, in steady rhythm to the heartbeat, in answer to the actuality within him, the relentless refrain: *They would die if they knew.*

When the clock struck midnight, Bruce became suddenly impatient and left. It was cool and dark outside and they gathered at the door to say good-by. When he had gone, they automatically returned to the living room to sit for a time in a sort of ordained family counsel before the evening was entirely lost.

Albert's footsteps were heard on the porch and in a moment the screen had closed behind him. He stopped under the arch that divided the hall and living room and lighted a fresh cigarette. He smiled vaguely to each of them, but made no move to enter the room. There did not seem to be any reason for him to speak. Unconsciously he expressed himself best through his physical presence. When he was silent it was not noticeable, because he always seemed to be participating, with his disturbing individuality, his preoccupied eyes, with the infinite patience of his certain and agile body. He was wearing brown trousers and a white shirt and when he took off his hat there was a red line across his damp forehead.

"Stranger," the father said with a sudden note of pride in his voice. The son's eyes turned to him and his brown eyebrows moved up slightly. Then the father laughed shortly, transmitting to the boy a snug knowledge of the vagaries of males. Albert's eyes did not leave his father's face; he stood motionless, gravely waiting for the mocking reprimand, the safe conspiracy which the father, in his solid conformity, must establish between man and man.

"Blonde?" Ted Coleman said softly, sucking on the cigar.

Albert blinked and before his lips pulled back over his teeth in his ambiguous, solitary smile, he looked suddenly forlorn. Without answering, he threw his hat on a chair and started for the stairway. They listened to his rubber-soled shoes hitting the steps as he went up to the darkness. When he turned at the landing, Lucy Coleman called out, "Good night, my son," and they heard his faint good-night.

It was cool in the house now. Marian went to the window and looked out at the dark sky. The moon was covered with a film of cloud. A column of moonlight touched the tree next to the house and the damp surface of the leaves gleamed slick and silvery. A chimney of the house beyond stood up, short, rectangular, and solemn, between an opening in the trees.

"It's wonderful out," Marian said, and her mother came to the window. The sharp cologne the older woman was wearing made the air about her seem damp and cool, as if a dew had fallen.

Lucy Coleman put her face close to the window screen and Marian could see her profile, the passionate reticence of her shadowed face. At the edge of her eyes there was an intricate mosaic of lines. "Yes, it's beautiful," she said, in her slow reflective voice. "The night is always nice. There never has been a night that wasn't beautiful."

Marian drew back from the window with a feeling of disappointment. The fluidity of the mother's life was like a rebuke. The streaks of moonlight shining on the trees she had known as a child were no more to her than a dark field in the West, or nights seen while the car drove slowly over mountain roads, or stretches of treeless desert. She looked upon the world with sight maimed like that of an insect; she saw patterns of tiny pieces whose tones and values were indistinguishable.

Lucy Coleman did not notice, apparently, that her daughter had moved away from the window. She stood there for a long time staring at the darkness, and when she turned around at last she seemed a little startled to find the other two still sitting in the room.

Lucy took the pins out of her hair and let it fall to the edge of her collar. Watching this, Marian noticed for the first time the gray streaks over her mother's ears. The woman unbuttoned the high neck of her dress and then turning toward her husband said, "He is nice, isn't he?"

"Yeah, nice fellow," Ted Coleman said. He rubbed his hand over his eyes and when he closed them the lids were faintly brown. Now that he was tired, he seemed to Marian to look a little fatter. He seemed almost to have gone to sleep, and his jaw was heavy and loose in relaxation. There was nothing to be seen in his face except a kind of pleasant indolence and the fact that for him another day had passed. In the exclusive stillness of his body, he was a striking contrast to the two women who seemed to be sitting there, watchful and tense, and thinking: *Is this all?*

It was Bruce's departure that had left the painful emptiness. He had made them feel bright and attractive. For each one of them his presence was a sort of innuendo.

"Do you like him?" Lucy said. Her eyes stopped for a second on her daughter's face and then she averted them to look down at her own hand.

"Yes," she said, thinking, Now it will come. Now they will become parents.

"That's nice," Lucy said. "He's a lot more interesting than most people around here. He can teach you a lot. Already he appreciates the way you play the piano."

Marian had known that Bruce would ask her to play. The piano itself was an article of orthodox accumulation, like a bridal dress. Neither the grandparents nor Lucy had played, but the instrument was there as if in readiness for the one the family would produce. And so at the proper time the daughter had played discreet pieces and the three heads bobbed up and down in simple punctuation of the rhythm. At the end, in a faint elation, the mother had whispered, "We must keep up the lessons."

After a while, the father went upstairs to bed. In a moment they could hear his shoes drop on the floor. A heavy quiet lay upon the living room and the night outside was still and black. A dog ran over the front porch and then they could hear him at the back of the house, sniffing in the garbage. From where she was sitting, Marian could see her own image in the mirror. The face there had no reality for her. She saw her age, her color and disposition laid out before her, though these things gave no evidence of the complexity of her emotions at this time.

"Your friends?" Lucy Coleman said suddenly.

"Friends?"

The mother smiled patiently. "I mean girl friends. People you know. Those you go to school with. There hasn't been anyone here. You know what I mean. Girls calling up all the time, telling secrets. That kind of thing."

"Oh," the young girl said. "Yes, I have lots of friends. Eleanor, June, Louise . . ." The names, like tiny wooden figures, stretched out in front of her.

The mother was smiling in affirmation. Eleanor, June, Louise . . . the names, simple and stripped, so unsuggestive that Marian felt she was telling a lie. There was nothing here of the prodigality, the outright furtiveness of growing up, no indication of the creamy faces above red lips, of the intense fright in the back seat of an automobile, nothing of the half-hearted criminality of certain years. Marian had a sudden memory, from some years back, of the damp floor of a grocery shop and its sour barrels and dusty potatoes and she could see the yellow teeth of the old grocer exposed toward the girls. While one raised her lips to be kissed, the others stole a jar of pickles or an unwanted cake.

"Your father makes friends wherever he goes. No matter where it is, after we've been there a week he knows everyone. I don't like to know too many people," Lucy said.

"Why?"

"I don't know. You don't have time to be yourself, I guess." She paused for a moment. A window had been raised in the house next door and radio music could be heard. The mother seemed to be concentrating on it, trying to pick up the tune. When she had got it, she continued, "I've been in so many places everyone is alike to me. Sometimes I think I want to get to the edge and to squat there like a cactus."

"Why have you been in so many places?" Marian said.

"Why?" she said. "Your father's business, naturally." There was an iciness in her voice, as if she were speaking to a store clerk.

"Why is his business in so many places?" Marian asked.

She was not conscious exactly of probing her mother. All reaction was suspended for the moment in a sort of intuition. She had better speak now or never.

"Why? I told you why we left. I wrote all about it." Lines formed between her eyebrows and in her eyes there was an expression of genuine astonishment. "The last job had no future. Ted had gotten as much as he could out of it. Then this other thing turned up."

"What other thing?"

Impatience, full and uninhibited, came into the mother's voice. She spoke out sharply, as if she had been attacked, "Another job, of course! It's not definite yet. We're waiting to hear."

"That's fine," Marian said, with a feeling of having escaped coming too close to something.

The atmosphere altered immediately, as if magic words had been spoken. It took only a moment for the shock of questions to fade away, only a moment before the shadow of reality had vanished like a thief who had tried the door and, while they prepared to face him, had suddenly changed his course. The two women sat looking at each other without speaking, as if it had grown too late for mere words. The daughter was thinking beyond the face of the mother, beyond the pensive jaw and pink lips, thinking that here before her was a woman who, like most women of her age, was a kind of sum total of climaxes. Here was one who had been a bride, an accustomed wife, had twice been through the shocking loneliness of birth pain and who now had reached a state of obscure privilege. She had the privilege of having had children and no longer needing them, of having been young, but not old. She did not know what the mother was like in any of these stages, because imagination is not often specific in the case of one's relatives. But here she was with thin lines on her neck, with her waist sloping imperceptibly into the abdomen, streaks of broken veins behind her knees and small ball knots in the calves of her

94

legs. Her body was full of pride and memories, as if it were a guide for the preordained destiny of the daughter. "When were you married?" Marian said suddenly. "How old were you, I mean?"

"Twenty, I think. Yes, twenty," the mother answered. She ran her thumb over the shining surface of her nails. Her daughter's voice was a kind of unfair interruption to her for she was thinking: What is this summer to her?, what is this stage?, how young and how old is she?

"Yes, I was twenty," Lucy Coleman repeated. Laughter rose in her throat. "How old will you be?"

Marian did not answer. For an instant there was something in her mind that she might have said, but it passed away too quickly.

"If there's anything you want to know, I can't tell you," the mother said, without any particular emphasis.

"About what?"

"About things mothers are supposed to tell daughters. I have nothing to tell. Nothing you would really want to know." She caught her breath as if she would go on, but she did not. Neither of them wished to say anything further. They had faced each other in the quiet of the house at midnight, alone without husband, brother, or friend, and for a time it might have seemed that the accumulated mud of the ages would roll back and that they might, for a small moment, reveal something of the store of their feelings, desires, and expectations, something that they as mother and daughter had always known. But the impenetrable insincerity, as automatic and instinctual as closing the eyelid against dust, threw its weight between them. Even if they might have spoken to each other, there were no words to work with.

Lucy Coleman got up from her chair. She brushed away a little heap of ashes which had fallen on the table beside which her husband had been sitting. They did not speak

95

again. When all the lights were out, they groped their way up the staircase. On the landing where the faint moonlight shone through the window, the flesh of their bare arms touched casually. And soon every member of the family had his private sleep which stretched out gradually into each one's private awakening.

CHAPTER SEVEN

$\mathcal{D}$URING the two weeks that followed, the weather was hot and dry. It began to rain shortly after dawn on the day of the parents' departure. The pleasant sound of distant thunder awakened Lucy. She saw that rain might come through the side window and got up to close it. She had slept lightly during the night as she always did before a journey. The sense of excitement came upon her immediately and the rain had awakened her so fully that she did not want to go back to bed. It was just light enough to look out of the window and see the rain in the gutters. She ran her hand over the damp window sill. On the table the clock was ticking away, but it was still several hours before they were to get up. Down the street a light switched on in one of the houses and she watched it shine through the darkness.

Remembering that the living room window was open, she crept down the stairs to close it. The rooms in the lower part of the house looked very peaceful. The brass andirons reflected the rays of early light and the chairs and couch looked comfortably used. In the halls the gladiolas were still fresh. It was pleasant to wander about the house in this stillness. For a moment she feared someone upstairs might hear her and think she was an intruder, and so she kept her ears alert for any sound of movement. Softly she stepped about the house, picking up an occasional match from the floor or stopping to look moodily at something she hadn't noticed. Suddenly she had the feeling of touching the core

97

of the house, of being part of the family tread that was beaten into the dark wood of the floors. She felt it now as something vast and yet private, and she loved the familiar evidence of long, distracted living in one place. I really shouldn't leave, she kept thinking. The thought ran through her like an endless refrain, and yet, at the same time, her mind retained its unwillingness to accept the past and the future which is what living in this house would mean to her. To stay here would surely mean that what she had now was all she would ever have. The excitement of new plans, the belief that this time, this move, this decision, would alter everything overpowered her. She imagined some far-off and obscure triumph which would be relayed back to this house and which would represent something grand to them. She believed that she still had the power to establish a state, both personal and material, which she and her family could always depend upon, always retreat to, like a comfortable and ceaseless inheritance.

While she was wandering about the house, the sun came out and the rain clouds disappeared. The fresh fragrance of the trees came into the rooms. In the quiet, she heard footsteps near the back porch and the rattle of newspapers. She listened and when there was no other sound she began to think it was only a dog. Then, unmistakably, she heard a low cough. She was frightened and held back a few moments before going into the kitchen. There was no sound at the lock of the door and since the footsteps did not actually come up on the porch she decided to slip into the kitchen and look out of the window.

Last night's newspapers and a few magazines had been placed beside the garbage pail. She stood behind the curtains and watched a Negro man go through the papers. The ones on the top of the pile were damp and he carefully laid these aside. The others he put into a burlap sack by his side. The first thing Lucy saw was his black hands sorting the papers. She watched them work slowly and without hesitation; they shone when a ray of sunlight passed over them. The man wore trousers which were the dark green color of an overripe avocado and a brown workshirt. His face was shaded by an old hat. Lucy could see the brown of the collar of his shirt against the deeper brown of his neck. The burlap sack picked up some of the damp earth as he dragged it toward the garbage pail. He was going through the cans now and taking out a few clean ones to put into a bag. She had lost all fear and stood watching him as if he were a child at play. Unconsciously she had moved away from the protection of the curtain and he must have been able to feel her eyes upon him, because she saw his body suddenly straighten. His posture was rigid, even formal. He isn't old, he's young, were her first thoughts. She wondered why she had thought him old. His face was long and the skin was pulled tightly over his prominent forehead and cheekbones. His lips were thick above the short fuzz of his beard. Lucy had her hair pinned flatly against her skull and a robe was loosely thrown over her shoulders. They looked at each other without speaking. His gaze was solemn and unhurried, as if it were too early in the morning for anything except looking. He was holding a can in his hand and, still gazing silently at her, he dropped it into the bag. In the back of the yard she heard the shuffling of feet and the sound of a child's voice. A young girl and a child were standing beside the bushes. The girl was very slight and though her shoulders were bent in the direction of the ground, her eyes were anxiously looking upward at the woman in the window. The little girl had her finger in her half-open mouth and her other hand grasped the front of her dress as if it had been frozen to the cloth. They were so still that the sparrows jumping about on the green bush behind them seemed to be making a clamor. The man turned around, in a reflex way, to look at them. Their faces did not alter in any way, but they seemed to communicate with him by some private language in their large eyes.

He took off his hat now and Lucy heard him say in a resonant voice, "It's nobody's. Actually, the stuff is nobody's." He pointed to the sack on the ground. "Things throwed away don't belong to no one." There was a startling rationality in his voice, and he talked as if he were stating some irrefutable proposition.

"I suppose you're right," Lucy said, somehow amazed at the sound of her voice. She wondered if the two people waiting so silently could also hear her.

"If you'd a wanted these things, you'd a kept them in the house," the man went on. He did not give any special inflection to any of the words in the sentence. Nothing could be inferred except a deep stubbornness.

"I don't want them," Lucy said, "but it isn't right to go snooping around people's houses before they are up. Why didn't you come later and ask for the papers? We would have given them to you." The words came so patently from her mouth that she was annoyed with herself. It made her feel old. She did not like to lecture anyone, and yet she felt it necessary to protest the presence of the three strangers in her yard. At the same time, she did not want anyone in the house to hear her.

The man looked at her with restrained bafflement on his face. His stern eyes looked bored, as if by some useless disturbance. "Did I understand you to say to come around later? Did I understand you to say that?" he repeated insistently.

"Well, yes," she answered, feeling that she had gone too far, but not knowing just what he had meant to say.

"I couldn't possibly do that," he said flatly. The sun brushed across his face and he moved into a shadow. "I couldn't come around here and knock on the door and ask for the papers and cans. This way, early in the morning, they don't belong to nobody and you don't have to ask."

She thought now that his voice was like a preacher's and she felt intimidated by an unanswerable exegesis. "This yard belongs to someone," she said, unable to control the lift in her voice.

The woman and child had turned their backs to the scene. Lucy felt a strong desire to see their faces. The two brown figures looked lifeless and stationary as pieces of garden sculpture.

"Do you want them back? I'd as leave as not take them out and put them right back here on the ground," the man said with a note of finality.

She scratched her finger on the window screen. "Of course not. Take them. You've already got them," she said.

He drew the sack over his shoulder and walked away. In a moment he was reunited with the woman and child at the edge of the yard. He took the little girl's finger out of her mouth and Lucy thought she heard him whisper to the woman.

They were just leaving the yard when Hattie came in sight. She was swinging a bright red purse on her arm and trotting toward the house. She stopped abruptly and looked at the Negroes. By their faces, she seemed to be able to tell that someone was awake in the house. She did not speak, but something in the way she passed the intruders irritated Lucy. Perhaps it was the not speaking. She had passed them as if they belonged there, as if their presence was in no way unusual and she had no reason to note it.

The people did not seem in any hurry to get out of the yard. They continued walking quite slowly and Lucy saw the man's head close to the woman's. The sun was shining on the child's bare legs. The burlap bag was jostling up and down. The child stopped and let the wet grass tickle her toes. The others paused and watched her playing.

When Hattie came through the kitchen door, Lucy turned rapidly away from the window. "Good morning," she said.

"Morning." Hattie did not look at her, did not question why she was up so early.

Lucy felt very much a visitor in the house now. "Do you know those people?" she asked, pointing toward the yard. She altered her voice very carefully, because she was afraid Hattie might think she was angry.

"No'm, I don't."

"The man was very nice, but . . ."

"That's good. I thought he looked fine," Hattie interrupted. Her voice was a restless, hurried chirping. She moved away from Lucy Coleman without comment and started to boil the coffee water.

Lucy went once more to the window. The three people were still visible in the distance. Now they were walking rapidly and the static quality of their bodies had completely disappeared. She could see them swinging along together, young and alert, and she imagined that they must be talking and laughing. Perhaps they were laughing at her. When they turned the corner and were quite alone, Lucy felt as if something had passed which she had not understood, something she had badly mismanaged.

"What will they do with the papers?" she said to Hattie.

"I don't know no more about them than you do," Hattie said. She turned around from the stove. "I reckon they got something in mind." She stood there staring patiently at the older woman and Mrs. Coleman felt annoyed that her hair was pinned tightly to her head and that she had on no make-up. Hattie's round, glaring eyes made her uncomfortable. Lucy had a need to look her best before her inferiors. Well, what else? Hattie seemed to be saying. They were more or less caught in a moment with each other and Lucy was conscious for the first time of the stony frailness of the girl's figure, of her weird, ancient face. Hattie's hand was resting on her hipbone, the fingers spread wide. On the top Lucy noticed that a short gash was shining purple through the black skin and it reminded her of the hand of a monk she had once seen, the hand which had slipped through the door of the monastery when she had tried to visit without knowing that women were excluded. She remembered that the hand from working in the dirt had been almost as black as Hattie's and how amazed she had been at the open wound on the top. Hattie's face was a secret to her, like the faces of the monks.

"I don't guess they hurt anything," she said, unable to shed her random feeling of trouble. The day had started off badly and this superstitiously upset her.

"No'm, I wouldn't say so," Hattie said in a voice that seemed to parrot Mrs. Coleman's.

The wall clock showed that it was near seven and Lucy knew it was time to get dressed. Leaving the kitchen, she passed the nail upon which Hattie's hat was hanging. It was a round-shaped hat of tan straw that faded into brown at the edges of the green band. Seeing it there, she turned back to look at the girl with an amused wonder of how the hat would look on her. Hattie had not moved; she was still standing there with her hand on her hip and Lucy thought that her bowed legs looked like a black hoop.

Even as she went into the living room, the picture of the girl remained extraordinarily vivid. She felt vaguely frightened, but remembering the funny hat on the wall, the rickety legs and the brief cotton dress, she said to herself, "She really is good. A great help." And immediately the troubling picture was comforting.

She stopped to open the front door. Sunshine came rushing into the house. She could feel it warming her neck and arms. From the kitchen she heard Hattie say, "A few throwed out papers, don't seem a whole lot to worry about."

Lucy thought kindly, They are always talking to themselves.

Several young boys in Boy Scout uniforms were trailing up the street, obviously out for a hike. Already one of them had opened his lunch box and was chewing a sandwich. Though they were walking up a concrete city street, imagination and the early morning stillness had turned the streets into an unexplored wilderness. Lucy thought, I won't be here when they return in the evening, when the dream is over. She went up the stairs feeling rather proud of her own adventures and sorry for those who had not been awakened by the rain.

Marian was the first one to get dressed for breakfast. As she went down the stairway, she paused at the window and looked at her father's car in the driveway. It was clean and polished and the license plate was glittering black and gold. The car was the most permanent thing about the parents and the license plates were their heraldic symbol. As she stood there, Albert came down the steps.

He rubbed his hand over his eyes and yawned and Marian thought angrily that he was going to make all of them see how much effort it had cost him to get up so early in the morning. He would make them feel honored.

"I hope this hasn't disturbed you," she said sarcastically.

"You're crazy," he said sleepily. "I don't understand it." He needed a haircut and Marian looked at the way his hair, not properly combed, curled on the back of his neck.

"What is this business about Arizona?" he said. His eyes were fully opened now, set deeply in faint blue circles.

"You know what it is! Papa has a job there," she said sharply. Immediately she regretted her sharpness, because she was afraid Albert might walk away. His coldness toward the parents distressed her, but, at the same time, she was anxious to get his reactions.

"What sort of job?" he said. "It's rather sudden, isn't it? The last thing I heard was some foolishness about South America."

"They got a telegram from a friend. Someone they knew out West. But you know this, Albert. Why are you asking me?" She wondered why he thought she was keeping secrets from him.

"I thought you might have been able to get something definite out of them. You stick around them like wax."

"Do I?" she said, frowning.

Albert's eyebrows shot up. He was smiling. "What do you mean, 'do I'? Jesus!" He whistled through his teeth. For a moment she thought he was going to touch her, because he always wanted to touch things he pitied or which amused him. He drew his hand out of his pocket, but let it fall at his side.

"What sort of work?" Albert asked. "Insurance?"

"I'm not sure. Maybe it's something else." Already Marian could feel doubt sinking into her bones. She could foresee the car moving out of the drive, their final good-bys, and the trail of imponderables they would leave, like dust, behind them. She was aware that plans which seemed so promising and right to the mother and father were greatly embarrassing to others. Even she dropped her eyes when they started to talk about business, but, at the same time, she felt a vast need to believe in them. She felt that if she distrusted or laughed, this lack of confidence would fall like a curse upon them. They were before her like shabby waifs to whom she must give the surface of respectability and authority. She had to share and uphold the one thing her parents had: faith. They had no home, might as well have had no family, they had no certain talents, they were not even very young. But they had this childlike and religious faith in the new job and the new town.

"He'd be a fool to stop the insurance. You can always make a living selling policies to niggers. I guess that's what happened in Montana. There weren't enough niggers." Albert's tone was merely reflective; he did not judge. He accepted the inexplicable.

"What?" Marian asked, without having a definite question in mind. (She could see her father on a cold morning, bundled up in his coat and with a cigar between his teeth, rapping on the door of a little frame shack. And when the door opened and the black face looked into his, he would smile reassuringly, as if he were a doctor. He would be warm and talkative before the cold, silent house. When he laughed gruffly he would be one of them. "How di do, Tom. Think it will snow?" The black face would laugh up at him and then shuffle off after saying, "I'll be right back directly." Her father would stand just inside the door and make pencil marks in his account book and he would not be conscious of the muffled, undecided voices in the house.)

"I hope he's not going back into insurance," she said.

"Why, for God's sake!"

"Well . . . I don't . . ." She could not turn her random impressions into arguments.

"Of course, we really don't know what happened on all these jobs," Albert was saying. "One minute everything is going fine and they are borrowing money to buy a house or God knows what. The next minute the whole damned thing's been called off and they say they never liked the town, didn't really like the business and feel sure that something else would be better. By now the whole thing's a joke. The only thing that bothers me is where they get the money to make all these changes. They must have a flock of bills in every state in the union!" He took a cigarette out of the pocket of his shirt.

"Albert! They're your parents!" Marian said hoarsely.

"Well?" His eyes looked at her over the match flame.

It was not a social whim that made the young girl draw quickly away from her brother. His blasphemy struck fear in her heart, because her parents were to her the equivalent of a savage's totem. She derived her being and power from them; she stood in an unalterably intimate relationship with them that was beyond question. She could no more escape from their troubles and sins than from a god's wrath; she could not deny them any more than she could deny her own face.

With something of the proselytizer in her voice, she said, "I know he could get a job. Papa said they wanted him back in Montana. Mother says he's very good in any business."

She spoke very softly for fear they might hear her. She could almost see her mother's dismayed and confused eyes staring down on them.

"What difference does it make what she says? Naturally, *she* thinks he's doing all right. She's his wife."

"Isn't that enough reason?"

"I don't know," Albert said with a sudden look of wonder on his face. "I don't know. Maybe they'd be better without each other. You can't tell."

"But they don't want to be without each other," Marian said.

Albert was bored by the conversation. He had gone as deeply as he cared to go. He looked impatiently at his wrist watch. "I hope they get away before ten," he said. "I'm going down to the lake with Ray Appleton and I can't hold him off any longer than that." He had retreated into his old privacy. When he looked at Marian she felt that she vanished before his eyes. The sense of having a personal and mysterious destiny dominated him again.

"Who?" Marian asked. She had heard what he said, but she wanted him to repeat it.

"Ray Appleton," he said.

"I didn't know . . ." she began, but he was already going down the steps. She followed him to the porch where the breakfast table was set. As he went in front of her, she seemed to be seeing him for the first time. She noticed how slight he was and yet how strong. He was beautifully strung together like an athlete for whom the proper sport had not yet been invented. His hips were narrow and he walked with a light spring. He was wearing moccasins and no socks and when he walked she saw his white ankles, as thin as a girl's. But, on the stairway, he had ceased to look young to Marian, despite the agile beauty of his body. She could see him riding through the streets in Ray Appleton's roadster, and she thought what a contrast he would be to the

107

man with the obvious wig, the soft, fat hands and the loud laughter.

"Albert!" she called, but he did not seem to hear her. In that instant she felt anxiety for him. Suddenly she wanted to protect him. He had become part of the mysterious totem, like the parents. Without being conscious of any particular attack upon him, she was already feeling a fierce loyalty. Her mind, like the sudden vision of fireworks, was making a thousand unrelated excuses for him. He is my brother, she was saying to herself, as if this were a newly discovered fact. He was a part of her. She closed her eyes against the image of Ray Appleton and after a moment everything seemed quite without danger. It must be all right! It had to be!

When she went into the kitchen Hattie said, "Ain't you started crying yet! They're going away today and I thought you'd be too weak to get up out of the bed!"

"Why should I be crying? Papa is going to a new job and I should be happy about it?"

"There ain't nothing to be happy about in no job is the way I look at it. A job's about the easiest thing to cry over I can think of offhand."

"How about the coffee?" Albert called from the porch.

"Well, who's that hollering so beautifully?" Hattie said, flinging her hands out in front of her. "Will you tell Missy Albert I'll be right out?" She began to laugh in her mirthless way which was filled with a bawdy contempt, but even this contemptuous screeching rang gaily through the house. Her harshness was never acknowledged. Marian too began to laugh. "You know you're funny, don't you?" she said.

"Yeah, like a wreath on the door," Hattie answered.

Mrs. Gorman's footsteps were heard in the hall and Hattie's face changed. She whispered shrilly, "Here comes the dove! If she says anything to me, I'll let her have it!"

Marian looked at her in astonishment. "She's never said anything to you, Hattie! She never says anything much to anyone. She's the easiest person in the world to get along with." A frown came across her face and Hattie, seeing her earnestness, said, "Sometimes I don't think you know straight up."

Ted Coleman pushed his coffee cup aside and spread the map over the breakfast table. "Well, I guess we're about ready to circulate," he said. As he bent over the table, his thinning hair was noticeable. Mrs. Gorman was calmly watching her son-in-law. She ate almost no breakfast but had, in the past, consumed an enormous amount of coffee until, as she said, the doctor told her to cut it down. (No one had been in the house when she saw the doctor and they had no word of her having visited him in his office. She was unusually vague, even for her, when questioned about it and so the matter had been dropped.) She was holding a thin white cup edged with a narrow band of gold. She took very small sips, probably to make the coffee last longer, and after each taste she usually put the cup down in front of her and stared into the dark brown liquid. But, now, the map distracted her and she said, "Do you drive at night?"

"Not often," Ted answered, putting his pencil down on the table. "We try to get to a good-size town not later than eight or nine o'clock and put up there for the night." He smiled reflectively, but something in the grandmother's question had struck them all. The trip was no longer merely a business move, a temperamental journey: in that moment it became a possible disaster.

"Is the car in good shape?" Albert said. He was tilted back in his chair, smoking.

"Oh, yes," the father answered. "We take it easy." He frowned slightly. He was wearing the Palm Beach suit and when he adjusted his tie even his clothing seemed to be intolerable to him.

"How long will it take?" Marian asked and her father

mumbled something about several days. The days stretched out before them, mysteriously heavy with unforeseeable possibilities.

"Well, don't drive at night," Mrs. Gorman said and picked up her coffee cup.

Lucy stepped through the archway. She was wearing a brown linen dress and her face was filled with repressed animation. She might have been stepping onto a stage, so did her theatrical sense of excitement overpower her.

"Linen musses quicker than anything else," Mrs. Gorman said flatly. Lucy drew back as if she had been struck. Her fresh, excited face was reduced by the remark into a childish melancholy. "It's the nicest thing I have," she said. looking uncertainly about the table.

"But why wear the nicest?" Marian said.

Mrs. Coleman was unable to cope with the question. She sat down at the table and spread her hands over the blue and white tablecloth. "I don't know. It is sort of exciting, isn't it?" she said hesitantly. "I always like to dress up when we start out. It's a good sign."

Ted Coleman had picked up the map again. He pushed the point of the pencil into the spot that marked their destination. "Well, this is it," he said. "This is it in more ways than one!"

Lucy smiled brightly. "I'm sure it is! Yes, I'm sure!" She gave each person at the table a bountiful glance, as if she were telling them that everything was settled. Her eyes invited them to make their plans, also. The wildest dreams seemed capable of realization.

"You haven't seen much of your father, Marian," Lucy said, after a pause. "It's a shame too. You two always have so much to talk about."

"I haven't seen enough of you," Marian said softly. Mrs. Coleman blushed and Marian began to wonder if they had really been in the house for several weeks. It did not seem possible that they could have been here, because things

110

were so completely unchanged. Was this what she had dreamed about? She and her mother did not know each other better. Marian was suddenly anxious for the letters to be resumed. The letters with the new scenery and the new names had a reality and personality which this scene lacked. "You will write, won't you?" she said passionately.

"Of course, my darling!" Lucy answered.

The sky was clear and the streets were shining smooth and hot in the sunlight. The bags were in the hall; the car was ready. There was no reason to linger. Ted Coleman looked at his watch. "Getting started even earlier than I thought we would," he said rather sadly. All of them felt that the departure had been handled too easily. There should have been more bustle, more rush and happy disorder. Too quickly the leaving smile, the dressed, packaged, and tagged look had settled upon the parents' faces.

"I wish I could take all of you with me," Lucy said. "Perhaps I will someday." When her shining face looked at them in this way, she seemed very powerful. It was possible to imagine all of them abandoning this home and entering the wonderful life the mother would make. "I miss you very much. It's terrible to be separated from the little family we have." Tears appeared in her eyes, bright, beautiful tears which did not distort her face, but only made her eyes sparkle brilliantly.

"Maybe you'd like to reconsider," Ted Coleman said literally. "I hate to drag you away. I said you could stay here a little longer and come out when I get settled."

Lucy's lip began to tremble and the tears of emotion changed into deeper tears of anger. She did not cry out. She did not say a word. Her arms were folded over her chest and her damp eyes, large with astonishment, were fixed upon her husband's face.

They were all aware of the shock, not so much in what was said but in what had been implied. The father had given the family evidence of a private conversation on a level quite different from the usual talk. Only Albert had conceived of the possibility of the parents being separated from each other, but even he had not imagined that such a plan was under consideration.

Ted Coleman looked at his wife like a puzzled schoolboy. He had not known, apparently, that he had said anything unusual. He himself had no guilt and therefore was not aware of his wife's reactions. "Why are you crying, Lucy?" he said in a lost voice. His huge frame, his prominent placidity seemed to crumble into a kind of curiously unangered despair. "I never know why you are crying." He was a simple man and capable of all the hidden cruelty of simplicity.

Lucy picked up the glass of water beside her plate. No one looked at her until she had finished drinking it. There was a mirror over the china cabinet and she pulled her chair forward so that she could see her face in it. She brushed her tongue over her lips and absent-mindedly touched the crest of her hair. "It's such a beautiful day. I guess we might as well get started as quickly as possible."

Albert and Marian took the bags to the car and when they got back to the porch they were embraced by their parents. "Please miss us a little," Lucy said gaily. She adjusted her purse under her arm and climbed into the automobile.

The three people on the porch watched the car back out of the drive. When it was turned in the right direction, the parents waved and then turned their faces forward. In the distance Marian saw Mary, her mother's friend, running up the street to say farewell. The car passed her and she waved frantically. Lucy did not see her. The car plodded on through the sunlight.

"You didn't say a thing to them, Marian," Mrs. Gorman said sleepily. "You didn't find out a thing. What are you going to do—next year and the year after?" Her voice vanished strangely. She slipped away from them immediately and they heard her climbing the stairs to her room.

"I did tell them!" Marian shouted after her. "I'm sure they understand and will send me the money to go to school. I explained it!"

Albert said, "You don't seem to have discovered that they are a little hard of hearing."

Marian looked out into the street. The car was gone and the quiet of the house behind her was undeniable. As she stood there on the porch, her mother's face came back to her as strongly as she had felt it that day while waiting for them in the garden. This diffuse, unpredictable mother-image was again calling to her, asking for love and understanding. And round the mother was Bruce, the generous masculine image. She thought suddenly, He will take care of me! And it occurred to her that she had found the reason for the existence of two sexes.

Albert was staring at her. She felt sorry for him because he was not a woman and had no one to turn to. He said abruptly and with the disinterested flair he had for the correct thing in women's clothing, "You look best in a straight skirt with the fullness in the blouse." He paused and looked at her face and, vaguely smiling, said, "Now, if you'd let your hair grow a little longer . . ."

"And what then?" she said, laughing. When he did not answer, she felt troubled.

The sound of Ray Appleton's horn startled them. Albert ran down the steps. In a moment that car, too, was plowing its way into the golden sunlight.

PART TWO

CHAPTER ONE

*T*HERE were footsteps in the corridors. Clicking heels made sounds like the hooves of galloping ponies, and buttocks moved up and down rhythmically as the women filed into the reception room. From the noise they seemed to have come in groups, but each one entered the room alone and stood alone, dozens of single items like stalks of flowers enclosed in a garden. The great chandeliers were lit and fresh powder was visible on all the faces. The women observed the deep carpet on the floor of the reception room, the couches covered in chintz or striped linen, the clean white stems of reading lamps and their vanilla-colored shades. After looking around some of the women walked toward the couches and sat down; they crossed and uncrossed their legs, paid great attention to buttons and bracelets, snapping and unsnapping, clasping and unclasping. Some of the ladies took letters out of their pockets, soiled, obviously read letters which they began to pore over with earnest concentration. Conversations were abruptly attempted and abruptly discontinued. There were all ages and the faces were a composite of all possibilities: mere female, daughter, mother, wife, teacher, worker, dreamer. The room was large, modern and comfortable because they, the women scholars, had come late upon the scene and dwelt in ivyless, traditionless buildings with new comforts. But there was something double-edged about the place, as there always is in houses for women. One felt that they lived and worked reluctantly in this atmosphere and, at the same time, invested it with piety and reverence. In that way it had the paradoxical quality of some mildly dreaded, but sanctioned, religious ritual. Behind each of the women there was a phantom: a man or a family who was, or had been, or might be waiting. Impatience to capture or recapture the phantom surrounded them in the solitude of this first friendless meeting with their fellow scholars. At this moment, intelligence clung to them like some functionless appendage. White handkerchiefs came out of purses, eyes looked downward at glistening nails and perhaps gratefully remarked the polished, dustless floor boards at the edges of the carpet.

Marian walked into the reception room to wait with the others for dinner. Every eye turned upon her as she entered the door and remained upon her until another woman came up behind her and claimed the attention of the group. Gratefully, she joined the observers who were standing awkwardly in the middle of the room. She saw that many of the women were young, dressed rather nostalgically in socks and loose sweaters. Others were of indeterminate middle-age. They had strong, maternal faces, sober and unpainted, and they stood there in the room like titans without a conflict great enough to use the matured strength. There were yellow-skinned Orientals, and girls from South America with the poised expression of exhibition tango dancers. Marian had the feeling that these women coming out of private rooms to meet for a communal dinner must appear very comic. She was certain her own face bore all the marks of its origin: in the smile and that peculiar just-out-of-the-pasture friendliness that seemed to find a strange world merely an extension of the plot of grass and the rectangle of house "down home." Conversations gradually became easier and the sounds in the room were a speech map of America. Beneath the banal partylike words, restlessness and ambition lay arched like a powerful bow.

At last a square-hipped maid opened the doors of the dining room. There was a hurried sigh from the women and a faint trembling, like wind blowing through a bird's nest. No one moved immediately; there were no impolite signs of hunger. The maid, with an expansive gesture, pointed to the dining room and with great dignity the women marched toward it, their arms crooked to hold the ever-present purses.

Tables for six were placed throughout the room. The shades were drawn over the long windows. College boys in white waiter's jackets stood behind the tables. Their immobile faces seemed to look through the female parade. A prayerlike attitude accompanied the seating, which was unplanned. Marian found a table not yet filled. She did not yet dare look at the faces and pretended to be engrossed in the menu. They must know why they're here, she kept thinking. At this moment she wasn't at all sure about herself and kept remembering the old man at the newsstand at home. (Ain't you married yet? Not married yet? Going to school? Seems like you done been to school already. Done been and still going? I guess I'm not smart enough to understand that.)

Two lighted candles beamed proudly on each of the tables. Because the women were older and freer than college girls, the dormitory atmosphere was replaced by the tea room quiet and darkness. Marian thought, The candles are a bad sign, somehow.

When the orders had been given, the faces around the table began to take shape. The first one to speak was a small, plump woman with tightly curled red hair. "Just before dinner I was reading that there are four murders a day in America," she said. "I can't get it out of my mind." She looked around the table and then turned her eyes down to the cloth.

"What? What is it?" the woman next to her said. She had a dark face and rather thick black hair. Her eyes darted furiously from one person to the other. "My English is bad. What? What?" she repeated, desperately smiling.

"Of course there are almost four hundred burglaries a day," the red-haired woman went on. "Most of us never think of these things, but with four hundred I should think the burglars would soon get around to everyone!" Her face was the color of fresh ash and she had strangely alive blue eyes, stern as a fanatic's.

"You mean everyone here is robbed? Everyone?" the dark-haired woman said rapidly.

The red-haired woman did not look at the questioner. She fastened her eyes on the base of the candlestick. "I said everyone had a good chance." Her voice was very deliberate and emphatic and everyone at the table stared at her. She could not have been more than thirty-five, but she had a completely static quality and someone, much younger, could imagine growing older and leaving this woman at the prim, plump, thirty-five stage that might have been in-vented especially for her. Her body was apparently nerveless. Even when she ate or talked the static quality remained. She was wearing a dress of brown silk—the sort of silk dress worn so long that it seemed to be breathing. The dress was wedded to her and profoundly intimate.

When Marian turned to say something to the waiter, the woman's eyes fell upon her. A rather school-teacherish re-flection came over her. "It didn't say, but I imagine the South has more murders than all the rest of the country put together."

"I'm sure you're quite safe in assuming that," Marian said.

"I wonder how all of this compares with the rest of the world?" someone said.

"What? What?" the dark woman kept repeating. Her head was over the table and she held her fork in the air, in an attitude of desperate waiting. Her mouth was half open and she sought mercy from one face after another, as if she were a condemned criminal. A tall girl sitting beside her began to explain the conversation in a low voice and the little woman smiled and smiled and nodded her head ecstatically.

"I always associate stabbing with Europe somehow," an indifferent voice said, but the red-haired woman interrupted and began a long and well-documented lecture on the use of the knife.

A steady stream of neat and proper words flowed through the room. By some acoustical cleverness, nothing ever sounded loud. Instead the conversation in the other corners of the room sounded like whispers. Listening to the voices, Marian was reminded of a cold autumn day, a high school day, in which she sat in the wooden bleachers and watched a football game. The opposite team was the deaf and dumb school and on the field the mute, awkward figures stood out against the bright, alert high school boys and seemed to be going through a painful parody of the game. Across the way a little band of deaf and dumb spectators sat primly in the cold. They were stiff and uncertain and their heads turned mournfully back and forth following the direction of the ball. The afternoon grew colder and the silent figures became bleak and gray. And then, as the sun was dying, a great excitement could be noted. There was a strange stir and the hands began to fly in excited communication. Without warning, one of the boys got up from his seat and with a grimly rehearsed gesture began to direct the group. A wild, unearthly cheer, like strained owl hootings, broke through the air. The game stopped when the breathless, convulsive cheers started and everyone watched the little gray cheerleader do a handspring. The deaf and dumb team stood at attention and returned the same struggling sounds to their comrades.

At the table they were exchanging names now. The candle in the center was melting. It was past seven, but they sat a long time over the coffee. The dark, little woman told them her name was Gertrude. She repeated it several times, savoring its sound and watching carefully to see if it were condoned. "It is heard here, is it not?" she asked. The tall girl said she had a cousin with the same name and the little woman looked immensely pleased.

"Well, we must go up," the red-haired woman said, but made no move.

"Yes," the tall girl said. She smiled at all of them. When she left her chair and walked across the floor they felt a shock. She was much taller than they had realized. Six feet, certainly. Every eye was turned upon her as she left the room. She wore low-heeled shoes and took rather long steps. When she got to the door, Marian thought she saw her turn around to see if they were watching her.

"They grow so tall here? Is it desirable?" Gertrude said, her eyes puzzled.

Marian remembered the tall girl's face. It was fine and clear and she had beautiful hair.

"High pockets," the red-haired woman said.

Gradually the dining room emptied. The girls crowded into the elevators and went up to their rooms. Going down the hallway, Marian noticed the changes that had already taken place. Through an open door she saw that the floor had been covered with a mat of white, fluffy fur. In another, the bed spread issued by the matron had been stripped off and replaced by a brighter one with pillow cases of a matching design. She thought she saw a tea set in a window. When she opened her own door, the room looked, by comparison, almost primitive. There was the neat bed, the comfortable chair, the dresser, the clean white basin: all useful and anonymous. She had brought nothing with her except a few books and a picture of her mother. In the room next to hers, she heard a steady hammering and she knew she did not need to look to see the prints going on to the wall. She imagined the symmetrical placing of toilet articles, the casual arrangement of books and pencils. The halls were ringing with the noise of furniture being rear-ranged. She felt very homesick and humbled.

122

From her window she could see the streets and the apartment houses. She wanted very much to go out, but was afraid to go alone. Here there was no one to smile at her; she did not know a grocer or a newsdealer or a store clerk. She closed her eyes and began to dream of her own house. The water must be running in the basin and Albert was standing over it, drawing his razor up and down his face. A clean white shirt, crisp and important, lay on his bed. In the kitchen Hattie was doing the dishes. And her parents, what were they doing? She had not seen them for five years, not since that summer before she entered college. Perhaps her mother's fingers were curled around a wine glass and her eyebrows were drawn up to give her the startled expression she always had when she was happy. Or perhaps she was alone in a furnished room, alone and poor in a bare room that lacked even the comforts the girl next to Marian was making for herself. She put her mother's picture on the dresser. It had been taken some years before and the mother's hair was short and drawn in a loop over the left side of her forehead. A neat white ruffle encircled her long neck. Even the picture was lonely in the room. Marian wondered how much of her own life was understood by her parents. Did they understand that the grandmother had given her the money to go to college? They had never asked. And did any of the family members fully comprehend the fact that Bruce was paying for this year? She had not mentioned this to her parents, had not even fully acknowledged it herself. The eyes of her mother's portrait stared down at her and she felt they were disapproving. She longed to explain that this year was for her, the mother, a year to make the daughter independent and capable of taking the mother away from every possible discomfort.

The hammering in the next room went on, but Marian no longer noticed it. She was back again in her own home, back to the summer of her parents' visit, to Bruce's appearance. This was a day, a month after the parents' departure, and she was waiting to hear from them, waiting to receive the money she believed they would send.

Bruce had just left and Hattie was saying, "I think I know him from some place." She took a bent cigarette stub out of her pocket and held a match to it. The flame came so close to her face that it almost singed her eyelashes.

"Be careful," Marian said, watching the flame. When the stub had caught fire, Hattie held it very tightly in the tips of her fingers, smoking it passionately. She was wearing a cap made from the top of an old silk stocking. It fit tightly over her wild, stiff hair and was twisted into a knot at the top of her head. The slick, shining silk, and the smooth roundness of her head, gave the girl a solemn quality. Her great, liverish eyes stared through the smoke.

"Where do you reckon I could of seen him?" she said again, her eyes directed to Marian's chin and her voice low and suggestive.

"Just around here in the neighborhood."

Hattie slit open a bag of peas. She dumped the peas into her lap and began to break open the pods. Marian pulled up a chair beside her and they sat there quietly shelling the peas and letting them drop into a pan.

"I don't think it was around here," Hattie said.

"I don't know where it was then." Marian had a suspicion that Hattie well remembered where she had seen Bruce.

"You know how it is when you know you know somebody?" Hattie said, her voice trailing off and the stocking-covered head thrust back.

Marian felt resistance rising within her, as against an unidentified threat. Hattie's staring, exhausted eyes, the biting mimicry of her speech dominated her. There was an impersonal challenge in everything she said. Marian wanted very much to know what Hattie was thinking.

"You think you know everything," she said.

Hattie's rough laugh, more like a cough, shook the room. "I know beans when the bag's open!"

She stood up now and took the pan to the sink. Marian observed the way the mended blue uniform touched the back of Hattie's fleshless legs. "Bruce likes colored people," she said.

Hattie picked the cigarette stub from the edge of the drainboard. It had gone out. "Yeah?" she said, bringing a second match up to her face. The cheekbones of the sardonic, twisted face were shadowed black and gray above the flame. The afternoon sun fell on her shoulder. The autumn wind came through the window and ruffled the skirt of her smock. The wind seemed to chill her and pebbles of flesh rose on her arm.

"Here, take one of mine," Marian said, pushing a package of cigarettes toward her.

Hattie blew out the match. "Is my face still on or did it melt away trying to light this thing?"

They heard the mailman's footsteps on the front porch. The rusty box creaked when he opened it. "It's bad luck to run out for the mail too quick," Hattie said. She began to make a lot of unnecessary noise with the pots and pans. Marian absently opened the cabinet and began to rearrange the dishes. And then they faced each other, Hattie's eyes full of doubt and suspicion and Marian's face unable to hide a quiet anxiety.

"Only a couple more weeks," Hattie said, her voice hardly above a whisper. "God, I'd just as soon be waiting for Gabriel to show up!"

Marian did not answer. They had been through this every afternoon for a month. She walked toward the window and looked at the parched grass in the garden. The tree leaves were golden and red. The sunlight brought out golden streaks in her brown hair, making it near the color of the leaves.

"Those two crowbaits ain't even studying you," Hattie said indifferently.

"Maybe they don't know what time of the year it is. People, older people, aren't sitting around thinking about September and school and Christmas vacation and summer and then school again. They probably don't even know what time State commences." They didn't know. She was certain her mother and father had lost all track of a schoolgirl's seasons. "Maybe it's still hot as summer out in Arizona. They don't notice children going to school with satchels under their arms. They don't see the different clothes in the store windows."

"I don't even remember myself," Hattie said. She closed her eyes, as if trying to remember the school bags, trying to remember when time had been separated into manageable lumps on the school calendar.

"Did you say anything to them about going to State?" she said. She was both intrigued and impatient with this situation. "Did you come out and say it, or did you just piddle around, wishy-washy, hoping they'd see the point?"

The mail waiting on the porch was more important than this conversation and yet both of them felt they should hold it off as long as possible. "I didn't have to come right out and tell them. They know I'm out of high school. They know it costs money to go to college. I don't have to tell them. Any fool knows that." That they didn't know, that they hadn't even thought of school, ran through her brain painfully. "Maybe I ought to go to work," she added.

Hattie blew a long line of smoke out of her mouth. "Lord, what kind of messing do you think you could get paid for?" she said.

They heard the grandmother walking over her bedroom floor. "Hurry up and get the mail before old Charlie Horse gets down here," Hattie said.

A letter from her mother was waiting in the mail box. Marian studied the small, even letters of her mother's handwriting. Already she felt guilty for criticism. She could see her mother's hand moving slowly over the white page and the way she chewed on the tip of the pen when she paused to reflect over what she had written. She opened the letter and read through it quickly.

"No, there's nothing here," Marian said to Hattie who had come into the hall. Hattie didn't answer. She disappeared into the linen closet. Marian put the letter on the table for her grandmother and Albert to see. She kept wishing Hattie would say something about the letter. She herself felt calm and forgiving.

"She doesn't understand, Hattie," she said softly. "She doesn't know how old I am. She knows, I mean . . . but she doesn't feel it. Maybe they don't have the money and she just doesn't want to say that."

"Why not?" Hattie said.

Marian smiled. "She just wouldn't like to talk about it. That's all."

Hattie looked at her coldly. "I don't know what you're worrying about. You'll just get to do things some way. That's the way it is around here. Some way, things just happen. You don't have to lay eggs and set on them. Chickens just drop down out of the air." Hattie closed the closet door behind her.

A horn sounded in front of the house. Marian went to the window and waved to the girls. The open car in front of the house looked proud and busy. She could see the eager faces of the girls clearly outlined in the sun. The engine raced impatiently. "It's them buzzards!" Hattie said. Marian looked at her and saw that she was trembling. "I won't go, Hattie," she said.

The horn sounded again. "Go on!" Hattie said. "You're going and don't pretend you ain't!" Tears came into Hattie's eyes, tears for all the afternoons that were flying by while she was jailed in this house.

Marian realized suddenly that her eyes had been closed and that her room was dark. She got up from the bed and looked once more at the city spread out beneath her. The sky was dark and it looked as if it might rain during the night. There was a strong wind and the window shades were rustling in the room next to hers. She heard laughter in the halls and bedroom slippers slapped up and down on the floor. She opened the door of her room and looked into the corridor. There was no one to be seen just now and she thought she might walk from one end of the corridor to the other in order to become adjusted to the new surroundings. She went down the door-dotted passage and looked out the window at the end. Bits of broken glass glistened under the street lamp. Behind her a door opened and she turned around to see the head of the little foreign woman peeping through the crack.

The little woman stared at Marian's face and started to go back into her room. Then recognizing Marian as one of the girls at the dinner table, she laughed strangely and came through the door. Even though the window was only a few feet away from her room, the woman turned her key in the lock on her door.

"Oh, it is you. How pleasant! How pleasant!" she said. She took her place beside Marian at the window. Perfume clung to her hair like a fragrant halo. She was wearing a cumbersome robe of many colors which reminded Marian of the silk and satin quilts old women make. Gertrude pressed her nose to the window pane and looked down into the street. The edges of her mouth had a tendency to curve sharply downward.

"America is beautiful," she said. "It is the most beautifulest country in the world. But best of all I like the radio! On the radio everything comes, and I listen to it to improve my English. I understand almost everything except the jokes and some of the songs. I am not here long, you know. I come from Europe and now I will study the library science." Her eyes looked happily into Marian's. She spoke very rapidly. She asked questions when she did not understand, but when she herself was questioned or misunderstood she took it as a kind of insult. Marian had noticed that when the people at the table corrected her or disagreed with her, she nodded wildly and did not listen. She liked talking and the concentration required to assimilate each distinction of usage threw a blight over her natural conversational pleasure. About her speech there was a deep and nervous faith, and she seemed to expect English to come to her all at once by some secret absorption. "I am from Vienna. My brother is in France and his wife is in England. England is lovely too, but not so lovely as America!" She paused. "You don't speak German, I suppose?" she said hopefully.

"No."

"I shouldn't speak it even you did! No, no! I promise myself!" She smacked her hands against her chest.

"Now, darling, tell me where you are from," Gertrude said. She put her hand on the radiator beside the window. "Quite cold. I like it that way. I cannot adjust to these hot buildings, but I still wear my heavy robe." Her laughter rang through the halls and echoed at the other end. "I must not be loud," she said thoughtfully. "We will work very hard here at our studies, won't we? And we shall all want quiet!"

A man stopped in the street to light a cigarette and, as though reminded by this, Gertrude took cigarettes from her pocket for herself and Marian. She blew the smoke on the window and watched it crawl up the pane. Her hands were soft and brown and stained yellow on the fingers where she held her cigarettes. Her profile was outlined against the window. She reminded Marian of faces drawn on cocoanut shells.

"Do you know the little drug store up the street?" Gertrude said suddenly. "The one with all the bright things in the windows?"

"No. I don't know any of the places around here yet," Marian answered. She felt as guilty as if a foreigner had asked about a national shrine and she was forced to admit ignorance.

"The people are very, very nice," Gertude went on. Her animation imparted itself to everything she touched, and even gave a lively stress to her words. "The little boys. They are so nice. They smile and joke all the time."

"Yes, I like drug stores," Marian said.

The cigarettes burned low. From some draft in one of the rooms, a chill came over the corridor. Gertude drew her dressing gown around her. "Where are you from?" she repeated.

"From home," Marian said, smiling.

The dark eyes met hers and Gertude's head bobbed up and down frantically. Marian could see her storing the answer in her mind, leaving it there in an uncatalogued spot until she had time to fathom its meaning.

Gertude reached into the pocket of her dresssing gown and drew out a rather soggy vanilla wafer. She pressed it into Marian's hand. The sound of a radio came through the hall. An orchestra was playing in slow waltz tempo. Tears immediately appeared in the little woman's eyes. She began to sway back and forth. "Ah, these tunes ravish me! Is that how you say it?" Her thick hair flopped from one side to the other as she gave herself to the music. When the muffled sound of the announcer's voice drowned out the tune, Gertude put her hand wistfully on her chin and said in a very melancholy voice, "How lovely everything is!"

"The wind is getting stronger, I think," Marian said, again looking down at the street. A boy and a girl, running very fast, sped through the circle of brass-colored light and disappeared into the darkness. It was midnight.

"I believe it is quite late," Gertude said.

The door leading to the showers opened and they turned to see a girl in a long night robe. Her face was distorted by the rubber cap over her head. "Another night owl," Gertrude sighed happily.

"I must go," Marian said. She felt very contented and very sleepy.

"Good night," Gertrude said. She took her door key off the band around her wrist. Marian wondered why she had locked the door. She wanted to look inside, because she felt something of Gertrude's old life must be stored there.

"Good night, Gertrude," Marian said.

The little woman grasped the door knob. Her face was brilliant with smiles. "How nice! How nice!" she whispered. "You remembered my name! You are really my first friend!"

CHAPTER TWO

*F*OR SEVERAL weeks the nights had been the same: clear,
windy and intermittently starless. Waves of white
clouds drifted together and separated and the entire sky
seemed to be constantly shifting and moving. After the first
few nights, the city, even at midnight, had become remarkably bright and safe to Marian and she took to playing little
games with herself, forgetting cigarettes or papers, so that
she would seem to be forced to go out late. She turned the
corner on this night just as the clock struck eleven-thirty.
The air was cold and the endless river wind blew and blew
and made walkers faceless and bent. She was not wearing
a hat and blowing hair tickled her face. She passed a lighted
basement room in which several Chinamen were working
over bundles of laundry. Amazed that they should be in the
shop so very late, she stopped to look in on them. The man
nearest the window stared out at her, his brown eyes deep
with wonder and his lips parted over loose, chipped teeth.
The grave mask of the workman glistened with perspiration. Steam rose from the damp cloth he was ironing. His
body was rigid, cast in a facial and physical position which
seemed beyond relaxation. He was erect in an utterly time-
less and impersonal way, like a stick firmly thrust into the
ground. When Marian did not go away, the lashless eyes
flickered slightly and the lips curled back over the parted,
broken teeth in a wooden grimace, incredulous and hope-
less. The shop (it was only this one narrow basement room)
and the work done there were open to view. There was

no camouflaging vestibule and there was no place for lip-sticked girls to take orders and keep the books. There was only the work. The other man, shorter and rounder and wearing a white, short-sleeved shirt, looked at the girl's face on the other side of the window. He is the father and owner, Marian thought. She took her last cigarette out of her pocket and struck a match. The men returned to the work on the table and she stepped back a little from the window and continued watching them. She was smiling and thinking that perhaps she should go in and discuss the laundry business with them. She could tell them about her grandfather whose hands had never touched wash water or lifted an iron and about his wife who had never been beyond the laundry office, had never ventured into the steam rooms. She might introduce Albert to the young man with the chipped teeth and they could talk of sons and business. She could see Albert in his perfect clothing and imagine his orderly and serene face meeting these inarticulate masks which had only one expression, never having learned to adjust mouth and eyes to the person and moment in Albert's extraordinarily exact way. She wondered in what amazement the two families would meet: families which had lived off money earned from washing and ironing. And yet both families had moments of danger, both sons lived under expected attacks. She knew that the young Chinaman's stern equilibrium was shattered daily by white hands pointing at him and shrill, complaining voices shouting, "This shirt! This spot here! Ruined. No good whatsoever to me!" And while the voices bawled on in a ceaseless monotony, the dark-eyed boy had only one retreat, his work. His expert irons, adjusted and guarded like precious instruments. Albert, in his way, knew what it was to have alien eyes and to hear voices that could not be answered. He had been frightened by drunken mouths in small-town bars. He was never at home in these places he frequented, never looked right against the blatant paint on the walls. He was uneasy

133

among the adenoidal and curiously ceremonial bar faces and did not trust the constant whisperings of the waitresses. Marian had once seen her brother in one of these bars. She had watched him go through one of his hazardous moments and a terrible pain had come over her as if she were seeing a bit of her own mutilated flesh exposed. Albert had proceeded toward a table with hard, conscious steps, walking with great care as if an instrument were attached to his legs to record the deliberate, dramatic footfalls. His face beamed under the hat he wore, but it could not hide the tedious intensity around his eyes, the intensity of a cat waiting for a dog to advance. He had passed a table where a young boy with a wretchedly prodigal face had winked at him. She had seen Albert hesitate. He didn't stop and yet he did not move forward; he was inhumanly suspended between response and suspicion. A plaintive expression, which Marian had never seen before, came into his eyes. He was like a child before a smiling stranger, a child afraid to trust his own judgment and pleading to be dealt with honestly. After a moment he had turned his eyes away and had gone alone to the bar. Breathless and silent, Marian had watched him lift the glass to his lips. She had seen the pale gold of his wrist watch glistening above his hand. He wore the watch down over his wrist bones and it was unnatural, somehow cheaply ornamental. In some way his hand over the glass was a flash of revelation, complete, irrevocable and fatal. He was fair, he was native, but Marian had seen in him something of the gloomy mystery of the alien when his eyes had retreated and he had set his mouth in an expression of anguished defense.

The sounds of singing were heard in the street and Marian saw a group of young people coming toward her. They separated to let her pass. A girl's high soprano voice struggled for the tune, lost it, recaptured it for three notes, and lost it again. Obscured stars flickered in the sky before they were covered with clouds. The purple-pink of the sandwich shop sign came into view and Marian walked toward it.

"You! You!" a woman's voice called out behind her. She turned around and saw that it was the tall woman who sat at the dinner table with her. Her face was flushed and shining and her hair was blown back over her ears. With her was a man in a black coat and very light gray hat. The top of his hat came only up to the tall girl's ear.

"Are you going some place?" The tall girl was laughing for no particular reason. She was wearing a fur coat which had a sweet cedary scent.

"Only to get cigarettes," Marian said.

"You go with us and have some beer!" the girl said, still laughing. "I am Florence Roberts," she added.

"Yes, I know," Marian said.

"And this is my friend Jesse Burke," Florence said, bending forward slightly. The three of them walked toward the sandwich shop.

"Are you sure you want to be bothered with me?" Marian said.

"Now . . ." Florence said, lifting her eyebrows.

"It's cold as a witch's tit," Jesse said. "Let's go inside."

Florence put her arm through his. "I see you are going to show off," she said, smiling down at him as if he were a child.

When they stood in front of the door Jesse said to Marian, "Do you go out alone often?"

"I do now. At first I was afraid, though." Marian had not looked at him directly and had only the vaguest notion of his appearance. Damp glasses concealed his eyes, but she noticed his rather indifferent posture. His arm held hers awkwardly, just at the elbow bone, as they stepped into the foyer of the shop.

"All Southern girls have a rape complex, I guess. The presence in the community of what they believe to be a

135

beast gives them something to aspire to." His voice was declamatory, marked by a trained evenness.

"I won't ask you how you know I'm Southern," she said, smiling to relieve the anxiety on Florence's face. "There I'm defenseless."

"How do I know?" Jesse said, lifting his hands in a mock prayer. "I drank it with my mother's milk. She was the last white hope of the Confederacy." He paused and looked down at his shoes. "Even to this day, the thought of my mother gives me a chill!"

Florence's round, contented laugh interrupted him. "I'm sure she was very nice. It pleases you to pretend otherwise."

"Nice! She was a creep, as is every other member of my family." He turned to Marian and his face beneath the steamy spectacles was solemn. "I have two sisters. Twins. They have been in a hospital for years, because both of them have nephritis. But they don't speak to each other and though the state is footing the bill they make all sorts of demands, like insisting on living in different wards."

They sat down in a wooden booth in the shop. Florence and the man sat on one side and Marian was alone on the other. Florence slumped down in the seat and spread her arms over the table. Jesse removed the dark overcoat and the very clean and smooth gray hat. Without his hat and coat, Marian thought he looked strangely unimpressive. He had a round, soft face with a marked absence of planes. He cleaned his glasses and she could see that his eyes were gray. Brown hair, streaked with gray, lay very flat and heavy on his head and resembled a toupé. He was wearing a plain dark suit and above his white shirt collar his face appeared, bland, as untroubled as a basin of water, rather sterilized and pure looking like his truly pearly gray hat. His shoulder touched the silk of Florence's blouse and her vivid face hung just over his, like a lantern. Her hand fell lightly on his sleeve and she was still smiling. Her profile at this particular angle was astonishingly beautiful.

136

"Feel my face!" Florence said suddenly. "I'm sure it's on fire." It was glowing red from the wind.

Jesse touched his fingers to her face. "Hot as a junked-up canary," he said.

When the waiter appeared and the beer was ordered, the conversation dropped. Names were carved into the wooden top of the table at which they sat: sad and simple names like Bill and Jimmy and Audrey and Jean and Barbara. Marian saw Jesse Burke staring at the names and around the corners of his lips a smile of consternation appeared, something faintly elegaic and dismayed. This expression which conquered his face from time to time was not exactly sad, nor was it indifferent. It was private and inscrutable. Florence drew the glass of beer to her mouth and her eyes met Marian's over the top of the glass. There was an indication of indecision in her glance, as if she were looking for an affirmation of something unmentioned.

"You like beer, don't you?" she said offhand. Marian nodded.

"In a rainstorm turkeys open their mouths, swallow the rain, and drown," Jesse said. He blinked sleepily and brushed the black down on his hand.

"I hadn't intended to go so far," Marian said.

Jesse gave her an acidulous smile. He looked as if he expected her to take offense, but she smiled back at him, certain that his deprecating manner was a very recent substitute for timidity. Florence's warm face was hovering over him and when he looked at her, squinting his eyes strangely, Marian was certain he had never before known the beatitude of love. He was stunned by it, and still distrustful. His heart said, How easy it turned out to be, how easy! But his mind was still deeply shadowed in the defenses of loneliness.

"Do you like New York?" Florence said. Her arm was still on the man's sleeve and her voice was filled with cheerful and matriarchal kindness.

"Yes. I like it very much. It's a woman's city, isn't it?

137

The whole thing has been especially created for them, I'm sure—the stores, the streets, the clothing industry, the printing and publishing—it's all for women." She paused. Jesse was looking at her over the rim of his glasses. The pinches of fat on his cheeks stood out like balls of dough.

"It's not accident that the Bible speaks of the city as a harlot," he said. "Its days are spent on lotions, bangles, patent medicines, ribbons, clips, oils, puffs, scents. It creates every possible dye to deepen further the female disguise."

"Protective coloring perhaps, like the white bellies of birds and fishes," Marian said.

"Yes. Special banners to signal to the rest of the flock in time of distress."

"Nonsense," Florence said dreamily.

"You cannibals, you cannibals," he said to her, picking up her hand. "My little Sedna, mother of the sea-mammals. I am one of your cut-off fingers." He laughed.

"What am I supposed to say to you?" Florence said. Her bright eyes were suddenly cloudy.

"You are not supposed to say anything. You are supposed to eat me silently." The preacherish, provincial tone returned to his voice. "It is not the female who is so splendidly depraved. In every way the male asks for this treatment. He has a special aptitude for tragedy. The first blow stuns him. He is delighted and falls down upon his knees to beg for more. He is not satisfied until he has been torn apart, bit by bit."

Florence looked tenderly at the soft line of his jaw. "How funny," she said reflectively. "I should have thought it was the other way round. I was sure of it." Memories of loneliness and uncertainty bathed her face.

The beer glasses before them were empty. Smoke hung like a fog over the shop. "Of course you thought it was the other way round," Jesse said. "The female always accepts the male with a pious revulsion. She finds no particular joy in destroying him. In fact, she finds no joy in him at all and God knows what reason she has for giving in to him."

"No joy?" Florence asked. "What reasons?" The nimble amusement on Jesse's face evaded her and she said quite seriously, "Darling, did you never hear of love?" A baffled frown came over her face. "I'm afraid Marian will not understand you as I do, Jesse."

Marian dropped her eyes to the spot where the two bodies opposite her parted; she saw the man's fist on the table and Florence's curved elbow. In the stigmatic relationship between the man and the woman, conversation was always threatening to scrape some vital center, but this assault was deflected by negating smiles. There was something in this like a frenzied bird song, a defiant announcement of possession of the nest made ridiculous by the fact that there was no transgressor in sight. Personal scenes and equivocalities always distressed Marian because they swept her back into her own life. Her home and her past became more and more vivid as the days passed and this vividness adumbrated the present and the new scene. Trying to wipe out the feeling of recall that was overcoming her, she concentrated upon the shop. But the young girls drinking Coca-Colas through limp straws, the red and green books wrapped like perishables in cellophane covers, did not distract her. Florence had moved her shoulder and it was no longer pressed against the man. The white of her blouse rested against the mud-colored wall. Marian's attention drifted away from this evening and back to an evening with Bruce.

The night was fading when the automobile turned onto the dawn-speckled country road. They faced each other, white eyeballs peering over the orange glow of the dashboard. They were alone, cut off from their own histories in the early morning bleakness. Sometimes in the distance there would be the fast and dangerous sound of a car passing over the gravel road they had left behind. In this solitude they were completely removed from the organic structure of all their other meetings: the first soft and personalized ringing of the door bell, Bruce walking into the hall, Marian emerging from the confines of the house and then the exchanging of polite, impersonal words that were followed by a lengthy silence. This particular night had no flesh or bone; it was composed of papier-mâché reproductions of emotion, constructed only for the occasion but remarkably powerful for all their falseness. Reality intruded momentarily and vanished the succeeding moment. She would think guiltily, We don't love each other, only to be overcome by a blinding feeling of passion cloaked in sacred, eternal garments.

And in the quiet sufficiency of the immediately past love, Bruce said, "You'll go away for me. I'll send you."

If he had said they would get married, they would have done so. Instead he had said affectionately, "You must not stay here. You must have a future. I feel it." She had answered that she would go, but that nothing would come of it. As usual, he refused to listen, hating all negations. He wanted the masquerade to be believed in, he insisted on wild plans and endless statements of individuality. He imagined he heard her saying that a career was the only thing she wanted. He kindled imaginary fires and when she began to cry he became more and more tender, as he understood less and less.

Florence's rosy, clean face was cupped in her hands. She never looked fatigued and her skin never lost its superbly healthy and childlike glow. What are you thinking, Marian?" she said. "You look like some of my pupils when they are supposed to be reading a book, but are actually miles away."

"Are you a teacher?" Marian asked.

"Of course," Florence said, smiling cryptically. "Of course!"

Jesse lifted his eyes to the ceiling. "She is the little goddess Neit whose inscription reads, 'I am everything that has been, which is, and which will be, and no mortal has yet lifted my curtain.'" The two women watched him in silence. Florence bent toward him whenever he talked. And when she did move toward him, when their breathing became regulated together, there was always something like a miracle surrounding them. An intangible solution of all contradictions was provided. It was evident that Florence needed him. Why and for what purpose did not matter. Both of them recognized this need and it stood between them like a banner. He was as transformed as she by it. He, with her love rising up in him, became lofty and objective, cynical and daring and immensely lazy about their relationship. She was, at times, rather stunned by her own emotion and seemed aware of the enormity of the accident that had thrown them together.

"I never know exactly what you mean by things," Florence said suddenly. She looked at him in a sort of fright, as if she were afraid of being thrown back to some previous state. Already she had lost the quality of a working woman. Her past dreams were unreal to her.

"The orangutan cannot afford to be too explicit," Jesse said.

A waiter came to the table. Jesse dipped into his pockets for the money. They went out once more to the windy street. Marian noticed the strange shifts in dominance between the two people. Inside, Jesse had somehow grabbed the evening and made it his. Now, in the open, he seemed to vanish. Florence, tall and grand, was bending over to take his arm and he looked shabby and far away, without romance in his stiff hat, clumsy clothing, and in the settled maturity of his body.

They ran to the corner where, under the demands of the weather, Jesse quickly parted from them to make his way to the kind of room one knew he must have: a room, lifeless and neutral, with a single bed and an unshaded lamp. The factual bachelorhood of his life had overcome him and he seemed remote from Florence. He was bare like the room in which he removed his indefinite suit, like the empty closet in which he would put his round-toed black shoes. Already Marian could imagine him asleep with his lips protruding slightly.

As they walked away, Florence seemed rather overcome by the picture of solitary life he had been in the last moment of the evening. She spoke hurriedly, as if to bring him back to her. "He is nice, isn't he?" she said. She turned her head toward Marian and tried to examine her eyes in order to make sure there was no criticism there. Her body trembled a bit when she repeated, "You liked him, didn't you?"

"Yes. He's very nice," Marian answered.

"Oh, he's much better after you get to know him. That's the way it is with so many people."

"Have you known him long?"

Florence smiled. "Only a month, really. But when you meet people away from your home, away from your work, that's a long time. Or maybe because you are away from everything you get to know people better in a shorter time."

"What is he? What does he do?" Marian asked. She was conscious that Florence enjoyed these questions. She liked having the opportunity to lay the new relationship out into neat sections.

"What is he?" she said reflectively. "He's a teacher. From Illinois, a small town there. He's in a high school and I guess he'll go back after this year. There's not much to do except to go back, is there?"

"Will you go back to your home and your school?"

Florence put her hands in the pockets of her coat. "I only asked for one year and I didn't tell them that I might not take the job again. It never occurred to me that I should want to leave the place." She bent her head down against the wind. Her chin touched the soft collar of her coat. "I always loved teaching and I can't imagine why I have changed. I thought I might go on and on, perhaps even some day get a college position. But I can't think of it now. How funny and far away it all seems. Forgetting it overnight is almost like amnesia, but maybe it will come back. Maybe I'll have to go on with it."

"What do you propose to do instead?"

"To do instead?" She suddenly stopped walking. "Why, I suppose I intend to get married!" The simplicity of her statement seemed to daze her. Apparently she had not faced her plans directly until this moment. She looked about her as if she expected Jesse to be standing beside her. Do I really know him? Have I gone too far? she seemed to be saying.

"That's fine. You should get married," Marian said.

Florence's laugh broke through the stillness. "Of course!" she said gaily. "That's the way I feel. I know it's right. I feel it so strongly, and isn't that the only reason one needs?"

"I'm sure it is."

As the two women turned into the gateway of the dormitory, they heard footsteps behind them. Thin heels tapped precariously on the pavement. It was the sound of a woman running awkwardly up the deserted street. They turned and saw that the woman was Gertrude. She was wearing a collarless fur jacket which came only to her waist. The wind pitilessly whipped the bottom of her black silk dress. Her hair was turned up in a roll around her head and earrings of white glass glistened coldly on her ears. Her shoes were fragile and open-cut and the little feet gripped the cold pavement in agony. Cold had settled deeply upon her face. Her eyebrows, like two thin pieces of brown thread, seemed to have been parted from the basic skull.

"My God, you must be freezing!" Florence said, looking angrily at the thin clothing.

Gertrude's eyes surveyed the tall figure in the heavy fur coat. She smiled. "No, no. This coat is quite warm indeed. It is thicker than you think. It is quite comfortable!" Her black-gloved fingers grasped the edge of the jacket.

Marian looked at Gertrude's sadly absurd shoes, sad not so much in their insufficiency or because they denoted lack, but in the choice they represented. Gertrude had other shoes, strong, sturdy ones, and a long woolen coat which buttoned from top to bottom. She even had a warm, drab suit to wear beneath the coat.

Florence said sharply, "It's so silly to be cold when it isn't necessary!"

Gertrude did not look at her. She turned her frozen face to Marian and said mysteriously, "I have been busy tonight. The gentleman told me that the women would be wearing fine clothing and so I thought this the most suitable of all the things I have." She paused and her nervous eyes waited for approval. Marian managed to smile without Florence's seeing her. "We went to a very fine place," Gertrude continued. "It was charming. The dancing they do in America is so amusing. It is quite different than what I know." She sighed deeply.

They walked up the pathway of the building and into the warm hall. Under the lights, Gertrude looked rather tired. Florence who lived on the second floor left them at the elevator.

"Does she walk up?" Gertrude said.

"It's only one floor," Marian said.

"But how silly to climb the steps when one can ride. How silly!"

When they stood in front of Gertrude's door, Marian said, "Do you know many people here? Many men?"

"A few," Gertrude said vaguely. "This one tonight was delightful! How witty he was. He had very light hair, cut

144

close to the head." She made no move to unlock her door, so Marian said good night and went to her own room.

She took off her hat and coat and sat down on the bed. The room was very warm, because the window had been closed all day. An unfinished letter lay on her desk:

Dear Grandmother, I have been working very hard and therefore have not had a chance to write as often as I'd like. I think of you and Albert . . .

She crushed the paper and threw it into the basket beside the desk. Music books were piled into the chair and she looked at them sadly. They were her excuse, her passport to this costly leisure. Gertrude had her library studies and Florence had the high school. There had to be something while one waited. In the building there were women who seemed to be deeply occupied. They got up early and returned to their rooms only when the library had closed. They did not smoke or gossip and lazy coffee-shop discussions were as remote to them as to a farmer's wife. They were like members of a cloistered order and were rather beautiful in their constant awareness of the difficulties of the dedicated life.

It was one o'clock and Marian left her room for the showers. As she walked past Gertrude's door, she listened to see if she were still awake. She heard her moving about in the room and whistling along with the radio. Marian knocked on the door. Gertrude opened the door only wide enough to let her head peep out. When she saw who it was, she stepped out into the hall, closing the door behind her.

Her black hair hung to her shoulders and her face was shining with grease. The innumerable toiletries which greedily devoured her life were evident.

"You should be asleep," Marian said vaguely.

"I know it, my dear. I know it," she said, shaking her head mournfully. "How much time it takes. If one were only a man!"

"Gertrude, where did you go tonight?" Marian said quickly.

There was no answer. The little woman ran her hand over her face to distribute the cream more evenly.

"You must tell me! Who asks you to go out?"

The plucked eyebrows shot upward. "How funny you are!" Gertrude said happily. "How sweet to be interested."

Marian tied the belt of her robe. "You must be careful," she said, trying to get a solemn tone into her voice. "You mustn't talk to strange people. They might not understand."

"Americans are very friendly," Gertrude said dreamily. "In all the shops and restaurants, very friendly."

"You shouldn't go places alone at night." Marian knew she had gone alone. She could see Gertrude's face beaming with curiosity and happiness in the half-darkness of a bar.

"I see. You think they might be interested in me, in my sort?" Gertrude said slyly. "Perhaps they are! And that is nothing to cry about." She gave Marian an impatient smile and abruptly re-entered her room.

CHAPTER THREE

*I*T WAS hot in the building and since she was already wearing her coat, Marian decided to wait outside for Leo Morse. She was standing beside the door and could hear the busy, contented voices in the corridor. Far up in the building, a typewriter was being manipulated by fast and expert hands. A violin student had taken over the music practice room which Marian, only a few minutes ago, had abandoned. Now two women approached the building carrying almost, so did he seem to be lifted along by their momentum, the lazy body of a man with a placid, coffee-colored Asiatic face. They stopped before the doorway and the smaller of the women stepped a little to the side. Her face was rapt and excited and she listened to the conversation the other woman was making. Whenever there was a lull in the talk, the little woman's eyes became anxious and she seemed to be saying, Now it is my time to say something and I shall sound very foolish. Thus far she was safe, however. Her companion's eyes were boring into the lapel of the man's coat and she was saying very briskly, "There's no love lost for the British here, not a bit!" She tapped her heart region with a gloved fist. "I know what India has suffered and what longings there are beyond physical suffering. But don't despair. It's just a question of time, now. The Empire is dead. It simply hasn't selected a shroud yet." She lifted her eyes from the lapel and looked into the eyes of the brown face before her. His eyes were large and sad like an old dog's.

"You are very understanding. You cannot know what it means to meet such understanding people," the man said. He took off his gloves and began to stare at his pinkish nails.

"No, no, don't say that!" the woman said quickly. Her green eyes snapped and she jerked her head impatiently. "It isn't a question of being understanding. How ridiculous that is! And this isn't a matter for personal compliments. This is not something between me and India. When you say I understand, you make the whole thing sound like a mathematical operation. This isn't something that comes with study, and it isn't something to be congratulated upon." The woman's face reddened slightly. She set her mouth firmly.

The man lifted his eyes from his nails. He turned in Marian's direction and coughed. "But for a lady, an American lady, to be so much interested in these world problems. Ah, Madame, it is something to be graceful about." The sun fell upon the black velvet collar of his coat. He brushed away the dust specks on his lapel.

The woman turned to him coldly. She seemed from her speech to be from the Northwest. "The devil with being an American lady," she said. She did not speak angrily, however.

The other woman started to speak. "I read . . ." she said, looking down at the small leather pouch she was carrying.

"What difference does it make what you read or didn't read!" the other woman said. She swarmed between the man and the woman like a violent wasp. "If one had never read any argument, it would be the same. It's so simple, one doesn't have to be corroborated."

"The magazines in America are very kind to our cause," the man said. He shifted his feet slowly and smiled in a mysterious way. "I hardly expected to find the country so well prepared to receive my position. My countrymen

148

will be pleased at the great kindness of your journalists."
His brown face twitched with emotion.

"Kind?" the woman said. "Kind?" Her voice became
dangerously higher. She is going to cry, Marian thought.
She is not going to shout or to reason; she is going to cry.
And the woman's eyes were blinking rapidly as she walked
through the door, after a hasty farewell. The other woman
looked shyly at the dark man and hurried after her friend.

The man stood there leisurely buttoning his gloves and
adjusting his black hat. Then he came toward Marian and
said casually, "It is not those two I love. It is you." Bowing
deeply, he turned and walked away.

As the man went through the iron arch in front of the
building, he passed Leo. "Am I late?" Leo said anxiously
when he saw her waiting.

"No. I just thought I'd stand outside."

He took a gold watch out of his pocket, flipped open the
case and said apologetically, "It's exactly four-thirty."

Leo was a thin boy of medium height. She noticed for
the first time the shallow cleft in his chin. "I can't imagine
you being late," she said.

"I don't like to be." He looked very closely at her face,
as if he were not yet reassured that she wasn't annoyed.
"This is the afternoon I box for forty-five minutes and
after that I had to shower and dress."

"You do a lot of things, don't you?"

"Well, no," he said shyly.

They walked toward the water. "Are you sure it won't
be too cold?" he said. "I'm sorry I don't have longer."
The sun shone upon the shining tip of the fountain pen
in his pocket. A yellow pencil was neatly placed on each
side of the pen.

As they walked along, Marian cast side glances at Leo.
He looked amazingly the same each time she saw him; he
was always at the same neat stage of dress without regard
to the hour. He was wearing a brown suit and overcoat,

polished brown shoes and a hat scooped down in the crown in college boy fashion. His small, well-formed face also had the same compact orderliness.

"You know I was thinking there must be lots of work for a pianist," Leo said when they were sitting on a stone seat in the park overlooking the water. "When you first think of playing the piano there wouldn't seem to be many chances for jobs, but actually it isn't as bad as that." He had taken off his hat. It lay on his knee and he ran his thumb over the hat band.

"Yes, there must be lots of things I haven't thought of," Marian said. Geometric trees were all about them. Leafless branches jutted out in strange and cold shapes. "The trees are sad, aren't they?" she said.

He looked up, his eyes vaguely puzzled. "You mean without the leaves, don't you?"

"I guess so," she said, smiling. "I always felt funny when I saw our house in the winter. It looked so barren when you came upon it suddenly, when there wasn't any grass and the porch didn't have any chairs on it. I'd always think that it wasn't my house, that I had made a mistake because it looked so uninhabited and forlorn. The inside was different, though. Even in the winter, you could always feel that belonged to you."

"I guess it's different to you here," he said tenderly. He had put his hat on again. His coat was open and she saw the way his brown vest fitted smoothly over his chest.

"What were you saying about jobs? Have you been investigating for me?" She tried to remember how this had started and could not. She couldn't recall having said anything about looking for work.

"No, I haven't been investigating exactly. But I feel certain there are lots of opportunities." From the way he was looking at her, Marian felt that he expected his earnest words to produce some immediate effect. "For instance," he went on seriously, "I know a girl who makes her way by playing for dancing classes. It's not hard. Instead it is rather interesting, I should think."

He drew in his breath sharply and she replied rather weakly, "Are there many dancing classes here?"

"Well, quite a lot I suppose," Leo answered. "And not only dancing classes, of course. There are some athletic places that use a piano player. And then lessons for youngsters, too." He stopped suddenly and seemed irritated with himself that he could not think of more possibilities. He fumbled with his watch chain. His face, set in this seriousness, looked very young, but Marian, sitting beside him, felt much younger in an embarrassing way. She knew that he wished her to be enthusiastic and the fact that she did not say anything about the jobs or her work gave him a feeling of frustration which he imagined was due to his own lack of resourcefulness. Every moment of his life was taken care of. He lived as if by the ringing of urgent bells. His innumerable duties, his studies, his pleasure, and his exercise were like parts of a puzzle fitted snugly into shape. She felt that he was trying to pull her along with him, that this smoothly functioning machine had her by the hand.

"I think I'll call this girl who plays for the dancing class," he said quickly. "I don't know that there will be anything at the place she works, but there might be something she'd know about. If you're working at something, you seem to hear about similar things all the time. I'll call her tonight." He paused. "I'd do it this afternoon, but she's probably working now. No, I'll have to wait until this evening."

"But that wasn't exactly what I had in mind, Leo," she said.

He was stunned and dismayed. "It wasn't?" he said.

His eyes were on her face. His head was motionless and almost splendid in its stillness, as he struggled with bafflement. The boy approached Marian as if she were an in-

151

habitant of another world, an enigma he was mysteriously compelled to understand and to please. She had met him only a few days before when, during a heavy rain, he had held his umbrella over her while they waited for a traffic light to change. They walked up the street together, their shoulders touching intimately under the umbrella. When she had reached her destination, he had said, in a nervous voice which shattered his childlike composure, "Will you be busy at eight-thirty tomorrow night? No, maybe I could make it earlier. Eight twenty-five?"

Fat, lascivious pigeons strutted up the walk. An iron-colored boat broke through the gray water. Marian wondered what she was doing here. She did not want to be with Leo and yet she did not refuse him. He was young and serious in a way that made conversation difficult. His methodical nature silenced her. She wondered if she might tell him about her grandmother and her discovery that the old woman could not write more than a few words and could probably read little better. (After a dozen or so letters in which Marian had implored her grandmother to write, she had received a fantastic note, illegible, confined to the repetition of a few misspelled words.) Could Leo imagine all the old magazines in the grandmother's room, her mountain of faded pictures and cut-outs? He would ask Marian why she had not known of the illiteracy before and she would be unable to answer. Could Leo ever be made to feel the paradoxical grandeur of Mrs. Gorman's indolence? No, it would be foolish to speak to him of these things.

"I don't know you at all, Leo," she said. "Where are you from?"

His body twisted slightly and he looked as if she had asked him a question of monstrous cleverness. Immediately she was sorry she had questioned him. He was inexperienced in these matters and she saw that he was frightened. Fearing perhaps some unconscious endogamy within her

152

and knowing that he had no clan or caste, he said with studied carelessness, "Here in the city. The usual thing, I guess." She waited for mention of mother or father, for childhood or house, but Leo said nothing. He might have been born only yesterday, born with his appointments, the duties of this morning and the consciousness that he would eat dinner at a certain time, go to another one of his jobs and then reach the time which he had allotted to sleep. There were no faces about him, no faces recalled from a long lost summer or winter. There were only the people of this period and she was one of those. Leo had not stored up any junk; he was as fresh and contemporary as a new apartment building. Marian was ashamed of the sudden feeling of anger she had. She wanted to break through his organized surface and to shatter his solidity. This passed and she felt a pity for him. She almost wanted to warn him that he might be torn into the shreds of his own identity, that the past and future which he had woven into a smooth, flawless cloth might at any moment be unraveled into its fragile strings. Sometime he might have to try to put the threads together again and would possibly find them knotted beyond help. She looked at his firm, small face and saw the innocence which lay behind his eyes and she felt sorry that he would, like everyone else, in time reach for something beyond his grasp.

"I don't want to pretend that I know everything," Leo said. "It's only that you haven't been around here very long . . ."

His solemn little face was gloomy with indecision. "You're just what I need," she said. His tireless blue eyes brightened and Marian began to laugh. A frown settled on his mouth as he tried to tabulate her laughter and then slowly he too began to smile. It was one of those infinitely sad smiles that come from those who laugh only at a patterned joke and it was very close to tears.

153

"I must go. I'm sorry that I can't stay longer, but I have to be at work at six," he said.

Leo walked her to the door of the building. When he left her the late afternoon was disappearing from the sky. She watched him go away and saw that he was running. The brown coat flapped against his legs, and in his body that firm promptness of his mind was evident. He was going to work at one of the many secret jobs he had. And she thought that he had always worked, had worked in the summer and winter, in the afternoons, and at night before studying and perhaps after that until the time to go to bed. He had no knowledge of the passion of laziness. She wondered if seeing her might be complicating things for him and, if it were, whether she should allow it.

CHAPTER FOUR

*M*ORNING light, gray as old winter vines upon a stone wall, came through the windows. Enameled white door numbers stood out in the steamy gloom of the empty corridors.

"Merry Christmas!" Marian said outside Gertrude's room. Her voice echoed through the hall. She was dressed in coat and hat and ready to go out, because no meals were served in the dormitory during the holidays. "Gertrude!" she called. Marian was especially anxious for Gertrude to have breakfast with her, because she did not want to face the elevator man alone. He always smiled with exaggerated warmth in these deserted days and tried to make the girls left behind feel better. He succeeded in making Marian, at least, feel like an orphan. His fatherly concern filled her with melancholy and homesickness. During the holiday season he had magically concocted a special expression for his face; his watery eyes and the stiff white hair on his head had become emblems of sanctified family life.

There was no sound in Gertrude's room and Marian knocked on the door. She heard Gertrude's body moving under the bed covers and she knocked again. After a moment, the door opened several inches and Gertrude's pallid, unrouged face slipped through the crack in the door like a disembodied head. "Oh, it is you. Merry Christmas," she said sleepily. The odor of stale perfume came from the room. Gertrude wore a white crocheted cap over her hair. She rubbed her hand over her eyes and Marian saw that they were covered with little white mittens. "To keep my hands smooth. It is so important," Gertrude said, holding her hands out in front of her.

Gertrude's eyes suddenly fell upon the sweater of blue wool Marian was wearing. "You look very beautiful," she said, carefully observing the sweater.

"A present from my grandmother."

"Your grandmother! How lovely. The dear old lady! Did she make it for you?"

"No, I'm sure she didn't make it," Marian said, smiling.

A frown of uncertainty came over Gertrude's face. "I have no sweaters. Are they especially popular?"

"They aren't necessary, if that's what you mean. You can do very well without one." Gertrude's grave eyes still appeared unconvinced and Marian began to laugh.

"Why do you laugh?" Gertrude said. "What is funny, my dear?"

"Nothing. Nothing. I just laughed. Hurry up and eat breakfast with me."

Gertrude too began to laugh in her rather distressed way. Her laughter itself was a reminder of the old days when she must have known humor and gaiety intimately, but her eyes could no longer participate. They never lost their battle with confusion and strangeness. "Wait downstairs, darling," she said. "Down in the nice chairs. I'll only be a minute."

"It won't be necessary for you to take much time dressing," Marian said. "We won't see anyone so early in the day."

"Oh, I will indeed hurry," Gertrude said. "Christmas. And the next is New Year. How wonderful!" She disappeared behind the door.

Marian faced the elevator man alone. He seemed to have had rather a bad night and was no longer concerned over the girls who hadn't gone home. His old hands trembled as he opened the door of the car. The odor of alcohol hung around him.

Cream-colored shades were drawn in the reception room. The place was tinted with a pale golden light. An enormous Christmas tree, heavy with ornaments, stood in the center of the room. It had been there for two weeks and now that Christmas had arrived it looked very much out of place. The management of the building preserved without difficulty a collegiate feeling. Gray heads willingly perpetuated the spirit of the sorority house. Grandmothers, potential doctors of philosophy, transformed the Coca-Colas and cookies taken in their rooms into a surreptitious boarding school repast. The feeling of "playing house" crept into the atmosphere as softly and permanently as dust.

Marian liked the building without the other residents. There was a kind of excitement in its solitude, as if those left, she and Gertrude and the girls from South America and China, had a secret society. She was proud that she hadn't gone home, because she had wanted so very much to go. Knowing there was no money for the trip, she had written early in the month that she had work to do and couldn't make it. And yet money was never real enough to her to be a motive. If she had tried, the money would somehow have come into being. Staying here of her own accord was a feat she did not understand, but which made her feel noble. She took this lonely Christmas as a mysterious punishment for thinking so much about home when her thoughts should have been on her work and the opportunity this year represented.

She heard the maid tripping across the floor. "Miss Coleman?" she said in a rebellious voice. She was holding a letter in her hand, but did not offer it yet. "I wouldn't have thought you was here, somehow," she said. "The Lord knows I wouldn't be in this bone orchard on Christmas day if I had halfway good sense." She hissed her words through teeth that jutted out like an awning over her lower lip. "It's bad enough when the ladies-in-waiting are here, but like this I just can't hardly think for listening to myself breathe!" Her eyebrows, like bunches of white wool, shot up over her eyes. "Here's a special delivery for you!" She pushed the letter into Marian's hand and went away muttering, "This is my purgatory! It's surely old pugtown right here on earth!"

Marian saw her mother's handwriting spread across the envelope. "She did remember me! She did!" she whispered, half-aloud. She hated herself for believing that her mother was going to let Christmas day pass without a word. When she opened the letter her hand was trembling.

MY DEAR CHILD:

You really are not a child to me, because having so many advantages makes one very adult. Always I dreamed of going away to school, but my husband and children were given to me when I was very young and that made further education impossible. (What would have been best? I do not know.) Your father and I will not do much for Christmas. His boss—I have mentioned Mr. Rollie, haven't I?—has asked us to his house. His wife has no children and has plenty of time for parties, but I don't want to go. I like holidays to be private, don't you? Your father enjoys himself at parties and gets all the attention. (I wonder if you and Albert fully realize how popular he is.) And yet he too prefers to stay around the house, I'm certain. You know how agreeable he is.

There is a thin layer of ice on our sidewalk. I sit and stare at it, because the pavement is rough and the ice forms in funny patterns. Albert says it is Bruce who gave you the money for this year. I thought it was Grandmother. Does she still have a lot? It's nice to have a friend like Bruce—or is friend the right word? You have been extremely fortunate and I am happy for you. Your father and I wish you a nice Christmas. Thank you for remembering how much I love good chocolates.

Marian put the letter in her pocket. For a time she did not feel anything. She looked at the clock. It was already past nine and she wished Gertrude would come so that it would not be necessary to think about the letter. But it was too late. She was already lost in that section of her mind reserved for her mother. By now she was conditioned to a certain approach to her parents which was beyond her control. She continued to try to make them real by fitting them into an imaginary environment. Her mind had created a house filled with a certain sort of furniture; she had even given them specific clothing. Yet, when she distrusted them, she believed it was her own imagination at fault. She had them in the wrong room, under the wrong sky, and did not know under what stresses their decisions were made. Were they awake now? Were they sitting in a breakfast room and recalling other Christmas mornings? Did they know she was alone and in an enormous room and that she was waiting to have Christmas breakfast in a drug store? Slowly, the worst part of the letter jolted her reverie. She had never told them about Bruce and the money because she had feared their censure. They hadn't complained! They hadn't told her she was wrong. She could no longer pretend about their scruples. They were far away from right and wrong. Like worms in the earth, they accepted what they crawled upon without asking questions. And I am just like them, she thought with a shock.

"Is this dress suitable?" Gertrude said. She had slipped into the room. Beneath her short fur jacket, the skirt of a black wool dress could be seen. There was something wrong with the dress, something outmoded which did not immediately become definite.

"Yes," Marian said.

"Are you quite certain? For Christmas morning?"

"It's fine."

"And I look agreeable, if that is how you say it?"

"Yes."

"Well, let us go, then."

They walked out of the building and into the windless

street. For all the lack of the wind, the air was heavy with coldness. The streets were empty except for a few people returning from Mass. The lusterless pinnacles of the empty school buildings vanished into the dark sky. They saw a drunken man coming toward them, his reluctant legs pushing slowly onward. The man stopped by the frozen corpse of a dead dog. The head of the dog had been smashed and the matted hair of his body was stuck to the pavement. The drunken man, his legs astraddle the mashed animal, stopped. His head was bent low and the words dripped down from his mouth, as if he were saying last rites for the dog. Actually, Marian heard as she passed by, he was telling a complicated story of last night's intrigue, of stolen money, of conversations in alleys, and brawls in saloons. As he stood there, the sun came from behind the clouds, then disappeared again.

The drug store on the corner was open, but did not look very inviting. The window display was partially dismantled. Papers and cigarette ends cluttered up the doorways of the bars that dotted the block. The violent end of Christmas Eve revelries could be seen everywhere in the business section. A piece of pink silk underwear lay in the gutter.

"Let's go to a restaurant. A nice one," Marian said.

"Yes! Yes!" Gertrude replied. Any pleasure excited her, no matter how small it was. She had a fine flair for social activity. This very gregariousness that was so native to her was, at the same time, her betrayer. Marian felt that Gertrude's happiness was built upon a dangerous impulsiveness, but she did not know how to warn her.

They entered an almost empty restaurant. A round bell made of red paper hung from the ceiling and they took the table beneath it.

"Order coffee, will you?" Gertrude said as soon as they were seated. "I must make a call."

"Nothing besides coffee? Oughtn't you to have something else? A complete breakfast. You're as thin as a split match, you know."

"Yes, I am, thank God! Like Papa! Exactly like him. His waist was so small he had to wear little boys' belts!" Gertrude picked up the red and green menu. "Perhaps I will have a little more. I'll celebrate the holiday. Take care of it for me, darling." She winked mysteriously and got up from the table. Marian watched her make her way to the telephone booth. Before she entered, she took an address book from her purse and pondered over it for a time. Then, vaguely waving toward her empty seat at the table, she disappeared behind the glass doors. The waitress filled the water glasses and took the orders. The food was on the table when Gertrude came out of the booth. She was not smiling. Her narrow shoulders were bent and her high, tightly bound breasts were almost bursting through the snug black dress.

"Is it too early in the morning to call?" she asked. Her voice was a shade more anxious than usual.

"A little perhaps. Whom were you calling?" Marian could not resist the question.

Gertrude did not answer. A crafty, female hesitation followed. She brushed loose hairs from her shoulder. "A charming boy I know. Quite charming! He was very nice and didn't at all mind me getting him up, though he was sleepy." She drew the coffee cup to her lips, looked at it for a moment, and then, as though it were dangerous, she put the cup down. "Do I eat like Americans?" she asked. That painfully earnest expression was on her face again.

"So far as I've noticed," Marian said. She did not like to look at Gertrude when she asked such questions. "You really don't need to change everything, Gertrude," she added. She did not know how to tell her that she who was so unused to the foreign liked Gertrude's accent and the funny things she did.

"No, no!" Gertrude said vehemently.

"A little eccentricity never hurt anyone."

"You must tell me everything I do that isn't right. Promise!" She waited until Marian had nodded and then, with her eyes sadly cast down upon her plate, she said, "Most people are not like you, darling. I don't know how to explain it, but I feel it. The least little thing unusual makes them angry and cruel."

Marian was disturbed by Gertrude's analysis. She was also ashamed of herself, because she knew the other girl was right. She had a vision of taking Gertrude home on a day such as this. She could see the frightfully alert dark face among the fair, acclimated faces. "Here is my friend from New York," she would say and the slow voices would murmer, "Pleased to meet you." And Gertrude, almost mad with watching every eyelid and with listening until her head was filled with a roar of words, would answer eagerly, "How do you do," giving the answer the upward lilt of a question which would in some inexplicable way set her off. She could see her grandmother and Albert become, as Gertrude had said, strangely angered. Their silence would be cruelty.

"What is the boy's name?" Marian said.

Gertrude took a mirror out of her purse. "I always smear my lipstick when I eat. Is it too soft? Is that it? Yours doesn't do that way."

The lipstick was still unsmeared and she put the mirror away. "His name is Robert. Oh, no. Bob! Bob!" She gave the nickname a low, full sound. "Bob!" she repeated, relishing the word. "It's a nice name for a boy, isn't it?"

"How do you have time for this with your studies?" Marian asked.

"My studies! Oh, I work very hard. My library science is very difficult, but I must get a nice post and without a certificate one cannot. I have had it all explained to me."

Marian could not imagine this woman in school classes, could not conceive of her taking examinations and doing the required things. She imagined her sitting sideways in her classroom seat with that uneasiness of mind clouding her face. She thought that Gertrude probably laughed loudly when the others laughed and that her pencil flew or rested in imitation of the students around her.

"I love my studies," Gertrude said. "Women must do something just like men. They say library work is very suitable for women in America."

"I don't know," Marian said thoughtlessly.

The fork crashed into Gertrude's plate. "Perhaps I am misinformed!" she said aghast. "Perhaps it is not so good for women and I should do something else. Go into other studies that will lead to an interesting profession. I do want something interesting and dignified!"

"I'm sure you have chosen the right thing."

"Ah, what a relief, my dear! I was frightened." Outside the church bells began to ring. "I do not yet like church bells, but I shall learn to do so," Gertrude said seriously.

An old woman and a girl, not a young girl, stopped tentatively in the foyer of the restaurant. They stood with locked arms and read the menu pasted in the window. They were obviously mother and unwed daughter existing in a hallowed, iron union. They came into the restaurant and Marian noticed how strongly alike their faces were, except that the mother's long chin was covered with a light fuzz. "Here! Mother! Here!" the girl called out. "By the window so that we can see the people on the street!" Her voice rose in the loud, habitual oratory that association with the deaf brings. They sat down and the light touched the tops of their hats as they proceeded in a noisy, formal way to have breakfast. "They have stewed kidneys!" the girl screamed. She reached over the table and pointed to the proper spot on the menu. "We haven't had kidneys for a long time! Do you like that, Mother? Do you?" The old woman nodded. When the waitress had taken the orders, the two women settled down to an earnest conversation. The girl patiently repeated every other word in a high, strong voice which never lost its urgency and tone of great excitement. The mother acquiesced silently to the booming of her daughter. Gertrude, whose present life was devoted exclusively to achieving the inconspicuous and the normal, showed not the slightest interest in the mother and daughter. Marian suppressed her desire to comment upon them. Instead she said casually, "Gertrude, have you no family?"

"I have a large family, very large." She was eating rapidly. Her long fingers, covered at the nails with red polish which had started to chip at the tips, broke toast into tiny pieces. She picked these up one by one, like a chicken after grains, and swallowed them. "But it is not good form to talk about one's family, is it?"

"You worry too much about good form," Marian said abruptly.

Gertrude's body suddenly became rigid. She sucked in her lower lip and a mole, no bigger than a pin point, trembled on her chin.

"I'm sorry, Gertrude. Forgive me." The face before her had become older than she had ever seen it. Gertrude could not, in this sadness, disguise the fact that she was in her late thirties. She dropped her head downward, like a duck slipping its bill into the water. Throughout the rest of the meal, she stared at the tablecloth. When the waitress came with the check, Gertrude seemed to revive and her dispirited eyes fastened firmly on Marian's face. "Please," she said in a voice that showed no inner feeling, "please, my dear, I am in your care." She smiled and the old optimism returned to her eyes. With the smile, she again looked quite young and Marian found it difficult to recall the way Gertrude had looked when she had started to cry. She did not look old now and she did not look helpless; her superb, almost wicked, sanguineness had recaptured her. The obstacles to her happiness seemed to be small and weak, only short hurdles in her path which she could jump over, effortlessly. She had no knowledge of high, thick walls.

164

"And, now that you mention it, your family? How are they?" Gertrude said.

"I had a letter from my mother this morning."

"How nice! How nice! A Christmas letter!"

Marian found herself agreeing with Gertrude. "Yes, very nice," she said sincerely. Her distrust had vanished as it always did.

"Didn't you want to be at home?" Gertrude asked.

"Yes. Yes!"—Marian paused—"Don't tell anyone, Gertrude, but I want to go home all the time. I'm not really here." Why do I want to go? Why? she kept asking herself. There was no answer. It was mysterious and profound, like a wish for death.

They did not speak again until they were several blocks away from the restaurant. They became conscious that an automobile was following them. When the car was parallel to them, they heard a cough. A man sat behind the wheel, crouched into the seat, sejant, with his head jutting out like a balloon from his shoulders. "Ah, these American Quixotes!" Gertrude said. The man coughed again, but they did not answer and he turned a corner, looking perhaps for other prey. Gertrude stumbled upon a broken Christmas candle and Marian took her arm. The eleven o'clock bells rang out in the air and the two girls walked slowly back to the silent building.

In the afternoon the maid rang Marian's phone to tell her that Leo was in the lobby. When she came downstairs he was leaning against the wall. He had on a new pair of gloves, his face was very smooth and a thin film of talcum powder lay in the creases of his nostrils. He was holding his hat in his hand and his suit looked very new and very special like his gloves. And yet there was little of the fatigued holiday spirit about him. He did not appear stuffed like a boy who had had Christmas dinner at home or like one who was pleasantly nervous after a night's celebration. Instead, he looked like an affable and neat bellhop just off duty.

His hand trembled when he gave Marian the bottle of perfume he had brought. He said, in a strained, comforting little voice, "Was it so bad being away from home on Christmas day?" She knew immediately there were no special days for him and that he was trying, rather desperately, to feel what he expected she must be feeling.

"No, it wasn't," she said. "I'm sure I wouldn't have had nearly so much attention at home. Even the Chinese girls were disturbed about me and, as a result, I have a shelf full of candies."

"They must have missed you at home. Is this the first time you've been away?"

"Yes."

He held her coat for her. "A new dress?" he asked, blushing. The dress was gold silk and had a belt covered with sparkling red, green, and topaz imitation jewels.

"Oh, no. This is one of the things I got on Grandmother's charge account! I always tried to make myself believe that things bought in that way didn't cost anything," she said, rather wistfully. He was looking at her strangely and she added, "I've worn it many times before."

"Really?" he said, annoyed he hadn't remembered.

When they got to the door she said, "Can't we go down town for a drink?"

"Oh, yes! I thought of that. We must do something special." He seemed a little put out that he had not been able to make the suggestion himself. On this day he wished to be her family and her entire holiday.

The down town streets were more crowded than Marian had expected. Girls, each in something undeniably new, walked about in pairs. Their feet were cramped into tight shoes and their hoarse laughter was old far beyond their years. There was gaiety everywhere and the feeling that the day must not pass unnoticed.

"Those girls look tired, don't they?" Marian said. Leo looked at the face directly in front of him. "I guess so," he said. Marian could see that he was diligently asking himself, "Is that girl the one she had in mind? Is it the girl with the large mouth or perhaps that one in the green hat?"

It was getting dark when Leo led her into a bar. The bar was built in a circular arrangement and the walls were decorated with turf scenes. The mischievous faces of jockeys wearing yellow and red caps beamed down upon the customers. Leo was not shy in public places and with rather proud adroitness he led her through the crowd of customers to a quiet corner table. It was dark in the corner, but they did not turn on the light. The lamp was made in the shape of a red-coated jockey with a raised right hand which contained the bulb.

"What did you do this morning?" Marian asked, when their drinks came.

"I was at the switchboard until twelve noon," Leo said.

"What switchboard?"

"At the apartment house I work in on holidays and some nights." He stirred his drink. He did not seem to want to talk about these jobs which he managed so punctually and so effortlessly.

"You have too many jobs," she said. "It isn't right to be working all the time."

He unbuttoned his jacket. "They aren't hard. Just a few hours at each one. It sounds like a lot, but it's really nothing."

They heard a tinkling piano in the distance. "It's not worth it," she said after a moment. "You need more time for yourself."

"But I don't mind," he pleaded. She saw his face in the shadow. His features were evenly balanced and smoothed over by a patina of innocence. A ray of light from another table fell upon the shallow dent in his chin.

They did not talk for a time and Marian wondered why

she wished to make him dissatisfied with his life, why she wanted to break down his rushing, his punctuality and organization. Why should she make him complex? He held a match to her cigarette and she could see how closely clipped and filed his nails were and how carefully the skin at the base of the nail had been pushed back. Even this filled her with an inexplicable irritation.

"Is there anything you need?" Leo asked. She could not see his eyes clearly, only the oval-shaped chin.

"Why, no. Of course not." The drink in her hand wavered. No one had asked her quite this before, or perhaps the question had not meant the same. Leo's offered her the returns of that ceaseless labor of his, the benefits of his hurried, routinized life. She was amazed.

"No, there is nothing I need," she repeated. The smoke in the room was making her eyes water and she rubbed them lightly with her hands.

"Do your eyes hurt?" he said. His own were still remarkably clear. "Do you want to go?" His attentive face moved closer to hers and she could see his sharp, white teeth.

"No, Leo, I don't want to go." She took a sip of the drink and turned around to look at the people. She was not thinking of them; instead she was thinking that when they got out on the street again he would take her arm and guide her through the crowds. And when they sat down to dinner, he would ask her more and more questions and say unspecific things about himself. During the meal he might even begin to laugh, because by that time an insidious comfort would surely have come over them. And then what? she wondered.

"I believe it's very cold out," he said, pressing his nose on the window. "Will you want my scarf?"

She said, "Yes, if you don't need it." Putting on her gloves, she added, "Well, we might as well go now."

They walked up the cold street. Marian could feel Leo's

arm and shoulder pressed against hers. Among the racing people, they were caught in this half-embrace in order to distinguish themselves from those rushing about them. His thighs slapped against hers. She could feel the happiness that radiated from Leo; he was warm in the excitement of being engrossed in something outside himself. From time to time he trembled and she heard him sigh, as if he were checking himself in the fear that he might bungle everything.

"You need a fur coat," he whispered into her ear. Looking at his profile, she could see the expression of sorrow around his mouth. Her lacks from the cradle onward had suddenly been thrown upon his shoulders. "It's too cold for you, I'm sure," he went on.

She drew her arm out of his. She thought he surely must be able to hear her saying, "This is the moment to cut myself off. Not later, but now." Actually she had said nothing. Being here with Leo gave her an intimate vision of the errors of her entire family. This is what happened to all of them, she repeated silently. Must have happened to my grandmother when my grandfather first stepped through the door of her house. Must have happened to my mother . . . No, that is wrong. It was my father who was baffled, my father who, on first sensing the flavor and depth of my mother's love, on seeing that singular smile she had for him, must have been tempted to cry out that this was not what he wanted. Fear came into her eyes. She was not at all certain that she could stop the momentum of this day.

"What is it?" Leo said. "Why did you stop?"

The green lights flashed on and the sound of starting cars drowned out her thoughts. Everything around her seemed bleak and uncertain except the little rectangle on the street that she and Leo inhabited.

"I didn't want my hat to blow off," she said.

They started on again and she did not touch him. But

when they came to a corner he again pressed his arm through hers and in this manner they entered a bright, warm restaurant.

Florence returned several days before the holidays ended. Her hair was cut short. She seemed to be especially made for cold weather and when she appeared with her cheeks dusted with rosiness and her eyes shining she looked like a throwback to some imaginary healthy and strong race. "She is a lovely girl," Gertrude once said to Marian, "but physically not the type I admire." Gertrude lived in a kind of feminine cocoon in which she seemed, without self-consciousness and even without vanity, to be watching herself grow into her own sort of perfection. She was at times unreal in that she was compounded exclusively of female traits. Events beyond her control had devastated the womanly prison in which she was best able to express herself; she needed a life in which everything from birth to death was regulated by family and household. Now that she was challenged with new life, now that everything was dominated by chance and she had no family or husband, she could only try, in fantastic ways, to rebuild the soft, protective prison. Gertrude was deeply moved to pity by Florence's height, even by the healthy and beautiful face that required no care and no disguise. "She is not a man's type," she said, sorrowfully.

Florence was still wearing her coat when she came into Marian's room. "Look," she said, holding out her hand. She was wearing a small diamond on her finger.

"It's beautiful," Marian said. It was a very new and very young looking ring. It sparkled weakly on Florence's energetic hand.

"Jesse gave it to me," she said. "He didn't want to spend the money on it and I think it's silly, but I just couldn't get out of it." She brushed her hair back nervously.

"What do you mean?" Marian said. She picked up a book on the bed and made a place for Florence to sit down.

"I had been writing them at home about Jesse. I told them I was engaged and, of course, they started talking about a ring. My mother and sister don't look at things as I do. We also have lots of aunts and people like that around. You know how fussy such women are. I didn't want the ring, but I couldn't let them down. Anyway, it will give them something to talk about with their friends." She took a cigarette from the pocket of her coat. Her face had lost some of its calm.

"I don't suppose Jesse will ever stop kidding me about it. I guess he's kidding. Do you think I did wrong?" She was not looking at Marian.

"You wanted it, didn't you?"

"Yes, I suppose I wanted it myself a little. Not for here, though. Not for the city. I wanted it for home, for my family, my friends. Can you understand that?" She seemed in some way diminished, as if she had lost a very dear part of herself.

"Of course."

Florence's long, well-shaped legs were hanging over the edge of the bed. The desk lamp was shining on her face. "Would you have done it?" she asked.

"No, not that particular thing," Marian said shyly. "I wouldn't have needed to, because we aren't that sort. My family is not sentimental. Maybe that's why nothing shocks them." She was thinking of the money Bruce had given her.

"I wouldn't have thought that," Florence said. "I wouldn't have thought they were that advanced, somehow."

"Advanced?" Marian laughed self-consciously.

Florence crushed her cigarette in the ash tray beside the bed. "You do understand that Jesse wasn't selfish about it," she said, as an afterthought. "It was only that he didn't think such symbols important. The ring is practically worth-

171

less in terms of money, so he thought it was foolish to have it all. I agree. Really, I do. But . . ."

"Gertrude will approve. She'll be very excited about it."

"I know," Florence said. "I know." She smiled cautiously.

Florence kept saying that she had to leave, that Jesse would be downstairs. Yet, she did not leave. She sat there silently gazing at the wall. She might have been afraid to meet him again, afraid that, through the ring, he had found out something about her that displeased him permanently. She felt altered and uncertain.

A dense cloud of cigarette smoke lay over the room. Marian raised the window and a layer of cool air shot through the smoke. There was a strong feeling of Florence's private struggle in the atmosphere, and the eyes of the two girls refused to meet. Sitting on the narrow bed with the dark green cover and the dark green pillows behind her back, Florence looked, under the yellow light, like some Amazon court mistress. Even the bare floor and the simple furnishings of the room were softened by her transformation. There was nothing left of her past; nothing of the schoolteacher remained. Where had the other self retreated? In the quiet of the room, it seemed strange that Florence had ever known an impersonal life. The years she had spent in preparation for her work, her ambition—where were they? How could they have been erased so quickly? She was now simply a girl with an engagement ring on her finger. Downstairs a man would soon be waiting for her and that was the prime fact of existence. Soon they would be only shadows on the pavement, hers taller than his and hanging over the outline of his body like a cloak.

When the clock said eight, Florence got up and threw her fur coat over her shoulders. "Do you want to go with us?" she said brightly. "Jesse likes you very much. I want you to know him better." She began to talk very rapidly. "He's very nice and very gentle when you've grown accustomed to him. He only pretends to be cold and cynical. Strangely, that's the young boy left in him and his tenderness is the man." She repeated, "I'm sure you'd like him." The buzzer on the wall rang. "That must be Jesse. I told the maid to ring me here. Are you sure you won't go out?"

Marian shook her head and Florence disappeared down the hall. When the door was finally closed, Marian felt a painful loneliness. She longed for the winters of her childhood, for that which, whether good or bad, kept crowding out the reality of the present. Her home and family retained a mystery that made her solitary life pale. She was always returning from her new friends and thinking of her parents. Strangers did not baffle her; only her relatives. The image of her grandmother, the hermit old lady whose limp hand hung from her sleeve like a child's empty glove, was more unfathomable than all the foreign faces on the streets. Florence's voice ringing out, "You'll like him! You'll like him!" reminded Marian of Bruce and of one of her earliest disillusionments. The night outside was as clear and still as the night she and Bruce had passed under the heavy trees, over gravel and dirt and uneven pavements. "There are so many things I want you to know," he kept saying. The streets were silent and his voice was hushed, but his steady speech, the ceaseless anecdote and enthusiasm rising and falling, droned on like a motor. Hatless, tall and energetic, Bruce pushed her onward. Beneath the occasional street lights, his face was white and dramatic. The ground under their feet became soft, indicating they had passed beyond paved streets and had entered the dried mud paths with names she did not know. The lights in the houses became dimmer, and children played in the half-dark streets. As they walked, people sitting on the porches stared at them glumly. Danger flowed under the streets like a sewer. At last they came to the viaduct and he led her beneath it, into the unhoused dump yards. In this dark, subterranean world even the moon was sinister. The desolation was evil and alien and she felt it could not possibly be

173

a part of the town in which she had always lived. "You have never been here before," Bruce said. "It's the sort of place people are always pretending to know without ever really having seen it." He was breathing heavily and his voice was almost drunken. Across the way stood a school building, a dark prison-like structure surrounded by iron railings. So this was the bad school, the home of the evil pupils she had heard so much about. "In the daytime you can see more," Bruce said. "But there's something special about the nights here, also." He waved his arm over the desperate island. A solitary tree loomed up in the distance. It was as unnatural, in these surroundings, as the threatening school building. Bruce crushed her hand in his. They were almost running.

"It's not far from here. Just around the bend," he said. "I'm sure you'll like her. She's amazing."

"Are you sure she won't mind?" Marian said. He chuckled and did not answer.

They were drawing close to an appalling formation of dark shacks. With the approach of the destination, Bruce became more and more impersonal, as if he were facing an impolite audience. His protestations became louder and Marian kept saying yes, yes to everything he said, because she knew he wanted the adventure confirmed. He had a horror that things would not come off, that this present event would not be as exciting as the one before; and, so, he was always protecting himself, always saying that things were wonderful if in their proper form, but, if they should seem less than he had promised, he was not to blame. There was noise on the porches they passed. Bruce's voice became more insistent and he managed a weird colloquialism that matched the voices on the street. His laughter was harsh, suggestive and ebullient.

"It would be just my luck to draw a blank tonight," he said. "She may have hit herself upside the head with a jug and we won't be able to get a grunt out of her. But, believe me, she's funny when she gets going. I just hope she'll talk tonight."

"It will be all right if she doesn't," Marian said.

Bruce stopped suddenly and his rich laughter struck her again. "Certainly, it's all right! It just won't be worth anything, though! I want you to see her at her best." He stared rather angrily at Marian.

They turned a corner and the darkness deepened. "It's right over there," Bruce said. The house he pointed to was a tiny brown shack. The moon touched one side of it and it seemed to be tilted. The door was half ajar and a kerosene lamp was burning in the back of the house. There was no grass on the strip of ground between the house and the road. The two front windows were stuffed with newspapers. The moonlight flashed over a tin can on the porch, making it shine like silver. The steady sound of howling dogs punctuated the muffled voices behind them. Bruce stood for a moment in the doorway. A scrap of newspaper blew against his leg. Several people passed the house, and he drew Marian into the corner of the porch and they hid there until the street was empty. The little shack was silent and private and Bruce seemed momentarily disconcerted, but soon he began to laugh loudly. There was nothing to laugh about, but he seemed to want to make noise, to give the place a gaiety it lacked. He looked through the door and into the square, dark room. A narrow ray of light from the back divided the room. When his fist beat upon the door, they heard a sound in the back of the house and a deep, lazy cough. Marian followed him through the light ray and into the second room. A woman was lying on a brass bed. A gray blanket was thrown over her.

The Negro woman put one hand over her eyes and coughed again. She turned away from the light, threw off the cover and sat up on the side of the bed.

"Hi, you all," she said vaguely, looking without recognition at their faces.

"You remember me?" Bruce said, smiling. The woman smiled in return, or at least her lips came back automatically over her loose teeth and she shook her head. "Yeah, I do. I sure do." The bewildered expression did not leave her face.

"I've been down here lots of times," Bruce said slowly, patiently.

"Sure, sure," she cackled. "I know you been down here just lots. You was here not long ago. I member the very time."

She stood up now: a thin, old woman with skin drawn tightly over her facial bones. The left side of her mouth was misshapen. The lip turned downward at the edges and revealed a square of her gums. The entire face was emaciated and helpless; feverish eyes shone over the sooty surface of her cheekbones. Feebleness was rampant in the body, even in the loose, crazed, reflex smile. She was wearing a dress of red silk, the blackish red of blood. It came down in folds at her ankles and ended in a ragged scallop just over the tops of the old black men's shoes she was wearing. Brass earrings, little gleaming circles, hung from her ears like spectators at the movement of her incredible head.

"Spect I look like a turtle turd," the old woman said indifferently. The crazed smile did not leave her face and she mumbled on unintelligibly. She did not look at Marian. In fact one could not tell where she looked, because the tired eyes wandered all about the room, apparently seeing nothing. Besides the bed there was no other article of furniture except a clock painted green which stood on the window sill.

Marian did not hear much that Bruce was saying. She watched, almost in a state of catalepsy, the silent laughter on the woman's damaged face, the bald nakedness of the arms hanging down at the sides of the red dress, the dark, wandering eyes imprisoned in the forehead.

"You know that story you were telling me," Bruce said. He held out a package of cigarettes and she took one.

Laughing still, she took a match out of her pocket and struck it on the floor.

"Yeah, yeah," she said hoarsely. She licked the end of the cigarette. When she brought the match to it, her hands shook violently with age and illness.

"That story about the man down here. The man who said he owned part of a railroad that ran under the Atlantic ocean. He told about the railroad and . . ."

The woman laughed shortly. A gust of smoke blew around her face. "Yeah, yeah. About them railroads you say. Them railroads."

Bruce turned to Marian for a moment, but she did not look at him. Standing there in the center of the room and looking down at the woman's face, he looked even taller than usual. He held a cigarette in his red-skinned fingers and he pointed the glow at the woman who sat quietly staring at him, without moving, as if she were trying to read his lips.

"I know you remember about the doctor . . ."

"Doctor!" she said quickly. "No, man, you at the wrong place. I don't want no doctor looking up my ass to see if my hat's on straight. No, not me." Her hands shook more violently.

"I'm not a doctor," Bruce said.

"You ain't?"

He spoke more sharply to her. "But the funniest story of all was about the white man who moved down here. The man with the small feet and the straw hat which he wore summer and winter." He turned to Marian. "Maybe you saw that house down the street. The tall and empty one with the moon shining on the attic window. It's two stories and they say it was once a fine house, but you can't tell now." Marian nodded, trying to visualize the house and the man with the small feet. "This man, rich they say, moved down here of his own accord. Stayed twenty years and the white people forgot all about him. Then some more whites came down and they're still here."

"About twenty years, you say," the woman said, slapping her hand against her leg. The sunken cheeks, the dark, deadened skull were thrust up at them. The lips were shaped into the crippled smile and the voice was mechanical and compulsionless.

"About twenty years," she repeated.

"You knew him, didn't you?" Bruce said.

"I knowed him I reckon. I knowed him sure if he was here."

Bruce was now standing sideways, looking half at Marian and half at the woman on the bed. "You see, this man was a real character," he explained to Marian. "You've got to imagine what it means. This white man, down here in the big house, lost to everything in the town, to his childhood. The old booger just preferred this, I reckon. He wasn't anybody down here, anonymous in the way the ordinary mortal can't bear to . . ."

The woman on the bed moved. "You got anything to eat or drink?" she said, running her hand over her scarred lip. "I ain't even got the time."

"Are you hungry?" Bruce said. She began to shake her head vaguely, and her phthisic body rocked back and forth, crazily, childishly. "Naw, naw," she said.

She reached down in the neck of her dress and drew out the black shoulder strap of the underskirt she was wearing. "I got to git this hitched up someways," she said. She made a knot in the black string. When she saw they were looking at her, she began again to laugh. "I come close to hanging myself on this rope," she said.

Bruce laughed too, a short, mysterious laugh. "You look fine," he said.

She pulled the rags of her clothing up and looked down to the floor to see if the black undergarment was visible over her shoes.

178

The air in the room was stale and cold. The front door had blown shut and they stood there in the semi-darkness of the strange surroundings known only to the old woman. There was no evidence that anyone shared the house with her. There were not even many pieces of furniture to share her complete and frightening habitation of the shack. She slept and sat in the house as a dog would lie on a back porch at night. She did not for a moment allow the strangers to become a part of the room. When she turned in the spot in which she stood, or looked to the floor or ceiling, the room was as intimate with her as the clothing she wore.

"You wanna do it in front of her?" she said at last. The impervious and very old voice filled the room. It was a woman's voice, a voice that asked questions flatly and did not have any reply to the answer. She was waiting, unreproachful, in an impenetrable, blank acquiescence.

"We just came to talk to you," Bruce said. Marian, without knowing why, smiled at the woman. She had to smile; there was nothing else to do. To be nodding and smiling and looking into the drained eyes, and showing her white teeth and smiling into the black room—that was the role in which she had been cast.

"We've got to be going," Bruce said. He twisted the toe of his shoe around on the sodden, sinking floor.

"You all come back," the woman said. Spit seeped out of her twisted mouth. It ran out of the corner and down below the lip and into the deep wrinkle on her chin. "You all come back."

"I don't believe you mean that," Bruce said, hurt.

"Sure. You all come back."

They left her standing in the light ray of the kerosene lamp. Her outrageous head wobbled from side to side and on the scarred face there was an idle acknowledgement that someone had come and gone.

The street outside was dark. Urgent, quarreling voices rang out in the black shadows. The dogs continued to yelp.

A plane cut through the sky. "She's amazing, isn't she?" Bruce insisted. "I couldn't get her to talk much, but you could get some idea of her."

His hand was holding Marian's arm tightly. This strong grip somehow dissolved individuality and made them one. In one of the houses they heard the deep growls of an argument and in the moonlight these heavy human voices were filled with terror of themselves and of each other. Out, out the voices came, doomed and dooming, and then the sharp, hard sound of a scuffle, of body against body, could be heard.

They were walking very fast, almost running toward the dump heap so that they might pass through that and over the viaduct and see the first gasoline station whose redness and whiteness announced the dividing line between this valley and the town. There was a light in one of the shacks and Marian glanced at the living room it illuminated. She saw Hattie; other faces were around hers. They sat over a table near the window: a group of dark faces indistinguishable except for age.

"Oh, there's Hattie! Down here," she whispered.

"Where did you expect her to be?" Bruce said.

"Down here! This is where she lives."

She could not tell what Hattie and her family were doing. She did not clearly see the inside of the house and she did not hear their voices. But she had seen the street and the dump beyond, knew the danger that surrounded Hattie's house, the blackness and darkness, the startling fragility of every roof, the inconveniences. There were no carpets here, no telephones, no bathrooms, or bedrooms. There was only space enough to hold the people while they slept and while they were not in someone else's home earning the rent for this place.

"She's a real character, isn't she?" Bruce was saying. "She knows stories about everyone in this town. You weren't disappointed, were you?"

"No," Marian said. She felt his arm tightening upon hers until it was almost painful. In answer to this she repeated, "No, I wasn't disappointed."

When they reached the forked street beside the gasoline station, Bruce said, "You don't think I'd have anything to do with her, do you? It's too silly even to think about. I suppose she said what she did because she wasn't sure who I was. You know how they are . . . They forget." He was engrossed in Marian's face. She saw that he was telling the truth and that he had to be certain she believed him.

Marian began to laugh softly. He stopped stiffly and anger mounted his face. "What are you laughing at? I think you should know people of that sort."

"I think you should *know* them too."

"What?" he said. An ironic smile flashed across his mouth. "All women should get around more than they do. Being allowed to go to bars makes them think they know what's what. But I don't know why she said what she did! You can't explain those things. For Christ's sake, I don't know what the old idiot brought up such a thing for!"

"I know why," Marian said. He heard her and the sides of his mouth drew down in a strange grimace. She thought that he might strike her, but his face cleared suddenly. He never liked to get very deeply into anything. They walked on into town. She could feel a warmth rising up in him, as an inexplicable accompaniment to this misplaced evening. He became more and more exhilarated and more and more tender.

CHAPTER FIVE

ONE NIGHT toward the end of March Gertrude did not appear for dinner. She had never been absent at the evening meal before, though it was a common enough occurrence in the house.

"One of our sheep has strayed," the red-haired woman said. Now that spring was coming she had returned to the brown silk dress she had worn in the fall. A smile of calculated indifference was on her face. "Perhaps she is wandering by the docks and sighing for her homeland."

"What do you mean?" Marian said.

The woman pulled her salad plate closer to the edge of the table and posed her fork over it thoughtfully. "Nothing is so good as Europe, you know," she said, looking up from her plate and glancing at the entire table with the easy innocence and half-surprise of the guilty.

"You know that isn't true," Marian said sharply. "For Gertrude America appears more beautiful than any country can be in reality.

"They are very tricky," the woman said flatly.

The others at the table were listening, alternately seeming to agree with both Marian and the woman, and then suddenly and cautiously retreating into themselves, admitting to nothing except the existence of all possibilities. Florence was sitting at the end of the table and had not heard the first part of the conversation. "Where is Gertrude?" she said abruptly.

"Flown the coop," a timid young girl said.

"Have you seen her all day?" Marian asked. "I haven't."

Florence said that she had not. The meal went on.

A woman, close to seventy, with hair dyed jet black, brushed past the table and hobbled over to her own group. One of her feet was slightly malformed and it made her walk strangely, as if she were constantly trotting. She seldom ever spoke to anyone and seemed deeply engrossed in work of enormous importance. Even with her silence, the woman's presence particularly annoyed the younger girls. Her fingers were stained with ink and she carried countless papers in an ever-present purse. As she ate, she thumbed through the papers. For all the ink stains and the business-like purse, she reminded Marian of the old women on the porches of America. Her face was dry and wrinkled and full of comfortably circumscribed wisdom, like the face of a country woman whose children are grown and whose burial expenses have been taken care of. The woman apparently had only one dress, a dark blue silk covered with a small white design. The dress was as rectangular as a drawing board, except for the rounded hole at the neck and the bell sleeves which came just above her elbow. Between the library and the dormitory she passed her last days.

"She has been here since 1925," the red-haired woman said.

"So long?" one of the women gasped, a giggle rising up in her throat.

"What does she do?" another girl said.

The red-haired woman hesitated, apparently anxious to take her time and to enjoy the full depths of her knowledge. She twirled the empty water glass in her fingers. "She does just what the young girls do. She whiles away her time waiting. This is as good a place as any, don't you think?"

Marian felt the woman's sardonic eyes upon her. Disdain faded gradually into boredom and a forced remoteness. She went on, "There is one great difference, however. The poor old lady has been here so long that she actually works. She goes to the library at nine and stays until dinnertime. I have seen her shelf there. By now she has been through hundreds of books and she has surely filled thousands of cards with notes."

"How remarkable," a middle-aged woman said.

"Does she know what's on the cards? Do the cards represent anything?" a chemistry student asked.

"I doubt it," the red-haired woman said. "Yet she has the illusion of progress and I for one forgive her. But the young girls don't even do that. They don't go through the motions of study. They get their satisfaction by being able to say they are working on a degree."

"Nonsense," the chemistry student said and ceased to listen to the conversation. The red-haired woman was daunted by this girl; she feared the scientific eye.

The waiters filled the water glasses. A sense of failure, crystallized in the industrious old woman, had settled over the table. Each night, with the melting of the candles and the disorganization of the dishes, the women seemed conscious of being away from home. This hour was always heavy with nostalgia and each face became self-absorbed. The career for which each one hoped seemed enormously difficult and precarious. When this passed a frantic hurry settled upon them. (*I must write that letter. I must catch up. I must get the courage to speak to the head of the department.*)

"I was informed today that I have a good position for next fall," the red-haired woman said. "I shall be in college work now."

There were smiles around the table, though no one spoke. They did not hesitate to believe her, nor did they ask for details. She *had* got a good position; they knew it. She was to be a success, and there was no way it could have been altered. Behind her self-confidence lay the recognition that she had to work next year, the year after and presumably until she died. They bowed to her acceptance of this eventuality. It had given her equipment most of the others lacked, because, despite their plans, they didn't fully believe in the lonely future. They couldn't admit this year was to be followed by another like it and that such was to be the continuity of life. They pursued imaginary knights-errant who promised release from this planned and consciously constructed existence.

"You are in sociology, aren't you?" Florence said. "That's what I taught." Seeing her own former plans realized by the red-haired woman made her remorseful.

"This year is almost over," Marian said softly. The others said, Yes, yes. Marian began to feel sick inside when she thought of the money Bruce had lent her, the money which in retrospect seemed so valuable. She remembered the dreams she had for her mother and with pain she imagined her father telling the office men about his daughter studying in the East. And then, without warning, another thought came to her: they, her mother and father, were behind the meaninglessness of this year. The thought startled her so, she wondered if the others sensed what she was thinking.

"They'll never know," the red-haired woman said brightly. Green ice cream melted in her bowl. She stirred it idly.

"Who? Who?" the women said.

"The people at home. Where women are concerned, relatives are easily satisfied. An attempt at something will last them a lifetime," she said cryptically.

One by one, the women got up from the table. They hurried up to their rooms where they would feverishly engage in some activity until the guilt of wasted time, or confusion, had been erased.

"Where do you suppose Gertrude is?" Marian said to Florence.

"I don't know. Do you suppose . . ."

"She's usually here. Let's go up to her room."

They knocked on her door, but there was no answer. They did not speak about her further.

Marian said, "I'm going downstairs to practice. This is my hour to use the piano."

Florence said, "I'll go to the library. I won't fool around here as I usually do. I'll go and stay until the doors are closed." She started up the steps and then turned back. "I'm meeting Jesse at nine. Would you like to take a walk or something?"

"No. Leo is coming at ten."

Early the next morning, Marian beat upon Gertrude's door. When there was no answer, she started to cry. During the early part of last evening she had forgotten Gertrude, but when she went to bed the thought of the little woman troubled her sleep. She rattled the door again, but no longer expected it to have any effect. She already felt the shock of Gertrude's disaster, without knowing what it was.

She was still sobbing when she went into the director's office and suggested that Gertrude's door be opened. A look of acute pain came over the director's face and Marian knew she did not want to open the door. She was afraid she might find Gertrude dead there.

"Who is the girl again?" the director kept saying. A locket hung down over her breast and she pressed it between the palms of her hands.

"Gertrude . . . I don't know her last name," Marian said. She could feel the older woman glaring at her, somehow connecting her with the disorder.

"Gertrude?" she said sullenly. Helplessly she began to thumb through the files.

"The room number is 692."

"That's a little more definite," she said coldly. "Let's go."

The girls were just coming down to breakfast and Marian looked into the dining room to see if Gertrude might be there. She was not.

The director's keys jangled. She was breathing heavily. This tall, stout woman with a high reputation for executive ability was made very shy by emotional matters and any direct dealings with the residents.

In the elevator, the woman smiled vacantly at the residents. She did not speak again to Marian until the car had stopped. "What is your name?"

"Marian Coleman," she answered, feeling very small.

"Oh, yes. Oh, yes." The locket bounced up and down on her breast.

"Is this woman a friend of yours?"

"Yes."

As they turned the corner of the corridor, an alarm clock went off in one of the rooms. Water was running in the basins and these homey sounds gave their journey to Gertrude's room a kind of unreality. When at last they stood before the door, the director's face was expressionless. Slowly she ran her thumb over the endless number of keys until she came to the right one. Taking a deep breath, she slipped it into the lock. Marian stepped backward. From the open door, sunlight filled the hall.

"She's not here!" the director said, her voice shrill with relief. "Not here!"

Marian stepped into the doorway. The heavy odor of bath powder, perfume, and incense tickled her nostrils. The window was closed. She felt as if she were walking into some famous courtesan's burial vault.

"You see, she is not here!" the director repeated. She pointed to the bed over which a quilt of peach satin was spread. The room was so compact it did not seem to have corners. Everything blended into everything else, rug, chair, ceiling and floor, odor and color, as if they had entered a scented globe.

"I never saw so many things," the director said. "It does not look at all like a student's room. I don't know what it is like!" She was trying unsuccessfully to place Gertrude in her mind, to remember which of all the faces that had come and gone could belong to such a room.

The sunlight was filled with dust particles. They stood there without seeing each other. The room had overpowered both of them. It was a few moments before they noticed that the radio was playing softly. The director turned it off. She looked about the room in a sort of trance. On every available flat surface there were little boxes, each carefully marked pins, clips, needles, buttons. On the dresser there was an old-fashioned ivory hair-receiver with Gertrude's name written across the top in fine gilt German letters. A little jar of coins stood beside the ivory container. Gertrude's bedroom slippers peeped out from under the bed; one of the toes turned outward. Several heavy silver spoons streaked with tarnish lay on the desk. The sunlight was not proper for the room; it should have been lighted with a thousand tiny candles that gave off a faint odor of tallow to mix with the weighted and perfumed air.

"Where is her family? Nearest of kin?" the director asked timidly.

Marian pointed to the pictures on the wall. Among smaller frames, a large family portrait was hanging. They looked at the dark, vivid-featured group. The mother's eyes gleamed at them as if the eyes were artificially illuminated; the father's large nose and thick lips extended prominently. The children, boys and girls, were grave and solemn within the frame. They had thick, black curly hair, fine noses and dark eyes and a similar lower lip that puffed out slightly, as if bruised. Gertrude was there, a small figure, with intense eyes. She was shadowed by the family group, but held safely and proudly by them in the tightness of the frame.

"Do you know her family?" the director asked.

"I don't think she has any relatives here."

"What a situation!" The baffled woman sighed.

Marian felt the room closing in on her. It was a secret, remote self which Gertrude had guarded against the modern, clean, unreminiscent building. It was Gertrude's past. The little trinkets and pictures were the only things salvaged. Marian understood why she had never asked her into it. It was a part of the old world.

"Where is she?" the director asked.

"She's just gone off," Marian said. "I'm sure that's all. She's just gone off some place." She started to say that Gertrude was wearing a short fur jacket and high-heeled shoes and that she was probably sitting in a restaurant, talking to people, listening very carefully to what they said and to the dismaying echo of her own accent. Or if not there, she might be in a telephone booth and her laughter was going over the wire to some astonished person on the other end.

"Someone must be notified," the director said.

"There is no one."

She trembled. "The police then." Her large white face became flushed and speckled and she left the room.

"Close the door when you come out," she said. "Perhaps you can find a clue."

Marian hated to leave the room unoccupied. It was like deserting a cradle. The director had opened a window and the odor of Gertrude's perfumes was vanishing. This monument to her majestic memories was already being defiled by the wind that swept through the room. Where is she? Where is she? Marian repeated. Perhaps Gertrude was asleep, her black hair spread fan-shaped around her head and the sharp curve of her nose pointed up toward a strange ceiling. The images of Gertrude, all the places she might be, came to Marian like a gallery of pictures with Gertrude's optimistic face the central figure on each canvas, her unalterable face surrounded by various glooms which she did not understand. Perhaps she was sitting in a bus station, one foot drawn up under her and smiling at the crumpled faces around her; or she might at this minute be drawing a green shade in a hotel room and looking out upon a rusty fire-escape. When she remembers, she will think of her library

189

classes and of the rows and rows of white paper laid out carefully on the desks, of the pencils flying across the sheets and she will say, "I shall get a position in a library. Everywhere there is a library." She imagines herself in a black dress standing behind the clean desk with a sharpened pencil in her hand. There are rows of books on the shelves and to them she holds a magical key.

Marian closed the door and went to her own room. The maid was there. "She has gone?" the woman said. She leaned against the wall and stroked her sagging chin. "When they go like this, without taking anything, they are never found," she said. "Them that takes things comes back, because their minds ain't made up. They're still trying to keep something of what they've left. I've always noticed it. Mark my word, this one won't be coming back."

"Have many gone like this?" Marian said. "Many girls from here?"

The maid's eyes were glazed with fatigue. She blinked them wearily. "Not from here that I know of. But lots of people go. Turn on the radio some night and you can hear about them. It makes you wonder where all of them are."

"Perhaps they find each other," Marian said.

"What?" the maid said. "Find each other?" Her face was exalted with imagination. She seemed to see before her a vast, unfurnished room into which, in a perpetual twilight, these figures drifted and met their mates. "Do you think they let each other know when they get together? No, I don't think they would hardly do that. They wouldn't tell each other they were both hiding away." She rubbed her cleaning cloth over the desk.

"Is that your mother?" she said, pointing to the picture on the desk. She had asked this question countless times before. This time she did not even turn around to see Marian nod affirmatively.

"Where is she?" she said, her voice mysteriously softened

by the morning's excitement. "She's at your home, I guess."

"No, she's out West," Marian said.

"Lunger?"

"No."

The maid ran her cloth over the picture. She left a streak of furniture oil across the mother's face. "Out West, you say. Out West." She paused. "You're lucky she's not dead."

"Dead?" Marian said. "Oh, she's quite young."

"Look in the graveyard and you will see some there younger than you," she whispered.

The sense of the departed tormented the maid; the dead and the wandering materialized threateningly before her. "You think they're just floating around in the air, those that ain't here? Some do. Some can even see them."

Marian was thinking of her mother and Gertrude: two among the missing. Both of these truncated histories were important to her, and it seemed that she was not to know the end of either.

The maid ran the mop over the floor and prepared to leave. "Well, it's not our fault," she said in consolation.

"I guess not," Marian said. The woman went out. In a moment she could be heard telling the girl in the next room of Gertrude's disappearance.

In the afternoon Marian shut herself up in her room to go through the books and papers of her courses. Rain clouds hung over the city and it was too dark to read without her study lamp. With the evidence of the past months' study laid out before her, she felt that perhaps she had learned a lot. Here were books she had not known before. Her desk was filled with concert stubs and programs. The year had not been completely lost. At the same time it had not been fully used. A shadow hung over everything she had attempted, a shadow which, without her willing it to do so, was beginning to take an ugly shape. The richness of her family feeling was slowly being impoverished by doubt. Even the mother's holiness was daily defiled by her mind. The filial devotion that had been her life's sustenance had, by long resistance on her parents' side, become a devouring poison. As the feelings increased she was surprised that she wanted more and more to go home. Perhaps she hoped for a new vision, some sudden reason for faith that would bring around another conversion, like a death bed repentance of atheism. Or, if that did not come, she might, by returning home to an undeniable waste, cast off forever the paralyzing bonds. She knew now that those who mourned violently over a relative they had just as violently abused in life were not dishonest. The denial of God is certainly no more terrifying than the denial of one's flesh and blood and it was this terror that changed hatred to grief. Self-revulsion always accompanied these recent challenges of her family's right to respect.

After dinner that night, Marian followed Florence up to her room. The news of Gertrude's disappearance had been much discussed at the table. Countless stories of white slavery rings were revived and before the meal was over each resident had recounted her own town's most mysterious and gruesome event. When they left the table they were all chilled and stunned and full of hatred for the city that had suddenly become so sinister.

"I have some work to do," Florence said when they had reached her room. "You just sit on the bed and talk to me."

She took off her dress and put on a robe in preparation for washing out her stockings and handkerchiefs. With the hot water steaming in the basin, the towel spread over the back of the chair for the stockings to be laid on, the cover of the bed slightly mussed and a soiled blouse hanging on the nail behind the door, the small room was like a haphazard apartment. It was laundry, study, bedroom, and living room.

"How cold it is outside," Florence said.

"Yes."

"It's warm in here, though."

"Yes."

They were not listening to each other, but the conversation went on until it was interrupted by the sound of running water.

"Florence . . ." Marian said.

Florence turned off the faucet. "What is it? I thought you started to say something." Beads of perspiration stood out on her forehead.

"I was thinking of something I've worried about for a long time. It's about money. The money I came here on." The words sounded strange to Marian, as if she were speaking in a new language.

Florence had been bending over the basin. She jerked herself upright very quickly. "What money?" she said cautiously.

"A friend of mine, a man, gave it to me. I don't remember taking it, strangely enough. Don't remember the moment the actual transfer was made. There must have been a precise moment. A minute when I must have recognized what I was doing? Isn't that right?" She was shocked when she had first mentioned "money" to Florence, but now it didn't matter. Why had it ever mattered, she wondered.

"Is that so bad?" Florence said carefully.

"No. He had the money and he wanted me to come. That isn't the point. I do think I ought to have admitted that I was taking it, though. My grandmother knew it, my brother knew and I knew, of course. Yet, we didn't mention it to each other. My parents have never had anything much to do with my own finances, but I was afraid they would be shocked by this. When they found out, they didn't mind. They were pleased, I think. It shouldn't have pleased them, should it?"

"I don't know, Marian," Florence said humbly. "How can I say?"

Marian thought that if she looked at Florence, she

wouldn't be able to say anything further. She kept staring down at her stockings. "At first I was worried about the man. It seemed to me that I could never face him again, knowing how little is to come from this year. However, I'm sure he doesn't really care. When he remembers it, he is glad I'm here. He probably thinks, occasionally, that I may do something fine and that would be nice. If I don't, he'll forget. What is wrong is the fog in which it was done, the sly refusal to look at the accomplished fact. That's the way we are about everything."

Florence was spreading the washed stockings on the back of the chair. "Isn't that the South?" she said tentatively.

"The South? How silly!" Marian frowned. "I'm sure we would have been the same if we had lived in Pittsburgh. No, I'm afraid you don't get the picture at all. Maybe it's just that none of us is very smart; could that be it? Certainly we appear to be respectable people. Do you know . . . ? I'm afraid my grandmother is deficient. All of us have acted as if she were brilliant, because she was quiet and self-centered. How is it possible to be so much mistaken? And not only are we mistaken, but everyone else. She's very much admired and yet her reading and writing ability is not far beyond the second grade." She did not think it possible to describe her grandmother to Florence, to communicate the picture of the serene, empty face and the incomparable poise that grew out of a blankness deeper than anyone would ever know.

"No! No! You mustn't, Marian," Florence said. "I'm sure it isn't right to speak this way."

"I suppose not. Perhaps it's changed now. Maybe I am wrong. Before I left home I couldn't bear to think anything unpleasant about my family. Strangely enough, that's the only change I can see in myself after this year. I expected so much and it's passed me by, somehow."

"Yes, years do that," Florence said in a very remote voice. "I've had many of them and this is your first."

Marian said, "What am I waiting for? What were you waiting for? What did we expect to happen? What does my mother expect to happen?"

"Your mother?"

"Yes. I know something is wrong, but I don't know what to do about it. When I came here I wanted to work very hard and to be in a position to take her away from her troubles. As foolish as it may sound, that's what I wanted. Underneath, though, I rather believed some third party would come around the corner and save both my mother and me."

"What is wrong with your mother?"

"Wrong?" She adjusted the pillow at her back. "Maybe there isn't anything wrong. Perhaps I only dreamed she was unhappy."

"Why did you want to do so much for her? Why was that the reason behind everything?"

"I wanted her to love me."

"But mothers always . . ." Florence said. She did not finish the sentence. Marian got up and walked to the window. After a moment, she said, "I forgot my cigarettes. Do you have some?"

Florence made a great clatter opening the drawer to get the cigarettes. "Did you care very much for the man who gave you the money?" she said, as she held the match for Marian. Her voice had the special brightness she reserved for conversations on love and marriage.

"No, I don't suppose I did," Marian said. Florence's eyes became cloudy. "I expected to be scolded about him, just as I did about the money. I was sure my parents would object for a number of obvious reasons. Again, they didn't. If I had had to defend him, I might have fooled myself about what he was. You know how those things work. I had to defend him only to myself and in the absence of an opponent I suppose I was always too conscious of the darker side. Things he said and did kept troubling me."

"Do you think you ought to go so deeply into these things?" Florence said.

"I don't know," Marian said.

Confessions have their own formal limitations; if the ideas are discussed too carefully dishonesty creeps in and there is no confession at all. This one had come to an end. The room had become very hot with the last gust of evening steam. Florence's face looked empty, as if she had exerted all her effort and had nothing left.

The halls were deserted when Marian finally started for her own room. She undressed and lay down on the bed. It was still too early to go to sleep and she turned on the radio beside her bed. A tinny, cheap voice rang out through the darkness. The bored announcer talked on and on in a monotonous monologue:

"John William Brown; eight years, one broken tooth, four feet three inches, ninety-six pounds, scar on chin, a colored boy wearing blue trousers, blue shirt, last seen a year ago. Maria Scala; twelve years, one eyelid slightly drooping, five feet, one hundred pounds, wearing yellow socks, plaid dress and blue coat, missing since December. Gertrude Dorfmann; thirty-seven years, German accent, five feet three inches, one hundred six pounds, wearing black fur jacket, last seen . . ."

CHAPTER SIX

*L*EO's raincoat was the color of straw. His face was pinched into a frown of protest against the drifts of rain that splattered his cheeks. The smell of damp wool clung to the people on the street and chattering voices, like children muttering at play, rose and descended restlessly.

"I cannot believe it," Leo said. "You are going away so suddenly. Last night I kept telling myself that you wouldn't be here any longer, but it made me laugh. I knew it wasn't true. I thought I had been asleep and had dreamed it." The rain settled like dew upon his shoulder. He held the umbrella over her and his hand brushed against hers. It was cool and soft like a wet leaf. "Even now, I can't accept it. I keep expecting something to happen."

"Yes, it is strange," she said. She had got up at dawn this morning to reread Albert's letter. It was only a short note written with a scratchy pen and said that her grandmother was ill and she must come home. "There is no one to help except Etta . . . Etta is a friend of mine. You will meet her."

"What does it mean?" Leo said, his voice failing.

"I don't know." The illness of her grandmother had abruptly ended this year, and at the same time excused it. The event was beyond her control, and she was not certain that she felt sorry to be leaving. Already she was thinking of the house, of the wide, deserted porch, the untouched living room, of the way the rugs were spread across the hall floor. She saw her grandmother propped up comfortably in the bed and herself hovering over her, an attendant shadow in the darkened room.

As the taxi for which they had been waiting drew up to the curb, Florence and Jesse came running toward them. "I was afraid we would be too late," Florence said breathlessly. "I wanted Jesse to say good-by to you."

Raindrops dotted the brim of Jesse's hat. "It's too bad you have to leave only a few weeks before the end of the term," he said. He smiled in his dry, ambiguous way that always carried an unidentified accusation with it.

"It does seem a shame," Florence said.

"Yes. There is nothing I can do, however."

Leo opened the taxi door. "What a nice suit!" Florence said abruptly. "You look very pretty and I think that's what you want after you've been away. To look nice when you step off the train."

They were still waving when the taxi pulled away. "I believe they are to be married the end of June," Marian said to Leo. She settled down into the dilapidated leather cushions.

"Can I do anything?" Leo kept saying. "Please let me know . . ." She did not know whether it was a tear or a raindrop that clung to the lower lash of his eye.

Rain caressed the windows of the cab. The wide white expanse of the road before them contracted into a pinpoint in the distance. Piers of yellow brick concealed the tumbling river. The car dipped into a tunnel and sped onward through the city.

PART THREE

CHAPTER ONE

SEVERAL hours after midnight Mrs. Gorman was jolted out of sleep. A narrow band of moonlight lay, like an extra blanket, across the foot of her bed. Once awake, the bed beneath her began to rock violently and she had her now familiar sensation of being attacked by a volley of electrical shocks. Orange and white sparks flew about the room; a thousand burning needles pierced her flesh. Her eyes were stinging with the sight of imaginary fireworks shooting off around her. For a month she had endured these nightly terrors and each night at this hour she crept down the stairs to search for what she believed to be the source of her impending death. She imagined the source of these hissing, torturing rays was hidden in the house and that she might, by a cunning investigation, succeed in destroying the death current.

The nights found her with an enormous reserve of energy, which, perhaps, she had stored throughout her placid life in preparation for this boundlessly active death. She jumped out of bed, brushing away the brilliant pin points of fire that seemed to come out of the corners of her room. The streamer of moonlight fell upon her back. The house was silent. The odor of her room was sweet and heavy, like the milk-sweetness that clings to babies. She slipped through her open door. The stairs lay before her and to deepen the intrigue she imagined them hard and rough. With great caution she descended, as if she were moving down a perilous mountain slide. A strand of thin white hair fell across her face; the hem of her soiled night-gown brushed over her bare feet. She met her own vision in the mirror on the landing, but passed it without notic-ing the haunted eyes or the emaciated body and madly dis-torted face. Her whole frame was by now as withered and shrunken as her frail arm. Her carriage, however, was still grand and dignified and she held her decaying body, the fleshless, stiff bones, upright. The wild head was not bent. The street light was shining through the downstairs win-dow. It illuminated the brass handle of an umbrella that stood in the stand by the door. The gleaming brass agitated her furiously, but with great self-control she overcame her desire to seize it. Instead she knelt down on the floor and with extreme caution and stillness crept toward the um-brella stand. Intently she watched the light play on the shining metal. Gradually she drew closer to it. She touched the handle. It was cold. She moved it out of the light and saw that the glow vanished. This was not the source of the cruel lightning that plagued her sleep. In the shadows, masses of furniture stood out like piles of dirt, mounting upward and upward. In the corners there was a stranger, denser darkness. But she was not afraid. She swept through the house, sniffing, touching, listening for the source of her terror.

During her illness, slovenness had overtaken her. She was dirty in body and mind. The electrical shocks appeared only at night. During the day she had another form of horror. When she awoke in the morning, each awakening was accompanied by a mild, epileptic convulsion. Coming out of sleep, disgusting images, forbidden and hidden, swelled in the forefront of her mind, almost suffocating her. The weak convulsion she experienced each morning seemed to burst the images and she got partial relief. But, during the day, filthy, vulgar words, some of which she only half un-derstood, lay like a film over her tongue. At night, while she was wandering through the house, she experienced her greatest relief from suffering. The electrical shocks were confined to her own room and her hope of discovering the source in the lower part of the house gave her a feeling of control over the terror. The emptiness of the rooms pleased her; the countless places of concealment made her searching endless, for the terror was also her prime interest now. In the house disguised by darkness there would always be new crevices to investigate the next night and the night after. She did not experience cold, though her arms and feet were bare. She felt nothing except the intensity of the hunt for the origin of the death wire that made a connection with her body.

The rugs felt damp under her feet. When the nap tickled her toes, she would stop, rigid and furiously alert, thinking that the wires were hidden under the floor. When the breeze touched her arm, she would think the very air itself was the enemy. Yet the shocks were not sustained as those she knew when she was lying in bed and she proceeded through the house, cursing the walls she touched. In her madness, no member of the family, no recollection of the past, was outside the area of her curses. One by one they came before her and she poured a torrent of suspicion upon everything she had known.

The plants in the living room window cast off a strangely intricate shadow resembling crossed wires. She touched them. They too were cold. She dropped to her knees before the fireplace. It was like a great empty cave beneath the mantel. This place she had loved so well in her younger days became her special concern. She could never discard the evil possibilities of the chimney. She put her head against the stone and listened to the air passing up and down the column. It reminded her of the roar of a sea shell she had once owned and which she had held to her ear, hour after hour. The fireplace was cool and dark and she longed to go to sleep there.

The sound of the striking clock startled her. It was four

in the morning and she thought the room was getting lighter. The savage night was vanishing.

She was suddenly numb with weariness and defeat. But there would be another night. She had passed this one and therefore it was not too late to be reborn into her former tranquillity. Perhaps, tomorrow night . . . After a while she crept up the stairs. Her outraged heart beat madly.

CHAPTER TWO

HATTIE climbed the steps two at a time. All day long her shoes could be heard thumping and jumping on the stairs. She approached Mrs. Gorman's room as if she were entering a darkened theater. During the day the shades were drawn in the room and because of the illness it had not been cleaned for weeks. Hattie went in and out with pitchers of water and trays of food. Though she could have disposed of these duties quickly, she always stayed a long time, apparently watching the old woman. She had no real affection for the patient, but the shuttered drama going on in the room fascinated her. When she closed the door and vaulted down the stairs, her eyes were large and thoughtful. She might have been under a spell.

"If she lays a hand on me, I'm cutting out!" she said to Marian.

"How can you say such foolish things? You know she's too weak to hurt anyone," Marian said.

"Weak, my behind! I can see her getting ready to fly off and when she does just look for my dust!" Hattie, standing in the center of the center of the hall, looked like a dwarfed Cassandra denied garments and stature equal to the magnitude of the doom she forecast. She turned her head toward the stairs, as if she were listening for the beginning of a catastrophe. Her feeling for the sounds in the sickroom was astonishing. Whenever the old woman's cackles—they were soft, whispery and defenseless as a sick child's—were heard downstairs, Hattie did not run up to her. Yet, if she were in the kitchen when the noise was heard, she would appear dramatically under the archway of the hall and stand there while the others went up to the room. She seemed to hear something definite in these vague cries of discomfort which was concealed from the others. She filled Marian not so much with the terror of the grandmother's death as with the expectation that the old lady would commit some monstrous disgrace from which the family would never be freed. When Marian had gone up the stairs and tended the grandmother, she would return to find Hattie still standing under the archway. "Just wanted to be turned on her side, did she?" Hattie would say. She would shrug her shoulders as if this were a foolish understatement or as if she were scornful of Marian for not having understood the grandmother.

When Hattie herself had been into the sickroom, Marian, always vaguely upset by the mysteriousness of the girl's attitude, would go up after her. She saw only her grandmother's frail body stretched out on the bed. She watched her chest peacefully rising and falling, and was at a loss to understand Hattie's feeling of danger. Mrs. Gorman already looked like a corpse, but her fine features, when relaxed in sleep, had lost none of their cold, remarkable beauty. Her nose was still perfect and when her thin lips were pressed together her face retained the enigmatic calm. Marian closed the door with a sense of relief, but no sooner had it closed than she began to wonder if she had not made a mistake, if something in the face had not escaped her.

"I still say I'm bouncing out of here like a gum ball if she lays a hand on me. She's kin to you and you can put up with whatever she does," Hattie said. At that moment Marian, against her better judgment, could imagine the grandmother swooping down upon her and entangling her in a fierce and unbreakable net.

"Has something happened while I was away? Did she ever threaten you?" Marian said.

"No, she didn't. But she never was real right in the head, and she's even less right now."

"Never was right?" Marian said, hesitating.

Hattie said, pointing upstairs, "Well, would you call her just an ordinary person?"

"Yes. In a way."

"In a way. That's more like it."

They wandered about the house together, trailed each other in and out of rooms like children. The presence of the sick person had given everything a new standard and a new justification. One hour stretched into the other and the work, the quiet, even the meals were a sort of ritual. Impending change, due to the grandmother's illness, hung over the house, but it had not yet become actual. They were in a suspended state that did not require decisions. It was only necessary to watch the days come and go and to wait for the illness to do as it would.

"How's the colored people up in New York?" Hattie said when they were in the kitchen. She looked casually up at the ceiling.

"Why, I don't know exactly. I didn't see . . ." Marian said.

"You mean they ain't around every place? Just around wherever you go?" Hattie said rapidly.

"Well, they are and they aren't," Marian said, feeling sorry and ashamed that she had nothing more definite to say.

"Well, I'll be damned! They are and they ain't. I get it!" She slapped her hand on her leg. She began to whistle, as she always did when she wished to change the conversation.

"Hattie, who is Etta?" Marian said after a moment.

"She's no particular friend of mine. Don't be asking me."

"You could tell me a lot, but you won't do it. If she's been in this house, you know her."

"I guess everybody could tell everybody a lot," Hattie said sourly.

Through this haze the afternoon passed. Even Hattie seemed lost in the house. The ubiquitous quiet, the sense that the last authority had abdicated, had made the days slow and disorganized. Voices were automatically hushed and conversation lost its flavor. Sparrows collected on the lawn; the irises bloomed. Yet spring did not touch the inside of the house. The mailman's appearance was an event. He brought circulars addressed to Mrs. Gorman and bills from clothing stores for Albert. Once a day Hattie went to the grocery with a small change purse of frayed cotton stuffed in her hand, the market basket slapping against her legs. When it was time for her to return, Marian would pull back the window curtains and watch her walk up the street, plodding along like a tiny engine. Marian saw her kicking cans that came into her path, or putting down the basket to examine a piece of paper or an empty box lying on the sidewalk. She jerked and strutted along and her eyes drained the face of everyone who passed. She seemed to know every rock and ridge on the street intimately. If Marian was likely to be alone downstairs, Hattie came in through the front door. She slammed it when she entered and always said in her sharp, cheerless voice, "Albert would smack me in the mouth if he caught me coming in this way."

The first day she arrived, Marian had seen the foolishness and vanity of having Hattie in the house. There was no reason for her to be there; she was a luxury beyond their means. She wanted to tell her to go, but could not bring herself to it. She could not bear to think of the days here without her, could not imagine that life would go on if she were forever cut off from Hattie. And if the little girl ceased to work for them that would be the end of the relationship. Hattie would take nothing away with her except the sweater now hanging on the wall, but she would leave a void bigger than the house itself.

In the late afternoon someone rapped lightly on the front door.

"Here she comes," Hattie said flatly. "Don't be bringing her back here. I got no business with her." They were sitting in the breakfast room playing cards.

"Who is it?" Marian said. Hattie picked up the cards and disappeared into the kitchen.

Marian opened the door and a voice, muted to the illness in the house, said, "I'm Etta. You're Marian, aren't you?" Etta was wearing a suit of navy blue. The crisp white collar of her blouse lay over the neck of the suit. A small, blue cap covered her head. Her body was short and muscular and rather oddly unmatched with her small head. She had white skin and pink cheeks and eyes so well surrounded by white flesh they could hardly be seen. The girl passed by Marian and walked into the living room. She took long firm steps, and would have been graceful if she had not been so short. When she was seated, she spread immaculate white gloves over her lap. Marian kept thinking that there was some mistake. This girl was definitely not the type she had expected. What had she expected? she wondered.

"I always try to come in the afternoons," Etta said sweetly. "You never know when you'll be needed. I stayed away yesterday to allow you time to get settled. I know I don't like to be bothered until I'm unpacked and all that." She was smiling possessively at Marian. Even the way she had seated herself in the chair made her seem comfortably intimate with the family and its surroundings.

Marian said, "Albert wrote me about you. I'm sure you've been very good."

"There was no one else and fortunately I have plenty of time to help look after things." She removed her jacket. The blouse was molded tightly over her chest and shoulders. Without embarrassment she examined Marian's face carefully. "You don't look like Albert very much," she said. Marian noticed that she had a nervous way of putting her finger on her lips from time to time. Her voice was rather childish and its pitch altered without warning, yet there was a marked self-confidence in the way she talked. "What did Albert write you about me?" she said. Her cheeks flushed happily, but the way she put her hands over the gloves in her lap indicated that it had not been entirely easy for her to ask.

"He said you had been a great help. I hope we haven't put you out. I came home as soon as I could."

"I wasn't sure that Albert noticed I came over when Mrs. Gorman got sick. I knew he knew I was here, but I didn't think he thought much about it. You see what I mean?" She was smiling. Her nose was small and flat. She looked about her with an air of pleasant reflection. "I have known Albert two months. He's a funny boy until you get to know him." She paused and frowned and then seemed to reassure herself that she understood the essential things about him. "Of course, you know him well. Naturally, I don't mean to be telling you anything about him." She was suddenly ill at ease and for the first time uncertain and almost distrustful before the sister.

"I'm sure you know him better than I," Marian said.

Etta brightened. "Yes, yes. That's what I mean. It's never quite the same with a member of the family, is it? Well, as I said, I've known him for two months and we have had a mighty good time together." Her childish face had no connection with whatever she was trying to say. Marian wondered how in the world she had ever come to feel so at home in this house, how she had ever been involved in this family's history. She had slipped in with great ease and already she was potentially permanent, if for some fantastic reason that was what she wanted.

"You know Albert is working at Ray Appleton's. Ray's father died and now Ray runs the business. It's got something to do with tobacco. It's a good business and Albert seems to like it . . ."

"I'm glad he does."

"Yes, so am I," Etta said. She ran her hands over her

strong arms. They were covered with a fuzz of blonde hair. Her teeth were perfectly shaped, but short like the first baby teeth. From time to time a giggle shook her. There was a deep, if unmotivated, mirth in her laughter. Marian found it impossible to tell whether Etta's experience was advanced or retarded for her age. She started now in a solemn voice to go over her relationship with Albert. Sometimes it seemed that even the ordinary words were too big for her, but she struggled on with a profound faith in the validity of what she was saying. She was recapitulating the evolution of the overwhelming fact of herself and Albert, recalling the birth, the first signs of life, and leading up to the present stage for which she had no name, but which was nevertheless a natural moment in the life of the love plant she nourished.

She said, "I met Albert by chance. My sister knew him to speak to and we stopped one day to pick him up in the car. He sat in the back with me because there were lots of bundles in the front. When he got out, I asked him to come to the house sometime and one night, not long after, he came. He didn't call or anything. He just came up and rang the bell and luckily I was there. After . . ."

Marian was thinking that this had nothing to do with the Albert she knew. She could not imagine him in the back seat of Etta's sister's car nor could she imagine him ringing Etta's doorbell. Her brother relationship to him was so firmly set that Etta seemed to be talking about a stranger. Why did he go back? she wondered as the girl went on and on. Yet there was something in her firm, plain blondeness, her simple responsiveness, that made Etta possible for him. Marian was certain that Albert's decision to go to Etta's house had been sudden. Perhaps he was alone one night and he thought of the future and nothing came before him except that girl in the back seat of the car saying, "Come to the house sometime." He went probably because his loneliness terrified him. Marian had seen him in these moments when he realized he would not always be young; she had seen also that he was conscious of a lack in his life. Not that he needed this thing he lacked, but he had looked so long at other lives he knew a girl, a woman, a wife was almost mandatory. She was shocked that Albert had decided he could not face eccentricity. She herself had expected to drift into marriage naturally; she had even believed that for some unfathomable reason she would have a phylogenetic development precisely like her mother's—that marriage she had followed so very closely. But Albert had been far away from this. How much now he seemed like their mother as Etta talked; how shadowy he who was the central figure in Etta's drama became when she wanted him to be most real.

Etta's voice tossed back and forth through the room. She endowed her reminiscence with a richness and triumph and beauty to which the presence of the beloved's sister in some way contributed. "One night . . . and when we left, Albert . . . Albert and I . . . Albert . . . He . . . him . . . we . . ." The two figures, Albert and Etta, began to emerge from this reverie as the male and female dwarfs on a holiday card with caricature gaiety and cupidity on their diminutive faces.

From the grandmother's room, the weird, wordless cackle by which she made known the minute demands of her life could be heard floating down the stairs. Hattie appeared in the doorway. Her face was overcast with the peculiar boredom she always managed to bring to any family crisis. She had a small stew pan in her hand and she held it at arm's length, as if it were spitting fire. "I've got this hot milk and bread fixed for her, but if she wants something else I can't handle it." She thumped up the stairs, though not so fast as usual because of the liquid in the pan. They heard her pause in front of the door and then go inside. Marian knew that she was standing amazed and fascinated by the grandmother's bed. The quiet was ominous. Hattie treated Mrs.

212

Gorman as if she were already dead. She had always treated her much the same way and it had been reciprocated. It would have been impossible for the young girl to have taken on, at this late date, the hushed, infant gabble ordinarily used on the old and infirm. Hattie and Mrs. Gorman knew of each other's existence in the way one knows historical personages. To each the other was a series of manageable and separated traits, unencumbered with the contradictions and possibilities of a living human being.

"You are lucky to have Hattie," Etta said in a confiding whisper. "She's a sweet girl." She spoke secretly, as if she were recounting a bit of malicious gossip.

"Sweet?" Marian thought of the gooseflesh on Hattie's legs when she came in out of the cold, of the capricious face always new and always unpredictable, the stunted skeleton and the deeply extravagant iconoclasm that turned the whole world into a mad house.

"Isn't she?" Etta said, her eyebrows rising up comically like a clown's.

"Of course," Marian said, not wishing to discuss Hattie with Etta.

"You can never tell. They fool you."

They heard Hattie raising the window in the grandmother's room and if there were more sounds they were lost by Etta's voice saying, "My mother used to know your mother. Not very well, but she remembers her. She says Mrs. Coleman is most unusual and I would have expected as much from Albert's mother. . . . Albert says she is not at all unusual, but naturally his own mother would not appear so to him or to you. . . . Albert says . . . She will come back now to be with her mother, I guess. . . . Reunions are nice, though it's a shame sickness has to be the reason for this one. . . . You and Albert . . ."

"I have written her," Marian said. She felt certain the relationship between her mother and grandmother was some-

213

thing special and she took it for granted that her mother would hasten to the house.

Hattie was coming down the steps. She paused before the mirror on the landing, as if she were undecided which of her many masks to present to the girls seated below. When she appeared her face was expressionless.

"You'll stay for dinner, won't you?" Marian said to Etta.

"I have been staying once or twice recently. Just to help Hattie with the work."

Hattie was standing with the pan held out in front of her. At these words she put her finger on her lips and her eyebrows raised in imitation of Etta. Even Etta's expression of childish efficiency somehow managed to spread over Hattie's face. She stomped back to the kitchen and a loud rattling of pots and pans was her only audible response to Etta.

At five-thirty they heard Ray Appleton's car door slam and Albert came up the walk. When he came into the living room, he was humming. His face was fresh and his clothing unsoiled. He was smiling casually with the kind of elegance he had at odd, relaxed moments.

"Well?" Etta said. "Tired?" Albert did not look like a man who had come from a working day.

"No," he answered. "Not at all." The innocent smile vanished from his face. Seeing their eyes upon him, he seemed to lose his confidence. These swift fluctuations between pride and shyness were disarming. Even the loose grace of Albert's body subtly changed to tension. He spun around on his heels and started to leave them. Then, as if catching himself, he smiled again and sat down beside Marian on the sofa.

"How is grandmother?" he said, looking as if he had submitted to a trap. He sounded much younger than, Etta in these uncertain moments.

"She seems quite well, Albert," Marian said. "How are you?"

214

He lay back against the end of the couch. "I'm fine," he said. Suddenly he turned his head toward Etta and grinned. When he looked at her, Etta altered the position of her head. Confusion was visible on her face. Her hands gripped the arms of the chair.

"Marian and I are old friends," Etta said. "I knew I would like her, but I thought it would take us longer to get acquainted." Speaking seemed to dispel her perplexity and awkwardness. She stared at Albert's profile in her fixed, familiar way.

"That's fine," he said with no inflection. He closed his eyes and long lashes fringed his lids.

"Are you tired?" Etta repeated.

"Why should I be tired? The work isn't hard." With his eyes closed and his head against the couch, Albert's passionate self-possession seemed to return.

"I just thought . . ." Etta said. She sighed.

There was a short silence and then Albert, innocent enthusiasm rising in his voice, said, "Tonight, I'm afraid I must go . . ."

"Oh," Etta said, before he had time to finish.

Albert sat up quickly. "I must tonight . . ." he started, but his voice vanished and he looked at Marian in the forsaken way she could not bear. Tension returned to his body and his eyes were defensive.

Etta's eyes did not move. She watched him blankly, patiently. One of her gloves fell to the floor, but she did not pick it up.

"I'll take a shower and then we'll see," Albert said. Before they knew it, he was gone. Etta's eyes clung solemnly to the stairs up which he had climbed. In a few minutes they heard the water splashing in the shower. Albert resumed his humming. Etta looked about the room hopelessly, as if she were wondering if Albert had actually come into the house and if he had actually said . . . He appeared and vanished like some mythical creature, leaving Etta to wonder endlessly. She looked at the dent his head had made on the couch and shrugged her shoulders slightly. Marian had noticed that in some remote way Albert never completely rejected Etta. Even when he was embarrassed there was a part of him that kept remembering her, the way a drunk remembers his manners. He gave her just enough to justify the structure she was building.

Marian went into the kitchen, leaving Etta to wait in the half-darkness of the living room for Albert's reappearance.

"I ain't heard any kissing yet, have you?" Hattie said. The mock artlessness she could get into her voice irritated Marian.

"Hattie . . . please," she said. She had a sensation of ugliness and of life twisted out of shape and verging on the brutal and subtly cruel. She did not want to be with Albert and Etta again.

"He's scared spitless, ain't he?" Hattie said. A stray piece of lettuce clung to her wrist. She held the icebox door open and the cold air whipped through the room. "But he's as good as gone and knows it."

When she took out the ice tray, and held it under the faucet, water spilled on the red and green checked dress Hattie was wearing. She cursed. Marian said, "Why don't you wear one of the uniforms you used to have? If they are worn out, I'll get you a new one."

Hattie turned around violently. "I don't want no uniform," she said.

"But it would save your dresses. It's a shame to ruin them."

"I said I didn't want no uniform," Hattie repeated. Her hands were trembling and her eyes were flashing dangerously.

"But it would save you. That's all I want. I'm sure if you had a new one you would like it," Marian said, wondering why Hattie's face was so distorted.

The dinner plates were lined up on the cabinet. "I'm fixing the plates and putting everything on them. You can pass the bowls," Hattie said coldly.

There was no sound in the living room. "Do you suppose he's through dressing?" Marian said softly, as if she were afraid of being heard.

Now she heard Albert coming down the stairs, heard him rattling the evening paper. Etta's voice rose above the sound of the paper. And then her laughter rose through the house, and vanished as quickly and abruptly as it had appeared. Albert coughed.

"Tell them to come on!" Hattie said in a very low voice. Marian was startled by the voice, but Hattie's back was turned toward her and she could not see her face. For a moment, Marian had thought Hattie was crying. As she went out of the room, she managed to get a side view of Hattie's face. It was rigid and taciturn and Marian decided that she had been mistaken.

In the living room, she saw that Etta's hands were still on her lap. Her coarse, light hair was shining under the lamp. Albert had a short razor cut on his chin and it shone red against the smooth, light tan of his face. "I didn't know it," he said as Marian came into the room. "I didn't know it until . . ."

"It's all right," Etta was saying. There was nothing on her face and the lack of emotion was rather frightening. In her crisp, white starched blouse set against the dark blue suit, she looked like a model prisoner who sat primly in the dock, expecting to be doomed.

When they rose, Albert came closer to her. "Well, I guess we'll eat now," he said. She looked up at him and said, "All right, Albert."

They walked through the hall together. Etta's head came only to his shoulder. Her walk was firm and slow and Albert's body was light and alert with impatience. They separated and faced each other across the table, and Etta's eyes were level with his chin. There was little conversation at

217

the table. Marian tried to speak to Etta, but could not distract her. When Albert looked up there was a kind of nudity in his face. His eyes were ringed with blue and the skin around them was so thin that the blue half-moons were startlingly vivid. The silence oppressed him and he went deeply within himself. Here, with Etta, he was just as he had been with Marian and her grandmother. His stay seemed temporary and they were conscious of his strong preoccupation with his private life. His short bits of conversation were impersonal and revealed nothing of him. He had never belonged in the house and had been most real coming in and going out of it, most alive in his expectation and knowledge of the life outside.

"I guess I'll go and make a call," he said suddenly. "Maybe . . ." He got up from the table. They heard the click of the receiver and then his low, muffled voice speaking and speaking into the phone. He talked for a long time. When he returned he was smoking a cigarette and he seemed to be listening to the pounding of his heart. When his eyes met Etta's they were bright and hard, as if he were suppressing tears. He did not sit down, but leaned against the cabinet, smoking.

"You haven't finished dinner, Albert," Marian said.

"I don't want any more," he said.

"Aw, now . . ." Etta said. Marian noticed that she looked particularly young at this moment. Gaiety sprang up around her and she knocked her fork against her plate like an amused child. Albert looked at her rapt, happy face and he too smiled mysteriously. "You didn't have to," Etta said tenderly.

Outside it was dark. "I'll go have a look at Mrs. Gorman," Etta said. When she was gone Marian took a cigarette from Albert and they moved away from the table, into the darkness not illuminated by the round shade which covered the light over the center of the table.

"I have written Mother," Marian said. Her brother was

standing beside her and she could feel the furious way he smoked and the way his body had not given in to the evening before him. The muscles refused to recognize what the brain had accepted.

"Did you have the new address?" he said. "It will be forwarded, I guess."

"What new address? Have they gone?"

"Yes, to a small place. Very small. I don't think she'll come, though. What do you think?"

"For God's sake, Albert! It's her own mother! Of course, she'll come!" In spite of her affirmation, her heart acknowledged the possibility that Albert was, as usual, closer to the truth about her mother than she was herself. "That would be the end!" she said vehemently.

"The end? You mean if she didn't come?" He laughed softly. "Jesus, you still don't understand, do you? And, of course, there wouldn't be anything Mother could do."

She could smell his shaving powder. The glow of the cigarette illuminated his face and made him look like a bodiless head. "Well?" he said suddenly. He pointed to the stairs and Marian knew he was speaking of Etta. She had dreaded this moment.

"I don't know, Albert."

"No, I suppose you don't," he said hesitantly. "Well, I think it will work out."

His face was hard and determined, an utterly masculine face. The love he inspired in another person was to him a commodity that had its separate being, divorced from his own person and desire. Marriage was like one's birth: you do not ask for it, you do not make the circumstance with free will. You merely accepted it as an inevitable condition of adult life. "Yes, I don't see why it shouldn't work out," he repeated dreamily.

Marian said, "Do you think you are being quite fair to her?" Albert did not hear this. He was strolling across the room to meet Etta as she came down the stairs. He put out his cigarette and by that time Etta was standing beside him. Marian saw her hand fall upon his arm. His body went rigid and then limber again. Etta was smiling happily at his handsome face. There was a warmth about her, simple and comfortable as the warmth of a baking oven, and she talked about his grandmother, his house, and his life. They went into the living room and the conversation was lower, but it went on and on, like their breathing.

The sound of skates on the pavement made them stop short. Two girls flew past them. The scraping of the skates on the asphalt sent a shiver up Marian's spine. Cold, spring night winds touched her face. The sky was heavy with stars and undulant clouds. "I knew you'd want to get out of the house," Bruce was saying. They passed under low boughs and the moonlight seeped through the leaves and touched her hair. "Do you still like to walk?" he said. "We don't need to, but I remembered that you liked it." She had not seen his face clearly. He had slipped into the house, taken her coat off the stand in the hall and swept her out into the night. At intervals she turned her head toward him and observed his long jaw, broad nose and the wide span of his forehead. He fell unconsciously into walking very fast and she tried to take long steps as effortlessly as he did. He was talking rapidly and what he said seemed to stay around him like a misty formation around the moon. Happily he drifted onward amid the soothing haze of his own thoughts. The sense of well-being he had now was not in kind but in degree different from the contentment he had had in the past. She wondered what new adventure he had set out upon in her absence. "You must tell me everything," he said, his voice familiarly sensuous. "The concerts, of course . . . It was not a disappointment? I thought it wouldn't be. That's the place for a woman like you . . ." He stopped. "Woman? Let me see." He took her chin in his hand and turned her face toward the light. "Yes, I'm afraid you've reached your full growth."

His fluid half-monologue persisted and Marian wondered how the varied parts of his life were ever reconciled. "It hasn't been a year, has it? My God, almost a whole year! The best part of it, anyway . . ." He was almost running, with a childish elation that staggered Marian. He unbuttoned his coat and a white shirt shone over his chest. A roll of fat bulged slightly over his belt. When they reached the corner he took her arm and she thought fondly of his outrageous confidence and enthusiasm.

"You know you're much better looking," he said, laughing roughly. "The city, getting away from home, always makes women more beautiful. If you're passable looking to begin with the rest is just a state of mind." He grabbed the tips of her fingers and seemed to be pulling her up the street. They were not going any place, but he managed to turn the destinationless walking into an exciting evening. Now the center of town was visible and they walked past the bus station. It was dirty and busy, alive with activity and people as if it had been noon. Cash registers clanged at the lunch counter. The other shops on the street were resting peacefully behind locked doors. Chattering still, bending his head down toward her and then throwing it back in laughter, they passed the rows of cars in the parking lot. Bruce's laughter awakened the boy who was napping in the frame shanty office in the middle of the lot. Soon they were out of the center of town and back again on the darker residential streets. Bruce said, with no alteration in his voice, "There's a very smart little girl I met some place. Comes from a poor family, but she's very bright in the way you know some people are without having any specific evidence. Now if I can get the little bastard to settle down and go to college . . . who knows . . ." He grinned and sighed indulgently, "I suspect her idea of heaven is to be goosed by one of those tap-dancing chimpanzees she goes

221

around with." His coat was flying about him and with wonderful gracefulness his large body raced up the street.

Marian said, "Bruce, isn't there someone else? I mean someone besides . . ." She did not know exactly what she meant, but when he was talking about the young girl she had the intuition that Bruce could never be fully satisfied with the young. She kept thinking that his life was surrounded and fulfilled by something far removed from herself and the other girl. She imagined a woman with some of his own instinctive animality, a woman rather placid and dumb who lived in a little apartment that had lamps spread over every flat surface. She might even be the mother of several children, a talentless, relaxing woman. She could see Bruce sitting with such a woman, snoozing over a paper, not fearing silence. He probably told her about his business and forgot completely his peripheral intellectuality. And sometimes they had fights and she smacked him and he slapped her in return.

He stopped. "Why, you little witch," he said. "You must mean 'Mamma'—that's what I call the old tub. Who told you about her? You can't keep a thing in this town." He laughed and slapped Marian's shoulder.

They had now returned to Marian's house. The lights were still shining in the living room. "It's too damned bad about your grandmother," Bruce said. He was looking at Marian as if he were not certain of the next step to be taken. Moments of uncertainty were so irritating to him that they were particularly noticeable. She looked back at him and they both seemed to be thinking, Now where were we before this winter passed? How easy it would be to take it all up again and how easy not to. He lit a cigarette and she told him good-by without any feeling except relief.

When Marian entered the living room, Etta was putting on her blue cap. She stood in front of the mirror and fluffed the hair over her ears. "Are you ready?" Albert said listlessly. His face looked tired and strained. He took Etta

222

home and not long after Marian heard him re-enter the house and lock the door. The light switched off and on in his room and she knew that he was restless. After a time both of them fell into a sound sleep. They did not hear their grandmother descending the stairs and prowling through the dark house.

CHAPTER THREE

*W*HEN Hattie had not appeared by ten o'clock, Marian thought of calling her on the phone. She had even gone through some of the names in the book before she realized that Hattie had no phone. For the first time she recognized the possibility that she might never see Hattie again. She tried to believe that she was sick and would come the next day, but she did not honestly expect this to happen. And how completely and irrevocably Hattie was gone. She had left no clothing, no letters, no discarded powder boxes—not even any trash. There was nothing in the house to show she had been there for most of her waking hours during the past seven years. Even an over-night tenant in a hotel frequently left more evidence of his presence. If she were gone for good, there would be no replacement. It was much too late for that. It was already apparent that with Hattie's departure this way of life came to an end. The house was no longer a home; no one cared about it, not even Mrs. Gorman. All routine could be broken. The doors might be opened at any time, the shades might stay down all day. There was no further reason to pretend that one accepted and loved this life. Each member of the family was responsible only to himself.

All through the morning, Marian was obsessed with the idea that she was missing something, that a great part of her life had stopped. She fixed breakfast for herself and her grandmother. She made the beds and dusted, but these duties could not be prolonged beyond a reasonable time.

Stretches of idle loneliness followed. She tried to read, but the silence around her became more and more suffocating. Hattie's face seemed to appear before her. The face was accusing her and she wondered if Hattie had really been crying last night. She couldn't remember the conversation that preceded the coldness between them.

During this long morning she thought with emotion of her simple room in the dormitory and of the life there that now seemed, in retrospect, beautifully disciplined and industrious. Noon came and the sunlight shifted to a different part of the house. She waited for the mail and a letter came from Leo, none from her mother. Leo had little to say about himself. Most of the letter was concerned with best wishes for her grandmother and stereotyped thoughts he might have taken from a correspondence book on how pleasant it must be to be home again with her family. Yet she read the letter over several times and was amazed at the pounding of her heart. She answered it and when that was done the afternoon refused to pass. The sun was warm and the living room was uncomfortable. Around the house the grass was high. She thought perhaps her mother was on her way and, for that reason, had not written. She was again passionately looking forward to the visit, though this time her motive was largely boredom. It was about three o'clock in the afternoon when she had a thought that seemed to clarify everything. She thought quite simply that she must get married. Once the idea had taken shape in her mind she knew that the germ had always been there and it had not appeared suddenly. It had only crystallized on this afternoon. She was so much absorbed by the idea and the obscure liberation it offered that she wished immediate fulfillment. The realization that she must sit through this day and others like it became almost unbearable. The fact that it was Leo she would marry crashed through her mind, but she did not linger on that part of the dream. She kept pushing him back

225

and pretending he had nothing to do with this miraculous plan.

As the hours passed she saw her longing for Hattie had not diminished and she decided to try to find her again. She did not wish to ask her to come back; she wished only to show Hattie her feeling of loss. Etta came later and promised to look after Mrs. Gorman. The young girl was pleased to have the house for herself. As she stood on the porch and waved good-by to Marian, she looked like a sharp-toothed, clean, blonde watch dog.

The section under the viaduct where Hattie lived was much more ominous than Marian had remembered. Walking into it, she felt like an escaped convict. Actual terror came over her and she was ashamed of her squeamishness. How could Hattie, who brought a protection to Marian's secure house, who warmed and brightened it, live in this appalling terror? One delicate shack merged with another before her eyes. Even the ragged and copiously dirty children became aggressive enemies and she did not speak or smile to them for fear of showing ignorance of some secret and necessary code. Black and white faces bobbed up out of nowhere like monsters rising out of dungeon seclusion. The color line did not plunge down to this depth, apparently. At first she thought she might get courage from the white faces, that she might find some relationship to them, but she did not. They were even more remote to her than the blacks in that she could not imagine any of them working in homes or gardens; they were not, as she imagined the poor, fit to be street sweepers or garbage collectors. So impaired, isolated, and private were their faces that they seemed a new and unrecorded species. They had returned to dust, were raw, deficient, and incredible and maintained their breathing by the collection of iron junk that stood in all the yards. They were not even a horde, so little did their composite strength amount to. She remembered, as she had on the other trip, that this section was spoken of as a kind of Devil's Island from which there was, for the whites, no escape. She did not see any. It was impossible to imagine these bleached, slack-breasted girls in school. The only thing left was their ability to wrinkle up the face in a caricature smile which seemed to be remembrance of the state of mendicancy from which their parents had fallen. But this little gesture was remarkably reminiscent of the outside world and was, with them, sadly beautiful. The Negro houses were distinguished from the white in that they more nearly recalled a place to be used for living. Marian had thought she would remember the house in which Hattie lived and was terrified when she learned that she did not. She kept expecting to run upon it, but each place became more unknown to her than the last. The sun was retreating. She saw a dark face sitting on a step and she said, "Which house does Hattie Sipe live in?" When she had spoken, silence fell like a blow upon the man. Her voice did not seem to belong to her and she felt like a foreigner cast upon an alien, indifferent shore. The face of the man on the step did not move. Nothing altered the serenity of his possession of the house and neighborhood. "Can you tell me which house Hattie Sipe lives in?" she called again, trying to smile.

After another silence, she heard his flat, unanswerable words. "No, I can't," he said. A face appeared in the doorway, the face of a woman who jealously guarded her domain. Marian thought of the calm on these faces and of the way they sank into their houses before her, a stranger. As she went on, she could feel the two pairs of eyes upon her. She wanted to turn round in the hope that they may have changed their minds and would tell her the answer, but she did not dare.

The dirt of one yard imperceptibly became the dirt of the next yard. A red ruffled window curtain suddenly appeared in one of the houses and behind the curtain a middle-aged woman was standing, her broad face looking without expectation at the street. With a feeling of female kinship, Marian smiled at the woman. "Do you know which house Hattie Sipe lives in?" she said. The woman drew a package of tobacco out of her pocket and deposited some of it in a white paper. She ran her tongue over the paper to seal the cigarette. "I don't know," she said indifferently.

"Thank you," Marian said. There was no answer from the woman. At the end of the street she saw a white frame structure with a wooden cross at the top. Beside it stood a branchless tree, split at the trunk. She walked toward the church and looked through a cracked window pane. A flash of white cloth passed by the window. Faintly encouraged by the religious atmosphere, she knocked on the door. The paint was peeling and a colored glass transom threw a strange purple shadow over the door. She heard no footsteps answering her knock and she pushed open the door. There was only one room which ended in a raised platform. A short, stunted, red-haired Christ was painted on the center wall. It glared down like an angry pigmy at the benches below. A woman in a white gown that came up over her head in a hood was standing on the platform. Her face was covered with tiny moles of a darker color than the skin. The moles were like Braille symbols on the surface of her face. Beneath the shining whiteness of the hood her wide, oily eyes were swimming and her indigo lips were moving soundlessly. The face was so lost and so ruined that it was impossible to interpret her expression.

"Can you tell me where Hattie Sipe lives?" Marian said. The air in the church was damp, but it had a peculiarly weighted quality. The passionately cruel self-absorption of the red-haired Christ deepened as she looked at it. "Hattie Sipe," Marian repeated.

The woman lifted her arms. Even her hands were covered by the white robe. "I have no idea," she said in a voice as sweet and accomplished as that of a girl behind a reception desk.

"I must get in touch with her," Marian said desperately. And then hardly recognizing her own thoughts, she said, "It's not for anything bad."

The woman lowered her arms. The moles danced on her face. "I have no idea for good or bad," she said. The stillness that followed her speaking was like a pause in a prayer. A bird scratched on the window outside and through the door she could hear shouts which maintained a surprising intensity.

"I wish you could help me," Marian said, regretting that in this situation she had to use the same old words. The white robe gave the woman an indeterminate but sacred status which set her off from the people outside. "I wanted to tell her something I should have told her a long time ago. I just want her to know how I feel," she said shyly.

"Perhaps it is too late," the woman said. "I do not know the person." She had ceased to look at Marian. In what devotional attitude she had placed herself could not be said, but she was obviously patiently waiting for Marian's exodus.

Marian tiptoed out of the church. On the street the same unknown houses appeared. The smell of frying meat came through the air and she realized that she was hungry. She retraced her steps up the street and looked at the new faces that had appeared. A man was standing beside a tree, or rather a scrawny bush, in the front of one of the houses. He dug the toes of his shoes into the dirt. Gray, stiff hair stood up on his head, even though his body was young. Beneath the hair a heavy face the color of dough appeared, a face sprinkled with blackish freckles. Marian was walking very fast and hesitated to stop before the man. Yet she did, because she knew that if she could find Hattie all the terror and strangeness of the street would be forgotten. She thought that she had several times heard Hattie's voice, but when she turned around it was only a child, yelling into the dusky sky.

"Can you tell me where Hattie Sipe lives?" she said again. She thought the people must have seen her before. This recognized feeling made her seem wicked, like a rent collector. She kept telling herself that the people must know that she did not look like a collector or anyone bent on evil news. But when the man's indistinct gray eyes turned to her she was no longer certain how she looked. The dress she was wearing, the blue woolen dress, her hair flying about her face—none of this was a positive identification. She even began to believe that she had an expression of cunning on her face.

The man coughed and she saw how his eyes looked at the tip of her chin. "What's the name?" he said.

"Hattie Sipe."

The man kicked the dirt again. "Well, now . . ." he said, but before he finished he clamped his thick, dry lips together. He was again staring at her chin. A child, deepest black, came around the side of the house and stood next to the man. The child's body pressed against the man's leg.

"I saw her . . ." the little boy said. His father glared down at him.

"You say she lives down here on this street?" the arid voice repeated.

"Yes, I'm quite sure she does."

"Maybe she's moved away." The little boy reached upward and clasped the man's hand. There was a whistle in the house behind. They walked away and disappeared behind the closed door.

Marian continued her journey. She passed the same houses and saw the same cans gleaming in the late, withdrawing sunset. The orange sun faded into gold as it sank behind the city. Marian knew that Hattie was here. She could imagine that all the people she had questioned, even the woman in the white robe, had already stopped on Hattie's porch to tell her that someone had been looking for her, but had been outsmarted. And what was Hattie saying?

Was she asking if the stranger were a tall girl with brown skin and brown hair and does she walk like this . . . and talk with her mouth in this position? Marian tried to remember her own mirror image so that she could guess the peculiarities that Hattie was faithfully exposing to her neighbors. She could hear her saying, "Now this one has been to New York with money she got from the man, the tall, blond man who . . . And she didn't do nothing but come back here when the old scarecrow got sick and for all her messing she might just as well be back where she was. Her own mother don't know she's living . . ." And then Marian thought she was perhaps saying, "But she's a lot better than the rest of them." Was she saying that? She remembered Hattie's wicked, sarcastic eyes with that quality of the eternal judgment from which there was no appeal. She could see the fabulous figure dancing before her eyes, revealing nothing of her own world but imprisoning in her shaggy skull the last few years of Marian's world, the world that was lost and could not be re-lived in a better way by any of them. Marian remembered in a paralyzing whirl of images all the dishes, the vegetables, the afternoons and evenings when the kitchen was loud with the rattle of pots and pans. She saw Hattie's face and the way her hands pressed up the sleeves of the short flannel coat she wore in the winter and the collar of matted fur pinned tightly round her neck. Doesn't she remember me? Marian was thinking. I who meant to say and meant to show . . . Was it possible that Hattie didn't know how much Marian cared for her? She regretted her silences with Hattie and even with the lost Gertrude. And she thought of the great pain her mother's silences had given her. Life seemed to be an enormous subterranean existence in which nobody spoke and in which people died for want of a few words they needed.

She had reached the edge of the street which separated

this thickly populated abyss from the rest of the town. At the end, as if in a last attempt to escape before it was too late, she broke into a vigorous run. A pack of wild, hungry dogs appeared at her heels and escorted her to the edge of the town which was now busy over dinners laid out upon white tablecloths.

CHAPTER FOUR

*T*HE MOTHER'S wire said: SIMPLE TRUTH IS THAT WE CAN-
NOT AFFORD TO MAKE TRIP.

Albert found Mrs. Gorman dead when he got up one
morning. She was lying by the steps, her head tilted upward
in the direction of her own room. Her face showed evidence
of struggle and pain. Her hair was mussed and she was
barefoot. There was a streak of soot on her arm. They did
not know how she happened to be downstairs in the dead
of night. The doctor said she had died around four in the
morning. Her body was so frail it had made no noise when
she fell. Marian did notice that the lamp connections were
pulled out of their sockets in the living room and hall, but
she did not associate this with the death. By nine o'clock
the undertaker had come and put the body in a basket and
removed it forever from the house. By noon of the same day
Mrs. Gorman lay rouged and dressed in her coffin; she
looked like a woman of forty. Her white hair was smoothly
brushed and the pink lips seemed about to open and to
speak. Her rings were still on her fingers.

"Grandmother, my love," Albert said, overcome by the
sight of the cold, dead beauty. He put his finger on her lips
which were so like his own. "My love," he whispered. He
spoke to the old woman with such fullness of feeling that
Marian, looking down at the body in the coffin and then at
her grieving brother, saw a profound connection between
them which death had made plain. A sensuality, only partially controlled, lay on the two proud and handsome faces.

They were the two secret ones, so secret they could not speak to anyone or to each other. They, though so delicate, pale, and idle, should have been born in a colder, more rigorous world where the concealed passions might have burgeoned, or where the prudent blankness might have grown into an animal aggressiveness, perhaps even a common, satisfied vulgarity.

Brother and sister cried silently, their arms pressed against each other as they stood beside the coffin. A surprising number of people congregated mournfully about them. People they barely knew grieved for the fragmentary memories they had of Mrs. Gorman. Grim, commiserating faces came and went. Grief was deflected, however, by the shock of the absence of the children's mother and father. Albert and Marian were conscious of the undertone of criticism, particularly directed against their mother, that lay behind the solemn, sad voices. "She is too sick to come," Marian said to her neighbor. "The doctor said she couldn't possibly make the trip." The neighbor nodded, though her eyes remained unsatisfied by this explanation. Mary, the mother's friend, came to them. She did not question the absence of the mother, but when she embraced the children she seemed to be consoling them for a double loss. Her short arms clamped them to her breast and as they wept her maternal warmth came down over them and made them feel less homeless for a moment. Etta was there. Her eyes were hidden beneath eyelids that were red and swollen with shed tears. Her intimacy was boundless. She hovered over them like an inheritance. Albert seemed always on the verge of rejecting her tears and dissociating himself from her, only to find in the next moment there was something she could do. By his need of her efficiency, he was drawn back to her.

After the funeral, they came back to the silent house. Marian and Albert sat down in the living room gloom, unable to remove their hot clothing or in any way to make themselves comfortable. They did not look at each other;

it was too much like looking into a disastrous future. In the finality of the funeral they felt tied together helplessly. Each was now the sole protector of the other. Etta discreetly left them alone and went into the kitchen to make tea. They heard her puttering around, lifting the blinds, stacking the dishes: making life go on in her indomitable way.

"We both get five hundred dollars," Albert said suddenly. "I get the house. I don't know why. You'd think she would have left it to you, the girl." He flushed. "Mr. Logan told me this today. That's all."

The dusty furniture, the unwashed chair covers were there before them. They both knew why Albert got the house. They knew he was getting married to Etta and was going to live here. Mrs. Gorman had apparently known it also. Or at least she had felt he would marry, though she could not have known Etta when the will was made. The house was his life; the lawns, the bedroom, the kitchen, the domestic beginning—a tragic gift. Already Albert seemed to hear voices saying that it was a good house and would do for him and his family until he died. Already he and Marian could see it improved by young and interested hands, Etta's hands. They foresaw the new draperies, the new icebox, bright porch furniture, and new blossoms in the garden.

Albert got up restlessly from the chair. His face was distorted with impatient, rebellious tears. His body was rigid with irresolution. Darkness and anger spilled over his face as he listened to Etta clanging the teacups. Now, he seemed to be saying, she is opening the cake box, now getting out the napkins and soon she will reappear, silent and small, her face stained with tears but still comfortable and solid. She did come in with the tea presently, but she was not crying. She was a frightened child serving her first tea party. The black linen dress she had worn to the funeral was too matronly for her and she seemed to be struggling with the sobriety it demanded. Her earnest face was pitifully young

235

with anxiety. The future that went with the grandmother's death chilled her also. She looked into Albert's face, as if she were begging for some special sort of glance which she had not received and did not even fully understand. She was already conscious of an undefined and bewildering deficiency.

Soft footsteps sounded on the porch. The screen door opened and Ray Appleton walked cautiously into the living room. Perspiration dripped from his obese face. His eyes were large and glazed. He took out a handkerchief and wiped his face. Without looking at Marian and Etta, he proceeded clumsily toward Albert. His voice, soft and round like his body, could barely be heard, but they knew he was speaking. His agitated breathing filled the room. Albert's face was wildly surprised and he stared at Ray without speaking. He seemed sadly turned to stone in this moment when he was trapped between his two unwanted worlds. His arms hung like broken wings at his side. "Won't you come out for just a moment?" Ray's urgent voice was saying. "I want to talk to you." The car was standing outside like an inescapable destiny and Marian could see Albert and Ray furiously racing into a sudden darkness. Ray's chin had fallen in the utterly unrestrained desolation of his face. His eyes were stricken with emotion. They beseeched Albert like tears.

Albert's low, enraged curses burst forth like abrupt handclaps. The words squeezed their way out of his throat like a child's fussing at a fate beyond its control. He glided across the room in a singular fury. "Yes, yes," he said. "Let's get out of here!"

"Albert! Albert!" Etta's stunned voice called after him. He was gone. They heard the ominous humming of the motor as it pulled away from the house. "Albert!" the precise voice continued, as if she were an elder child calling to a younger.

There was no longer any sound of the car. "He'll be

236

back," Marian said weakly. She wanted to tell Etta that she should be glad for this meaningless rebellion. Albert would come back chastened and penitent. But she could not speak when she saw Etta's alarmed eyes. Her confusion seemed to have seeped through her body like a poison. She was twisted and blinded like one coming out of a horrible dream.

"Don't worry, Etta," Marian said hoarsely. Marian thought she saw Etta look at her with hatred, a dreadful, consuming hatred that had no other object to attack. All her instincts and proprieties were shocked and Marian had, irrationally, become the devastating instrument. And then, without motivation, the shock passed over Etta, as if by some act of the female, possessive will she were able to erase all ugliness from her consciousness. Horror changed to surprise, the surprise of ignorance and dwarfed imagination.

Etta said reprovingly, "It was nice of Mr. Appleton to come by. But do you think it's right for Albert to leave the house so soon after the funeral?"

Marian did not answer. She could not take her eyes from the face before her, the young, hopeful face full of profound belief in itself, its rights and its natural future, a face stronger than whimsical personalities and reinforced by the ages. "Good God!" Marian said. Etta looked at her for a moment and then returned to her cup of tea. Her skin was cool against the black dress. The round shape of her throat rose proudly over her collar. "Are you sure you love Albert?" Marian said hesitantly. "Do you think you will be happy with him?"

"Of course," Etta said, smiling. "Don't you think I will be?"

"No, I don't."

She giggled. "What a funny thing to say. Sisters never understand, do they?" She took a piece of cake and nibbled at the edge. "What will you do now?" she said, looking away. "I mean right now. It will be very hard for you."

"I suppose I will go find them first," Marian said, her voice clogging as if she had dust in her throat.

"Find who, for heaven's sake?"

"I must go to see Mamma and Papa! Where are they! They couldn't come." She had started to cry. Her mother's face appeared before her, begging her for help. She imagined the mother bent under a grief deeper than the grandmother's death, alone and lost. The sadness of this day had clouded her indifference and thrown her back to her fearful love for her mother. She felt that she had betrayed them in these last few months and that by some mysterious means they had known of her betrayal and she was paying the penalty. She wondered if they would ever forgive her.

"Do you really think you should bother?" Etta said. She was holding the cake between her teeth, ready to bite down on it. A look of wisdom came over her childish face. "They are grown and can take care of themselves. I don't believe they think much about what goes on here. Some people don't, seems like. They've been away too long."

"You don't understand!" Marian said. "She would have been here! I know she wanted to come! Her affection for her mother was very deep, so deep that she'll never be able to forget this. She'll always feel guilty about not coming to the funeral, not being here with her when she was ill and dying. Maybe Grandmother wouldn't have died if she had been here. That's probably what she is thinking right now. But he wouldn't let her come! That must be the reason!"

"Who?" Etta said.

"My father." Marian could imagine her mother sitting in a darkened room, suppressing her tears and grief. When her husband saw her he would not understand her sad, guilty eyes. Marian began to hate her father. She saw in him the useless, feverish flight of an insect that knows no satisfaction and denies peace to others.

"Are you sure about this?" Etta said.

"Yes."

Marian was disinclined to speak about it further and went upstairs to change her clothes. The grandmother's door was open. Her desk was still cluttered with the papers and pictures she had guarded so carefully before her illness. In the bed, the imprint of her body could still be seen for they had not entered her room since the death. Marian pulled the spread over the empty bed. She picked up boxes of buttons and pins from the floor. In the closet the grandmother's gray dresses and a lone pale blue one were hanging. Marian put her face into the dresses and thought for a moment they were all back on the breakfast porch in the summer, that Mrs. Gorman's eyes were staring at the tree next to the house and that Hattie was standing in the kitchen sighing and grumbling ferociously. Albert was there in a white shirt and they were all, in their diverse ways, waiting for the parents to come. The expectation and promise of these days had never been fulfilled. Numbness had replaced the nurtured warmth. What power the mother still had over the daughter's heart was based upon the fear of disaster, a negative thing. A wish that nothing bad should happen. She realized now that it was the vanishing scar of an old wound and not the wound itself that had appeared when the grandmother's death aroused the hallowed family feeling.

Marian went to the window and for no reason stood there waiting for Bruce to drive up to his house. Shortly after six he came and she could hear him whistling as he left the car. The weed-clogged garden lay before her and she wondered if her grandmother had often looked out of the window and what she had seen. There was no sign of life there now. The grass would grow over the path Hattie had made when she crossed the yard in the mornings. As Marian stood there she waited for the refrain that had recently never ceased to beat out in her mind: I must get married. Where was Leo? Perhaps at this moment he was racing up the street, a straw hat firmly upon his head, his body and dress as precise as his watch, running to some job, maintaining the rhythm of his life so persistently that even loneliness could not become apparent. She found that she was always thinking Leo could redeem her mother, that he, young and tireless, could bring her back into a manageable world. Marian no longer wished to live with her mother. She wished only to insure her mother's present life in the fear that should it be altered she might, by pity, be thrown back to her old responses. She was not certain her indifference could endure calamity.

The door opened downstairs. Albert had returned. Marian heard his light step on the floor and his voice saying rapidly, "I'm sorry, Etta. I guess I was upset. You mustn't think any more about it."

Etta's proud voice, streaked with her childish laughter, said, "But right after the funeral, honey. That was all I worried about. I didn't mind for myself, if that's what you think."

Albert was sighing, relaxing, sitting down with the presence of the girl creeping into his mind and flesh like a sleep to which he could not keep from yielding.

CHAPTER FIVE

*T*HE OLD car with "Taxi" painted on its sides rolled through a cloud of dust. "I can't hardly see out of this windshield," the driver said. Dust lay smoothly over the surface of his hoary face, as if he had put it on with a powder puff. They passed small houses and a three-block shopping section. "It's just a little ways out," the man said.

Marian could see the knots on the back of his neck. He adjusted the mirror so that he could see his passenger, but that not being sufficient, he turned his inquisitive face around and lost control of the car. With an old person's unconcern about machinery, he pulled the car back on the road and merely grunted at the danger. "You going to visit?" he said. She nodded. "Well, right yonder's your place."

He drove in front of a small frame house, almost hidden from the street by parched shrubbery. The driver did not let her out until he had turned the car around and while he shifted gears Marian could see the heads of her mother and father above the shrubbery. They were waiting for her on the porch. When the car at last came to a stop and she climbed out of the back seat, her parents descended the porch steps. In a sort of blind hurricane of emotion, she felt her mother's arms around her. The father stepped up from the side and the three of them were wrapped in a warm embrace. Marian and her mother began to weep. The mother wore a faded blue dressing gown that was in this worn stage as much a part of her as her features. The father, in yesterday's shirt, Marian, dusty and tired, the wooden, unreminiscent porch—these things gave the meeting a special, ordinary intimacy far beyond anything Marian had hoped for. The odor of cigars on her father's fingers and the faint suggestion of face powder that clung to her mother's cheeks were like cherished relics she had never expected to know again. Yet, when they broke apart something private and reserved crystallized in each of them. They stood awkwardly on the porch and watched the dust settle on the bushes. From that moment, Marian felt herself a visitor. She wondered where they would put her and if she had inconvenienced them. When they entered the three room house, she was immediately aware that everything was organized for two. There were two breakfast plates still on the table, two comfortable reading chairs with lamps behind them, two dressers in the bedroom. The father's dresser was bare except for an unused set of brushes she and Albert had once sent him for Christmas. She was rather ashamed that this gift was the only thing she recognized in the house and that it should be so very useless and meaningless. The mother's dresser was covered with nicely arranged cosmetics and boxes of trinkets that reminded Marian of Gertrude. When she put her suitcase down in the hall she wondered, uncomfortably, if they perhaps hated to have anything in that particular spot.

"I thought perhaps you were sick," Marian said when they were in the breakfast room.

"Sick? We are never sick, thank heavens!" she answered. Lucy Coleman poured another cup of coffee and raised the cup to her lips. She was crying, reliving through Marian's appearance the first shock of her mother's death. Ted Coleman put his hand on her shoulder. They had not yet mentioned the grandmother's name. Marian wondered if this were a repetition of the scene that took place the day they got her wire telling of the death. Did the knock on the door find them still at breakfast, the mother in the blue dressing gown and the father in the soiled shirt? She was not surprised they hadn't come for the funeral. Even if they had had the money she could not imagine them leaving this small house that was so indisputably theirs and which held them so perfectly. It was something like a play house for children and they had settled into it as naturally as dolls and as if it had been built for their special dimensions. The cheap white curtains edged in blue, the indifferent prints of imaginary landscapes on the wall were as ordinary as the bridal house of an impoverished couple. Everything was without history.

During the first and second day, Marian waited for her father to go out to work. He did not and she would not have questioned him about it any more than she would have questioned a stranger. On the afternoon of the third day they heard a knock at the door and a shrill, reticent voice called for "Miz Coleman." Lucy put her cigarette in the ash tray and she and her husband went to the door. "It's those Fralleys again," she said.

Marian stayed in the hall, but she could see the faces outside and hear the conversation. Mrs. Coleman stood calmly in the doorway; her husband's head peeped over her shoulder. "Good afternoon, Mrs. Fralley," she said in a rather grand voice. She looked down at the woman and at the four children clustered about her.

Mrs. Fralley's face seemed to alter when she saw Mrs. Coleman smiling coolly at her. She observed the way Lucy's hair was brushed so well that even the gray streaks had a fine luster. "It's that flue," Mrs. Fralley said. "We got smoke all over the house and it as hot as it is." Her eyes were gray and surrounded by yellowish whites. She had only three teeth left in the front of her mouth, though she was a young woman. When she talked she put her hand over her lips. Dry, brown hair was pulled tightly up on her head and she looked like a shy clown.

"What a shame!" Lucy said. "I thought Mr. Coleman

243

fixed the flue at your place." The children looked up at her and she gave them a sad and sympathetic glance. Their eyes lingered on her clear, calm face.

Ted Coleman coughed and he too looked down at the woman and children with sweet compassion. "I did fix it. You say it's not working again?"

"It's working plenty, but it ain't working right," Mrs. Fralley said. "I started to cook this morning and the whole place got right dark with smoke." She paused and brushed her hands over her dress. "That plaster too ain't right," she said, as if apologizing. The children began to giggle and the mother bent over them. She too began to giggle, as if they were engaged in a private joke. The sun had burned her face red up to her hairline.

"Can't Mr. Fralley fix the flue?" Lucy said in a thoughtful voice.

"He can, but he ain't got the materials. And also he ain't here!"

"Oh, I'm sorry. Maybe he will be back," Mrs. Coleman said.

"He's apt to stay away until Christmas if he takes a notion," she said gaily. "I don't expect you'd think I could go that long without cooking."

Lucy turned toward her husband and he stepped forward, his face brightly businesslike. He rubbed his hand over his chin. "Well, now let's work this out," he said pompously. "Would you rather have this flue patched up again, or would you want to wait until we can get a whole new one lined up?" Lucy nodded vigorously. "If you'd rather have the new one you wouldn't be able to cook for a while," he added.

"If I could have my ruthers, I'd ruther get a new one this here day," Mrs. Fralley said, exposing the three lonely teeth.

"Hell, I couldn't do that, Mrs. Fralley," Ted Coleman said. "I'd have to order it from Parktown. I'd have to find some way to get over there myself and pick it out. You know how they cheat you, if you don't pick things out."

"You're right there," Mrs. Fralley said, smiling. "They do cheat you if you don't make your own pick." She slapped the hand of one of the children. "These kids got my clothes nearly off my back." She adjusted the blouse of her dress. "Yes, they sure will cheat you every time, just like you say."

"Well, now just what is it you want us to do?" Lucy Coleman said precisely. She bent a patient head toward the woman.

"Well, I like to eat, but I don't like to smother. Seems like the way things are now I got to do one or the other. I don't believe patching up will last for more than one time. It'd be all right for cooking tonight, but then I'd have the smoke in the morning. And for a new one I'd have to wait you say how long?"

"I wouldn't want to set a definite time," Ted Coleman said seriously. "It might be a week and it might be longer." He made a funny face at one of the children and the child winked back at him. Then the other children began to grimace hysterically. Lucy Coleman's laughter caressed their happy faces.

"Did you ever see such crazy kids?" Mrs. Fralley said with giggling shyness. "I believe they cut up in their dreams, seems like."

Lucy was slowly moving away from the door. "You'll do something as quick as you can?" Mrs. Fralley said, suddenly retreating. "I sure do need it." She seemed baffled about the result of this conference.

"Just as quick as I can," Ted Coleman said. He remained in the doorway until the woman and children had disappeared beyond the shrubbery.

When Lucy came back into the living room she said to Marian, "Poor Mamma. I can't bear to think of her. She loved being alive so much." Tears flashed in her eyes and her thin shoulders sagged with grief. "How quickly it comes. It is over and there is nothing to be done. And my little Albert getting married. My little boy."

"Now he'll have someone to pick on," Ted Coleman said gaily. "Where are they going to live?"

"Grandmother left him the house," Marian said. "That was all besides five hundred dollars for each of us. Albert and me, I mean." She watched the faces of her parents. "Mamma, those people who were just here . . ." she said.

"It's a good house. I suppose you didn't get it, because you've never been the family type. I'm glad Albert will be there," Lucy said. "I couldn't bear for strangers to have it. Albert will be there, how nice!"

"Those people," Marian insisted. "Why were they here?" She reached into her pocket for a handkerchief, because she did not want to seem unusually interested. For some reason, she felt she would never find out things unless she pretended they didn't matter.

Lucy lighted a cigarette. "Didn't we tell you? Your father and I have a few houses. Four. We rent them." She smoked the cigarette vaguely and her mind was obviously not on the conversation. She implied that there was something ugly in Marian bringing up the Fralleys when she wished to discuss her own family.

"Well, it's like this," Ted Coleman said, expansively. "Business got awful bad where we were. There were just too damned many men selling coal which is what I went out there to do. I gave that up and went back to my own line, but there were too many men selling insurance. I hadn't lived in the town long enough and the other men sold just about all there was to sell. So, I thought we'd borrow enough money to get these houses in this town. We figured we could make enough to pay off what we borrowed. Once we really own these places, we'll always have something to fall back on. Of course, you got to keep chasing after the rents all the time. I'd fall down dead if somebody just offered it to me once without me going out after it. I don't expect they will though." He laughed.

Every word the parents spoke had the quality of an echo. Their words were twice theirs in this way and they seemed to have lost the sense of speaking to another person. The speech itself had slowed down and was without any urgency. The house in which they lived, the life they led had captured them at last, and if it was the end least expected they were not aware of it. It was clear that the truancy was over. They had run down like an old car and in this dilapidation were amazingly happy. Marian wondered if the people around here thought them queer. She certainly found them strange and wondered if they had always been so. How could she ever have imagined them an average couple capable of giving her the unconditional love and security she had craved? Even their faces had taken on an unremitting inwardness. Once they did not feel the need for more space or more adventure their casual, normal surface was shattered. They were frightening in that they experienced nothing beyond this house, this new, undistinguished and impersonal little house. Yet they might have been striving for this precise place and life in the way they accepted it.

Marian knew they would not succeed here any more than in the other places. The houses would not work out; the debt would never be lifted. But they would stay on and survive. The Fralleys would continue to knock on the door and they would meet all just demands made upon them with indolent good spirits.

"When will you marry?" Lucy Coleman said abruptly.

"I don't know."

"It's not a good thing to put it off," she said. "It's something we all do and all make too much fuss over."

"Oh, I'm sure people do it very easily. They only pretend to be making a fuss."

"That's right," her father said lazily.

247

The mother went out of the room and Marian was left with her father. His face and hands were quite brown from the sun. He looked a great deal older, now that laziness had appropriated his body. Not being in business, not continuing the office routine and perhaps the lack of masculine company had changed him drastically. He had never been so contented before. Now he sat for hours in a chair and did nothing more than look out of the window. These tranquil days and nights passed by as if they were something one heard about, not lived. Meals were an excitement to him and he always looked tired and hungry when they approached. When he got up from his chair and moved about the room, Marian noticed that his tallness and strength remained despite the inactivity. She saw the bulge of his arms and his wide, heavy shoulders. Yet he did not look strong. Perhaps it was that his face was so remarkably placid and inert when he read the newspaper or listened to the radio. He seemed at such times like an overweight child. When he was calculating and thinking about the unpaid houses, he was most like himself. Calculation was an unblemished pleasure to him. Money had no troublesome aspects. Even the recollection of the money he owed, the large, round figures, seemed to give him a pronounced satisfaction.

"Won't it take a long time before you will have any actual profit from the houses?" she asked.

"Oh, yes," he said pleasantly. He broke the paper on a cigar lying in the ash tray. He turned the cigar around in his fingers without lighting it. "Yes, it takes a long time to get things on a paying basis." He looked at her warmly, as if he were speaking to a trusted business associate. He enjoyed the very words of commerce, without fully understanding them. It was impossible to interrupt the irrational game he was playing. Marian did not listen to him. Instead she concentrated again on his alterations. What was missing? He was still handsome, but the potentially voluptuous

248

appetite had vanished. The bronze cheeks and the satisfied eyes, the heavier chin had taken his masculinity from him. Perhaps it was this neutrality, like a castration, that had turned this house into their permanent home. There was something irrevocably retired about him in a physical sense. This peace was omnipresent; it shrouded the wife, the home and all other relations. Even Marian felt he was no longer a force in the background of her own life.

"Money runs after money," he said after a long pause.

The days of the visit passed like a spool of slowly unwinding thread. Marian and her mother took walks down the dusty roads which at times would break off into a cool little clump of trees or sink down into a gully. Most of the soil around the town was hard and unpromising. The town itself was a succession of dull reds and greens, hot and with an arrogant instinct for ugliness. Marian was bewildered by the way her mother fitted into the place. When they walked down the street, her bearing, never very good, took on a regal quality and the few bits of clothing she had distinguished her from the other residents. When she loitered before a vegetable or fruit store, the proprietor was visibly pleased with her unrestrained enjoyment of the appearance and odor of an open crate of green things. The girls in the five-and-dime store treated her in a specially reserved fashion. She was a mysterious and noble stranger to them, as if she were a fabulous and infrequently seen landowner of a beautiful estate. Her own little house, her lack of money did not in any way deprive her of the quality of a slowly abdicating chatelaine. When she shopped an instinctive female dignity was brought out in her. In common with the millions of women who have little to spend she found great joy in the actual purchase of one inexpensive thing. This joy was not so much in the use of the article purchased, but that the buying of it gave her status in the world of womanhood. She moved leisurely around the stores and her eyes stopped at each counter. She picked up insignificant trinkets, turned them over in her hand and replaced them on the counter with a deeply amused expression. She would gaze at a row of brightly colored paper napkins, as if she were surveying a case of legendary jewels. She went into the drugstore and asked for rose water and glycerin in a tone that gave the preparation a magical power. The drugstore clerk looked at her in a kind of awe as he passed the bottle over the counter. She never spoke directly to anyone, but she was always on the brink of smiling and becoming friendly. It was apparent the townspeople felt she could not stay long in this ugly, hot, unproductive place. She seemed to be merely passing through on some brilliantly exciting errand and they must have wondered if the town did not have qualities of which they were unaware. But Marian, observing her mother and remembering the former nomadism, knew that by some accident she had abandoned the old follies and come to rest. She was as permanent a part of the town as those static ones for whom it might have been established. She would not leave these streets, but the people would always expect her to disappear and in that way she would no doubt retain her exotic and foreign aspects.

At night they sat in the living room. Lucy sewed and embroidered and listened to the crickets in the fields. Sometimes she would notice fireflies outside the window and she would watch their fickle lights break up the darkness. In her grape-colored dress, she was strikingly consistent with the cozy, bucolic darkness. As the days passed, Marian could hardly remember the mood that had dictated her visit. She did not know what she had expected to say and what answers she had hoped to receive. Biological fortuity alone connected her with her mother. She saw that the vast psychological superstructure of this connection was not inevitable. Her mother, despite the two children, was curiously barren. Her line was extinguished with her own life. Marian made no further attempt to establish imperishable emotions, though she knew she would retain certain fears. She would always fear for her mother's health and be deeply anxious that she should not suffer any irremediable misfortune. Even the slow aging she could already detect in her parents gave her an almost paralyzing regret. And this was all. How little it was when measured with the old things she had wished to give and to receive. She believed that she had misjudged her father, but it was too late to straighten her mind about him. Each time she saw his face it startled her in that it neither affirmed nor denied her previous imaginings. He was now dozing in his chair, anxious for bedtime and for the mornings that followed sleep. He loved those mornings in which he stood with the kitchen door ajar and let the sun beat down upon his chest. He enjoyed following his wife from room to room, from cupboard to cupboard. Lucy accepted his attendance upon her and was comforted by it, though she more or less ignored him. When he talked, she no longer listened with transported eyes. One had the feeling it was the man's presence she was soothed by and not the man himself.

Marian's stay in the house became more and more unnatural. Boredom increased acutely. She found that it was quite as hard to get away from a disunited family as from a congenial one. It was not that they insisted she remain, but rather that she did not know how or when to set a day of departure. This was as much her home as any other place. The other house had become Etta's overnight. Despair was softened by the five hundred dollars her grandmother had left her. It was the first money she had believed belonged to her and it carried with it the beauty and burden of choice.

She slept on a convertible couch in the living room and sometimes when all the lights were out she would lie awake and talk with her parents. They left their door ajar and in the darkness she felt closest to them. The parents remembered little things from their common past and in the intimacy of the quiet nights Marian felt included in their reflections. They could not see each other and the voices, bodiless and paradoxically more public, drifted between the rooms. The mother's laughter was rather theatrical under these circumstances and Marian kept waiting for it at appointed times. She felt that if she had not been too old these snug conversations would have meant much to her. In this half-sleep something of their lost bond was recovered. One night she was awakened by her mother's voice. What she heard was like a cue to the last act of their common drama. Her mother whispered, though without any note of conspiracy, "But five hundred dollars would be just enough to get us on our feet."

"That's all she has. Do you think we should ask her?" the father's drowsy voice replied.

In her leisurely, unreflective way the mother might have been saying a routine prayer. "It would be easy to pay her back. With the five hundred we could pay off the Fralley house and that rent would be pure profit." She sighed and her husband said, "That's right, Lucy." His voice was still pleasantly foggy with sleep. So phlegmatic had he become that not even this reasonable possibility of money could fully arouse him.

Mrs. Coleman said, "The moon is out. It is so bright in the yard it looks like dawn." Marian could hear her sitting up in the bed and adjusting the pillow at her back. "I'll just sit here a minute and watch it."

The father repeated, "I don't feel like asking her." He turned over and at the end of the sentence his voice fell with finality. In a moment he was asleep and his audible, rhythmic breathing rocked the bed like a light hand on a cradle.

Marian, as if she were facing an audience but was invisible to her fellow players on the stage, kept smiling. After a while, in a tone of natural exaltation, the mother said aloud, "It's so easy for young girls to get by. Something always turns up. It would be another matter to ask Albert. Boys haven't those hidden ways of getting things." She settled herself again in the bed.

"I'm not going to give you the money," Marian said to herself, enjoying the words. She felt only amusement at the conversation. She was not afraid she would relent. She did not dread meeting her mother's casual demands the following day. Shortly afterward she went to sleep, feeling very far away from this house, very much alone and quite safe.

A storm came up in the last hours of the night and they awoke to hear a downpour beating on the house. Rain was unusual in this hot, dry country and its arrival gave everything the festive overtones of a holiday. The family got up early. Heavy, swollen rain clouds seemed low enough to touch the roof of the house and to enclose it in a fairyland vacuum.

"The roof must be leaking in the Crowes' house. It hasn't rained for such a long time, I'd forgotten about that open space," Mr. Coleman said.

"Who are the Crowes?" Marian said.

"One of our tenants."

Lucy Coleman was bent over the table. The robe she was wearing revealed the sunken spot in her neck. "But how wonderful to have a leaking roof!" she said. "I wouldn't mind a whole house full of rain! I'm sure I wouldn't."

"The Crowes don't see eye to eye with you," her husband said.

Lucy straightened up and looked out of the window. She stared at the withering Norwegian pine tree by the house. The branches were covered with black needles which at the tip of the branch changed into a parched yellow color. She turned abruptly to her daughter. "You look very pretty this morning," she said. "The rain does that to some people, but I, who love it so, always look like a drenched hen." She put both her hands firmly on her waist and continued to inspect her daughter until Marian dropped her eyes. The blue, green, and brown checked curtains fluttered over the table. They were suddenly quiet as they broke the toast. And as the meal progressed those unpredictable changes that come over people on special days slipped into the atmosphere, as if the pleasure of the day made them melancholy because it was not greater. Taciturn moodiness came over the mother's face. She did not lift her gaze up from the table and was so self-absorbed the father and daughter looked at her wonderingly. The dampness made her hair straight and limp and she appeared older. Marian, sensing this sudden destitution, could say nothing. In the past it had been precisely these examples of the mother's spiritual invalidism, whether in letters or in her appearance, that had tortured Marian. Upon these portentous and excluding silences the daughter had built the persecuted mother-image. There was no discontent on the mother's face; she looked, rather, like a deeply bereaved *religieuse*. In her silent and inexplicable anguish, she asked nothing and yet the observer could not help but wish to remove the suffering. Marian felt again the obligation to find the proper spot for this misplaced woman. She felt challenged by the inadequacy of the little house sunken in the rain-soaked yard, the furniture just one step above ugliness, the chipped table top and the frayed napkins. This feeling of obligation was so old it was now a reflex response, but, like the instantaneous closing of the eyelid against danger, it was fleeting and could not be sustained. By this time there was a permanently stunted quality in the relationship of the three people, the final result of a lengthy short-changing.

"This is a hell of a place. The edge of nowhere," Ted Coleman said. Lucy's raptorial fingers were spread out on the tablecloth. The delicate twin arcs of her eyebrows raised and she smiled coolly at her husband, without in any way commenting upon what he had said. "You've got to be crazy to stay here," he continued, pushing the plate away from him. The darkness of the day made his suntanned face appear yellow. Reflection was so alien to him that it was always accompanied by a helplessness and shyness. Even his body seemed awkwardly heavy when he was examining his own emotions. Marian saw that he was recapitulating the dominant theme of his life. The quick, futile awareness that something was slipping by invaded him and gave him the only non-physical pain he ever knew. In such moments the changes, the seemingly unmotivated wanderings from place to place, had occurred. For the first time her father reminded Marian of Albert: both seemed to be physically restrained by an iron bridle.

"I think it's raining in the window in the living room," Marian said. She got up from the table and went to close the window. When she returned, they were still at the table but the feeling of disaster had diminished. "I am leaving tomorrow," she said.

"Of course," the mother said, shaking the ash from her cigarette. "I'd like to have you stay, but there's nothing here for you."

"It's all right for us, I guess," Ted said. "But I'll be damned if I'd have wanted to be young out here. Give me Florida for having fun." He began to laugh and all discontent vanished from his face.

"I hated Florida," Lucy said. She began to clear the breakfast dishes. Marian stood ready with the dishcloth. The father pressed his nose against the screen door and watched the rain beat into the ground.

When the water was running over the dishes, Lucy said, "I wonder if you'd be willing to lend us the money Mother left you? Only for a few months. We could pay off the debt on one of the houses and then the rent we get would actually belong to us." Marian felt that she had chosen this

255

particularly busy moment wisely. The simple process of dish washing somehow mitigated the extravagant request. Lucy gaily stirred up a soap lather.

"I couldn't do that," Marian said. "It's all I have. I must live on the money until I get a job. Without it I'd be lost. There would be no way to get out."

"Get out?" Lucy Coleman said attentively. "Where are you going, my precious girl?"

"I can't stay at home with Albert married. It wouldn't be right."

"How funny! I should have thought you'd like that. The girl—what is her name?—must be near your own age. Naturally, what you do is your own business."

"No, I don't want to stay there." Marian was thinking of herself as a spectator of interminable tables laden with food and of a lifelong observation of Etta and Albert and their fantastic history.

"I thought perhaps you and Bruce—" Lucy said.

"Oh, no!"

The mother began to laugh. "You are mysterious," she said.

"No, it's not mysterious! It's just that I couldn't . . ." Marian wished she did not have to spend this long day here. As usual meetings between them were of a clumsy length, either too short or too long.

"Now, girls . . ." Ted Coleman said.

When the house was clean, Lucy said, "Perhaps we can pull our chairs up to the door and enjoy the rain without getting wet." They sat there for a long time. During the night the dry dirt of the roads had been transformed into light brown mud.

The taxi came to the house early the next day. The sky had cleared and the air was cool. Lucy wore a blue shawl over her dress. It was draped rather primly around her shoulders and in this attitude of serene, decorous femininity Marian always remembered her. They said good-by with trembling lips. As the car pulled away, the daughter turned back and saw the heads of her parents. Their cheeks were touching as they looked at the empty road.

CHAPTER SIX

CLUMPS of snow-heavy bushes hugged the foundation of the house; vines not much thicker than spider threads clung to the cold brick. Premonitory winter winds seeped in through the window panes and gelid tree branches were outlined on the glass. Inside the house the grate was heavy with ashes and the heat from the furnace had died. The fireplace had been restored to usefulness by Etta since the family had not bothered with it for some years. Most of Etta's other innovations were cheerfully obsolescent. A geranium, encased in a bowl covered with green crepe paper, mixed a spinsterish, imperishable pink with Mrs. Gorman's ordinary plants. A bowl of dried rose leaves sat on the top of the piano and gave off a sweet odor. She had put up pictures in frames covered with scarred velvet. A leather chair and a sturdy smoking stand gave the room an hermaphroditic coziness. In the evenings Etta sat before the fire in her wine-red woolen dressing gown. Her face was always clean and bright, like the smooth, shining surface of a doll's face. When she sewed she brought the material up to her eyes and squinted happily at it, or perhaps, Marian thought, she sniffed it since olfaction was the most acute of her senses. The days and nights were ticking off with comfortable regularity. (Between the lighting of the morning fires and the banking of the evening ashes, Etta had her ceremonial house duties which she observed with a saintly ardor. She liked the big jobs in housework, loved the complete unheaval that preceded true cleanliness and was not perturbed by minor carpentry and plumbing repairs. The early evenings had their peculiar beatitude which was, in the presence of the husband, less strenuous than her private house devotions but equally consecrated. At times these holy evenings languished in a senescent drowsiness that could not be relieved by Etta's talent for serving the right food at the right time. She had an extraordinary sense of the precise moment that indicated a need for an apple and she had faith in the ability of hot chocolate to drown the fireside torpor.)

After ten o'clock it was too cold to stay in the living room and Marian followed Etta and Albert upstairs. She walked by their room or could see them from her own when the door was ajar. In the evenings she never actually crossed the threshold of the room in which their private life was lived and yet she could not escape glimpses and the hortatory echoes of the marriage-insulated voices. Albert, propped up in the bed with the collar of his red silk pajamas warmly brilliant against his white flesh, somehow perjured the immaculate conversation. Etta, on a footstool beside the bed, looked into his dreaming face and vainly tried to intersect the long, obscure nights with lucid, daylight corners. . . . Albert! . . . Albert! . . . On this evening she asked where he and Marian had gone on their walk and her question was answered. Albert said they had gone to the magazine store and from there to one of those unclassified confectionery-bars where they had a glass of beer. He told nothing of the cold outside or of himself in the short tan topcoat and green woolen scarf, nothing of the stained oak counter in the beer place or of the half-drunken boy with thick bushy hair that grew low on his forehead and the black tufts of eyebrows that hung over his surly brown eyes. Nothing of the beer foam hanging on the boy's lip or of Albert's own spotlessly conventional barroom talk and its insufficiency. No mention of the return homeward in which he had seemed anxious to unburden his mind to his sister but was checked because he did not understand the rudiments of personal honesty.

On these nights, before sleep and silence, the talk descended to a lower pitch, a key of soothing somnolence. A tone of trembling gentleness and wonder struck for the child that was to come. Back and forth they talked, elliptical, hopeful and proud of nature's benevolence that does not discriminate between the loved and unloved.

CHAPTER SEVEN

$\mathcal{W}$HEN the doors of the railroad station closed, it seemed that the building itself was outside the town and the houses and shops that had only a moment before been so real vanished. The streets outside were deep in a gloomy half-darkness; inside the rectangular station cold wind was battling with slightly steaming radiators. The ceiling lights glared down upon the red, green, and yellow tile that covered the station floor. The tall-backed benches looked dusty under the lights and in the quiet of the darkening day the sound of heels tapping on the tile floor seemed to come through an amplifier. The passengers clustered around the back door and watched the tracks beyond. Only the railroad employees were out under the ramp. A young Negro porter stood there clapping his hands for warmth and staring at the empty tracks. The air was filled with the promise of snow.

Marian was standing alone in the middle of the station and looking at Etta, who had gone to the magazine rack. Etta was talking with the man at the counter. She had to stand on tiptoe in order to see the magazines and her short, stocky body, wrapped in a brown sport coat just a shade too long, looked strangely like that of a wooden doll. Marian heard a familiar voice call her name and she turned around to see her mother's friend, Mary Wallace, standing beside her.

"Shh! Don't make a fuss," the woman said hurriedly. She

261

covered Marian's hand in her own brown and orange woolen mitten.

"You shouldn't have bothered to come," Marian said.

"This time you may stay away for good. I may never see you again." Pink, daisy-shaped earrings dotted each side of the woman's face.

"You have always been very kind to us," Marian said.

"You don't realize what great friends your mother and I were," Mary said. She was vigilantly faithful to this friendship of her youth, despite the fact that it was, in material ways at least, unreciprocated by Marian's mother. "I had hoped you might go to live with her now that your poor grandmother is gone."

Marian frowned helplessly and the woman, with a quick awareness of having said the wrong thing, continued, "No. No. It's too late for that, I suppose. I had always hoped you and Albert might some day live with your mother and father, but it didn't work out that way."

"No," Marian said, feeling very sad that to this devotion there could be no adequate response. Mary's coat was buttoned high over the ledge of her bosom. Her plain, unquiet face, for all its chasteness and simplicity of emotion, was without primness. The aureola of sentimentality came from her static allegiance to original perceptions now perversely lacking in cogency. Marian had no feeling for this woman's attachment to her remembrance of the mother as a young girl; she knew her only as a kind of unrelated aunt who had from time to time given a maternal warmth to her and her brother.

"That is Etta over there, isn't it?" Mary said, pointing to the girl at the magazine counter. "I never expected Albert to marry before you, somehow." She was staring thoughtfully at Etta's figure.

"She will be over in a moment. I'm sure she'll be pleased to see you," Marian said.

A baby could be heard crying in the women's waiting

262

room and they were quiet until the sound had died away. At last, Mary said, "I don't really know her. I will leave before she comes over." The black coat hugged her wide shoulders and short arms. She seemed rather frightened by Etta's unknown and disinterested face. "I never go past the house that I don't think of your grandmother. Sometimes I can't believe she's no longer there. She was quite young when I first knew her, though at that time your mother and I must have thought her very old." She smiled in her generous way. "I suppose your own mother must have seemed old to you," she added.

"No, she didn't," Marian said, turning her eyes away.

"Does she seem so now?"

"No. They are both quite young to me, even now."

"I'm sure that's the way it should be," Mary said brightly. She took a handkerchief out of her purse. "I'm afraid you won't come back again. The other time you left I was happy for you, but now that the family has broken up there will be no reason for you to return."

Marian did not answer. Her silence agitated Mary and she said with great emotion, "You do understand about your mother, don't you? That's really why I came down to see you this last time. When you came back from seeing them, you wouldn't say anything and I have worried about it. Was she changed in any way?"

"No, I'm sure she's very happy," Marian said, trying to sound indifferent. Etta was walking toward them and Mary prepared to depart.

"Good-by, my little girl," she said wistfully. Tears were standing in her eyes and she rushed away.

Etta was now standing beside Marian. She did not in any way indicate that she had noticed the retreating woman. Perhaps her small, green eyes, set in heavy white lids that narrowed strikingly at the edges, took her in, but the sternness of her face excluded everyone who was not directly connected with her present life. Marian could understand why this amazingly adult girl would distract the nostalgic Mary.

"Well, it's almost time," Etta said. She looked about the station and examined each face. Whenever she was in a large space or with strangers she seemed to be on the alert, like someone who has heard a noise in the night and goes valiantly, with a firm belief in his invulnerability, into the darkest part of the house to meet the threat. After she had examined the station, she turned back to Marian.

"I don't know whether I envy you or not," she said. For no apparent reason she began to laugh. When Etta laughed she revealed the last remnant of the placid girl she had been, a young girl with the usual lack of personality. She had moments of prettiness, even though her features were large for her small head. However, it was difficult to think of her face as a composite of features, because it was surprisingly varnished, for a girl just past twenty, with a relentless expression of betrayed zeal and peculiarly invigorating discontent. Marian, looking possibly for the last time at this face, realized that if Etta had not had her present challenge she would very likely have had another. Perhaps the past had been the delusion, the past, only a few months back, when Etta had certainly been sweet and shy with just the right smile, the right amount of reticence and thoughtlessness and without any destiny beyond the altar, the sink and the bridge table. Surely she had imagined nothing except a man with the same plausible surface, a man with whom she might edge a little forward every year by the tranquil activity of the ordinary and with whom she might achieve an unmarked position, neither high nor low. There were days when she seemed to have this stability with Albert, but these days turned into nights of unpredictable silences, nights in which her husband stood restlessly staring out of the window, as if he were waiting for his life to begin.

"I don't think you envy me," Marian said. She was uncomfortable with Etta. There was something ominous in the fact that she, the newest member of the family, was here to say good-by, and that she was the only one.

"I suppose I don't. I can't imagine not being married," she said. "Albert . . . it is funny, isn't it? I never knew anyone like him before. He's . . ." No word of description occurred to her and she began nervously to fumble with her gloves.

The first sound of the approaching train was heard in the distance and the two girls relaxed. The parting was now near enough for them to enjoy the last moments together. Etta put her hand on Marian's arm and for a moment she seemed quite affected by the separation. She seemed to be thinking, You are mine, part of me. She was most happy in definite relationships established by blood or marriage and her loyalty to these ties was as strong as her indifference to the rest of the world.

"You'll be glad to go," Etta said. "You won't miss anybody, will you?" Her fingers lightly clutched Marian's sleeve. "Of course, when you get right down to it, there's really no one to miss. That's the worst part. I wouldn't like it." Her precise, rather shrill voice was ringing in Marian's ears.

The train pulled in and people with tired faces climbed down from the coaches. Full shadows fell down upon the afternoon and conversation was halted by the noise of connecting cars. Two mail carriers with guns on their hips filed past the crowd to receive the mail sacks.

After she said the final good-by and climbed up on the platform, Marian watched Etta walk away. Her coarse hair was barely visible beneath the brim of her hat and she looked very young except that her body was already beginning to be awkward with pregnancy. She walked very quickly and as if every movement of her body were an expression of an insuppressible urge within her. She was anxious to return to the home Marian was leaving and to resume her struggle for the blue-print existence she had laid out for herself. Etta was prepared to fight with her husband for the mysterious symbols she wished to capture, but of the real mystery, the mystery of Albert her husband, she had no knowledge. It lay outside her understanding, but she could feel herself being altered by it. Marian wished to call to her and to tell her that she would win, because Albert needed her in a way she could never understand. But she must not go deeper than the surface—there she would lose.

When the doors of the coaches had closed, Marian looked out the window and saw Bruce standing under the ramp. He was smoking a cigarette and, in the cold, the smoke and his breath came out of his mouth in a long stream. He looked casually into the coaches, but the profusion of faces discouraged him and soon she saw him crush the cigarette, button his coat, and move away. He made his way through the Negroes loaded down with bundles and the few stranded women who were staring at the sky in bewilderment and waiting for the one who had brought them here. Marian saw the top of Bruce's hat above the crowd for a moment and then he vanished through the station doors so easily and with so little evidence of loss that she wondered how they had ever come to know each other.

The coach was immersed in its perpetual dusk. The weak glow of the wall lamp was functionless, except to deepen the carefully dull austerity of trains. The green plush seats were also overcast with this endless twilight and Marian felt that the air coming from the buzzing ventilators was surely the same she had breathed more than a year ago. She could not remember many of her feelings on the trip— that time she had left behind the grandmother, mother and father, and Albert and the ambiguous shadow of Bruce, the instigator. No, she hadn't left them behind; she had carried them with her and they had, even at the great distance, been the main figures in that fruitless year. She remembered now that she had sat in this train a year ago and tried to figure out the way in which she had got through college in the town, how those years in which there had been dresses and shoes and leisure had been managed. She hadn't been able to answer any more than a squirrel could give an account of the way he stored food for the winter. She felt curiously empty tonight and looked back with impatience to those days when her mind had been cluttered with the copious debris of family life.

Behind her she heard a young boy's insistent voice saying, "But you most certainly did take him seriously!" And a girl's voice, struggling and anxious, said, "Not really! It may have looked that way, but I really didn't!" Marian turned around and caught the boy's eyes. He looked at her coldly, and the girl's voice went on and on trying to give reality to a difficult distinction. At last she said, "Hell! I know what I felt, don't I?"

The train rushed through tracts of farmland that were dark and cold in the night. There was snow on the window pane. Across the way two nuns sat with their hands resting on black skirts. It was almost eight o'clock and the people were returning from the diner. Magazines and newspapers lay abandoned on the seat because it was too dark for reading. The round, expressionless face of the porter appeared in the aisle. A young girl who seemed to be traveling alone asked Marian for the time. After a moment, she moved into a seat beside her. With what appeared to be unpremeditated insolence, the girl sat down without speaking. When she had adjusted her dress and made herself comfortable, she boldly began to observe Marian. Her eyes took in shoes, legs, dress, and then rested for a long time on Marian's face. At last the girl said, without smiling, "Are you going to New York?"

"Yes," Marian said. Suddenly the girl was no longer looking at her. Her eyes were on the window and she seemed curiously inattentive, once she had started the conversation. She was wearing a felt hat with an arc of fur on the front of the brim. Light brown curly hair covered her ears. She had very smooth skin of the rather thick texture which conceals imperfections and her features were regular. She was not small, though there was a quality of delicacy about her.

"Have you been there before?" the voice, Eastern in accent, spoke lazily. The girl rested her head on the back of the seat.

"I studied music there for a year," Marian said. The girl's face did not change and Marian wondered why she had spoken at all. Then silence fell between them and Marian listened to the jerking of the train. They hit a level spot and the train again maintained the unbroken hum of speed.

"Are you going to study music again?" the girl said in a voice as level as the sound made by the train.

"No, I guess I'll get a job. I'm not a very good musician."

"A musical job?" The girl's eyes were on her face again and Marian thought that she might be short-sighted because of this unabashed gaze. She decided that this was not true when she observed the coolness of the girl's manner. Perhaps it did not occur to her to stop staring.

"I don't think so. Something else. I wouldn't want to make my living as a bad musician. I'll just play for pleasure," Marian said. Then she added hesitantly, "You see how I feel?" Suddenly she was relaxed. A short time ago she had feared the man across the aisle with the pack of cards was going to talk to her. She preferred the girl's laziness to the man's earnest vigor.

"Do you know what kind of job you'll get?" The girl spoke crisply, but a certain friendliness had come into her voice.

"I don't know and I suppose you'll tell me I'm foolish to go unprepared like this." Marian reminded herself that she did not care what the girl thought, but she admitted that it would be nice to go to bed without a pessimistic lecture.

The girl hesitated. There was a resplendent languor about everything she did. Now she was brushing her hand over the leather surface of her purse and it might have been some studied stage gesture. "I wouldn't say that at all. It's not foolish to take a chance." She paused for what seemed a long time, then she said, "I don't imagine you're as unprepared as you sound. People always have something in the back of their minds, don't they? Either something or someone. I imagine you have that last resort like everyone else." The girl's beauty, the old-fashioned perfection and clarity of her face were somehow shattered by the precise, cool voice. Marian looked at her clothing and the fineness of her grooming and felt surprised. Already she sensed something discordant in the girl, some personal drought not relieved by beauty and poise.

"Well, I don't think I have a last resort," she answered. At that moment the image of Leo, his thin body and busy face, came before her. Am I depending upon him? Is that why I'm not worried? she asked herself. She began to laugh.

"I thought so," the girl said with indifferent amusement. "That's always the way, with women particularly. There's always an out."

"I didn't say anything," Marian said sharply.

The train pulled into a station and stopped. The girl closed her eyes abruptly and seemed to go to sleep. Marian heard train conversation all about her. The window sills of the station building were lined with snow and a man wearing an enormous black hat was shouting at one of the train workmen. The train pulled slowly out of the station and passed a group of houses sprinkled with lighted windows. The houses looked lonely and cast off in the darkness. The lights seemed to flicker in the wind like lamps at the opening of a tunnel. In the secluded coziness of the train, where the destination of the traveler was the only reality, this vision of the houses appeared humbled. The great gaps of darkness between them were ominous as forests. Marian thought that a house in which you yourself have never lived always seems dead and unconnected with the rest of life. Not having a picture of the room through which the light was shining, one cannot imagine the loved and familiar objects in it. The structure and shape of the buildings were cold without the knowledge of the way life was distributed among the rooms.

When the train had fully started again, the girl opened her eyes. Her face was as vacant as an out-of-date portrait and it had the same inanimate, pearly surface.

"Where are you from?" Marian asked.

The girl said she was from New York and let her voice drop with a finality that made further questions impossible. She took off her fur-trimmed hat and brushed it with her glove. "I suppose your folks told you not to take anything off Northern Negroes," she said abruptly. Her eyes flickered then like an animal's under a light.

"No, they didn't tell me anything and if they had I wouldn't have listened," Marian said. Unconsciously she had adopted the same impassivity. A little game was taking shape between them. She sensed a repressed ardor beneath the girl's unruffled surface.

"That's good," the girl said a little wearily.

The game was involuntarily suspended for the moment. The girl was not going to say, "How did you get that way, being from the South?" She was not going to say anything of praise and there would be no mutual back-slapping. There wasn't even to be an exchange of atrocity stories.

"I do think the South is making some progress," Marian said. She felt an impulse to laugh at the girl's enigmatic woodenness.

"Do you?" the ironic voice said. She got up without another word and made her way to the rest room.

The man across the aisle was shuffling through the pack

of cards. Someone was using a particularly clandestine voice with the porter and Marian wondered what was being ordered. When the girl came back her face was newly powdered and her clean, wavy hair was freshly combed. It hung down to her shoulders. Several of the men turned around as she made her way to her seat. The heels of her shoes were extremely high and her hips wobbled up and down as she walked.

She sat down again and began to stare out of the window as if she were a stranger. Marian, feeling that perhaps she was expected to acknowledge the new entrance, tried to think of something to say. The best she could do was, "I like New York." She did not want very much to talk, but she felt challenged and hoped to make the girl commit herself to something, anything.

She looked up and said, "I suppose it's better than what you're used to, but I think it's a mistake to overrate anything. I suppose you intend to hide out there."

"Hide out?"

"Nothing, nothing," she said impatiently. And then, as if penitent, the first smile came across her face. The smile was like the rest of her, flashy in its perfection, but with a studied respectability and again old-fashioned in its reserve.

"I haven't any idea what you're talking about," Marian said.

The girl picked up the magazine by her side and seemed tempted to read. After a moment she put it aside and the expression which was precariously balanced between reflection and vacancy returned to her face. Without a trace of hurry or uneasiness she said, "I look back with disgust to the time when I was exactly where you are." Her eyes were frankly upon Marian's face in an unshifting gaze.

"For God's sake, where am I?" She realized that she did not expect a quick answer. A woman with a very young child went down the aisle. The jerk of the train threw them almost into the man's lap. He looked at them happily, as if grateful for this attention. His cards were scattered over the floor and with great contentment he busied himself with their recovery.

"I used to be so proud of myself. I felt that I had come very far and that I was amazingly good," the girl said. "I told all the lies happily and sat up all night arguing and I was very much alive. Of course, you probably weren't in college then and so you missed it. We had meetings all the time. I'll never forget the time a young German boy—he couldn't have been over twenty and he didn't have any teeth, neither uppers nor lowers—well, he came in and said, 'When do we begin!' God! I was frightened and I said, 'Well, we're having another meeting next week!' He said, 'Meeting? What is this meeting business!' " Her voice rose clearly and, noticing it, she seemed to go up in the air after it and to pull it back. The conquering placidity came back upon her like an unexpected darkness and she said, "I hardly read the papers now. And all of the people I used to know are worse than I am." She crossed her legs and began to look attentively at the shining tips of her shoes. "Where is she now? That old slut, the Revolution!"

So that's it, Marian thought. She recalled the boys from the East she had known in school and found it difficult to connect this girl with them. "I didn't know . . ." she started to say.

The girl looked at her with the resignation of a prophet whose visions had soon faded. "You just have that look on your face. That first blush of having overcome a lot of home training and blindness."

Marian's arm was on the window sill. She looked absent-mindedly at the weave of the cloth in her suit and wondered what sort of expression was on her face. She knew that she was smiling, because she was thinking of bringing this girl into her home, thinking of Hattie saying, "She just don't care for nothing that's been invented." And she could imagine this tedious, reason-stricken face glaring indifferently, but with a cold censure, at Albert and Etta. She did not allow herself to imagine how Leo and Bruce would fare under this scrutiny. The unmoving eyes were upon her now and she remembered a number of somehow humiliating things.

The porter approached with the bundles of linen and a drowsy relief fell over the coach. The man across the aisle was still, apparently, regretting the series of mishaps that had caused him to be left alone. By now the travelers were inexorably mated. He seemed especially irritated by a fate that allowed two young girls to be sitting together while he, a man, was stranded without company. From time to time he looked longingly at the seats across from him and a frown of concentration wrinkled his face, as if he were reviewing his errors and resolving never again to proceed in the same fashion. He took an inhalant and a box of nose drops out of his pocket and administered them carefully. The medications seemed to revive him and his trickling eyes blinked brightly at Marian. When the porter passed by him, he generously told him to take care of the other berths. Two women farther down in the coach had already taken their shoes off and they waved frantically to the porter, pointed down to their stockinged feet, as if the absence of shoes gave them a special right to his immediate attention.

The girl across the seat from Marian had passed into another of her private retreats. Her eyes were closed and her face was so utterly relaxed that even her features seemed to have fallen into a new shape. A man walked by and hesitated before the smooth, resting face. He was quite obviously struck by the girl's beauty and Marian thought perhaps he might accost her and ask if they might not meet before it was too late, before they were forever separated by green-curtained darkness. After a moment, he went on to the next car. Marian had by this time decided that the

273

girl's dramatic withdrawals were cultivated mannerisms. Her relaxation was as trained and skillful as a mystic's.

The drowsiness of the train passengers was slowly being changed to sullenness. Rows of initialed suitcases had vanished and the pink cotton covers of the berth mattresses were visible. The white coat of the porter moved around like a searchlight. He was mumbling with faked patience, "Just as soon as I can get to it. As soon as I can, lady! I've got eighteen to do and I'm two-handed like the rest of the world." The young mother stepped into the aisle. Her mouth was sunken into her face, giving her an expression of profound irritation. She stood before the porter without speaking. Her small, accusing eyes wordlessly reminded him of the dollar bill which Marian had seen her husband crush into his hand early in the afternoon. "I don't know where to put the baby's milk, unless in the toilet. The diner's gone off and I don't carry no refrigerator around with me." Other passengers, thinking of fifty cent pieces yet to be given, were glaring at him. The porter seemed to be suspended over them like a balloon, ready to swoop down, but uncertain as to where first to land. The car had again become a small house in which all the residents were strangers. People who had only a few hours before been cheerful now looked like tired invalids in a shadowed attic room. A little woman with a round black hat box around whose blue band the words SuccessSuccessSuccessSuccess were written in flowing, ribbonlike black letters sat primly in her seat, her eyes glued upon the porter's shoes.

The girl across from Marian abruptly aroused herself from her trance. She seemed unaware of the bustle and exasperation around her. Her eyes were clear and there was nothing of the usual traveler's impatience in her face.

She said bluntly, "Do you expect to stay away this time? Away from home, I mean." Marian had the uncomfortable feeling that the girl had been thinking about her all the time her eyes had been closed. She was disconcerted to be the object of this fantastic contemplation.

"Oh, yes," she said. The girl's eyes seemed to darken. She gave no indication that she accepted the answer; she suggested, by her manner, that nothing had been said.

"I have no home to return to. So I won't be tempted," Marian continued. She felt angered by the girl's imperious aloofness. "Why do you look as if you didn't believe me?" she said impatiently.

"I believe you." Her expression softened. "Have you no family?"

"I have a family, but that doesn't interfere at all with my plans." She did not say that she had gone across the country to find that family and that by finding them she was completely free. There were no ghosts in the background, none whom she must think of when she made a decision. The mother's mystery had vanished. What she had left of her was no more personal than a casual snapshot. They had no united destiny.

"They don't interfere?" the girl asked, in a suddenly agitated voice.

"It might be more true to say that I don't interfere with them. This was more or less settled by going home again, I guess." She knew that the girl was probably thinking of the situation in its usual terms, imagining that Marian had by some act of determination thwarted over-zealous parental protection. She did not tell her that she had, on the contrary, merely diverted her own ardent desire to supervise and protect her parents.

"But your father, does he allow you . . . ?"

Marian thought of her ceaselessly advancing and retreating father, the man of action, the devitalized animal searching for a triumph that had never presented itself; he too was shadowy to her.

"Yes, he has given his permission," she said, smiling mysteriously.

"Imagine that! You're a lucky idiot." Confusion and envy spread like a film over the girl's face. Her placid features were marred by the strength of her reaction.

"Do you live with your parents?" Marian asked.

"Yes," she answered in a small voice.

The girl sank down in her seat and stretched out her arms. She turned away from Marian, but slowly, as if drawn by a force, her eyes came back in amazement to Marian's face. She did not ask for more details and Marian did not offer them. The train was speeding through the night and, little by little, the summer and autumn and early winter Marian had passed were beginning to shrink into nothing except a small portion of her life.

The next morning snow lay on the banks of the railroad tracks. No sun brightened the flagitious landscapes of factory town. Houses of evil similarity appeared like rows of disciplined, humiliated orphans. Gloom covered the narrow streets and alleys. A patina of ice shone on the rusting tops of abandoned automobiles stockaded on the outskirts of the towns. The train dipped into the last tunnel and the porter switched on the station lights.

Marian could not find the girl she had talked with the night before. She had disappeared after breakfast and now even her luggage had been removed. When they reached the station and piled out of the train, Marian caught sight of the fur-trimmed hat. The girl was walking slowly, her head erect, the nose and chin lines clearly visible as she turned casually from side to side. And then Marian saw an elderly man and woman approach the girl and embrace her. The two bodies blocked Marian's vision and she saw nothing more of the perfect, smooth face or of the proud body the two were leading away.

On the escalator Marian's mind felt peculiarly blank because of the elaborate pretense she had fashioned around the trip, the mock isolation and friendlessness. She imagined she knew no one, expected nothing and was in full command of herself. The steps beneath her seemed to ascend with alarming rapidity; when she got to the top there would be no denying to herself that her eyes sought a particular figure and that she had faith in the presence of this figure as she trusted the fact that the city lay outside this half-subterranean station. When she reached the top of the stairs the people in front of her scattered and hurried away. She saw immediately the back of Leo's head. He was standing opposite her and intently watching the wrong exit.

She saw his brown hat and a coat of lighter brown and the dark trousers. "Leo!" she called. He did not turn. She did not call to him again or go toward him because she wondered what craft she would assume when they did meet, what fraudulent whole-heartedness she would manage. She moved to the side of the track exit. Leo looked at his watch. As he held out his arm, the dull gold of his class ring shone under the lights. He turned his head slightly and she saw his chin. His body was rigid with anxiety and his clothing hung on him as if he were a mannequin. Now he was shuffling through some bits of papers in his pockets, apparently checking the train time. She wondered what plans he had made for her. He had probably found her a job and a room. If she spoke to him she would, for the lack of any other plans, go to the job and in the evenings she would sit across from him in the room. It seemed to her that the cadence of her life was already established; the secure, unambiguous flow of her existence was already hypnotizing her. She found herself imagining that rejection and doubt would easily be vanquished by some mysterious means.

Snow evaporated on coat collars, voices echoed through the building and were accompanied by the muffled beat of overshoes. Leo took a cigarette from his pocket and Marian watched the way the straight brown line of his shoulders bent toward the flame. She thought how kind and strong he appeared, how fortified and warmed by his singularity of purpose. Even in repose his body retained the quality of a domestic warrior and she was reminded of all the plunder he would lay at her feet, of the treasures this carefully routinized energy would gather. Like some worshiped statue she might accept these sacrifices without personalized response. Frostiness blew through the station and Marian stepped into the doorway of a tobacco shop. At that moment Leo turned around and his eyes were angry with self-abnegation. No more travelers came up the track he had been watching and he walked toward the information booth. She did not follow him, because she knew that if she took one step in his direction it would be too late to ask herself what she meant and what her motives were. Going toward him, accepting him, would mean that she did not care about motives. She picked up her suitcase and went in the opposite direction, to the cold and crowded exit. All around her people were pairing off or gathered into group embraces. When the doors closed upon her she could not remember anything in the station except Leo's anxious, masculine image. On the steps she looked back once more, half hoping to see his comforting face and to feel his arm upon hers steering her through the streets.

He was nowhere to be seen. The great brown and copper doors upon which an icy ray of light was shining separated her forever from him and his shelter like the forbidden gates of Eden.

AFTERWORD

MY FIRST NOVEL, *The Ghostly Lover*, brings to mind the period in my life when I decided that I would try to write fiction. I say "try to write"rather than "to become a writer". Even now, many years later, each compositional task turns out to be an ambiguous challenge of curves and hills and almost never the straight road ahead one hoped to have earned from perseverance. The work of writing is so peculiar that I am still not quite sure what sort of activity it is. On the one hand, writing often appears to be an effort any curious, educated person with the inevitable good stories and unique adventures might undertake on behalf of his own experience. But, no, a day at the desk shows it to be elusive in execution, confounding in demand and altogether mysterious. In a way it is tiresome that the years of starting to write are so like the years of continuing to write.

I remember the details of my own beginning. Two landscapes were what I knew and these two appear in my first novel. One was Kentucky where I was born and the other was New York City where I went to Columbia University to do graduate work in the English Department. It was the 1940s and I stayed at Columbia for about three years, had a very good time and learned a lot. The course of study then was intimidating, rather proudly along the German lines, and more punitive than it later became. I smiled when some years ahead I was asked to read a doctoral dissertation about the novels of Iris Murdoch. In my time that would have been thought perhaps too easy, and certainly unsuitable when one might have been working up the forgotten pamphlets and sermons of a seventeenth-century divine. The idea, of course, was to learn how to do scholarship rather than to be interesting, a sound and, above all, a practical limitation.

In any case I decided to flee the dreaded History of the Language examination and to take a sort of midnight reprieve from the executionary "orals". Daunting as these matters were, the obstacles were not insurmountable, as one could judge from the number of modestly inspired scholars who actually had their degrees in hand. So, I left not from certain defeat but from a contrary desire, the desire to write. I felt some guilt about it, too, the sense of a surgical amputation; also something of a fraud and more than a little hysterical. It was hard to explain to my family and to the old neighbours nodding on their porches that I had what was spoken of as "all that education" and I still didn't plan to be a university teacher. So, among other things, trying to write made one as defensive, nerve-wrung and spiteful as one of those disagreeable clerks in Russian literature who has, in a moment of vainglory, spit in the face of a bureaucrat.

It was possible in those days to leave New York, pack up, vacate, and come back as you liked. The city was not then the residential tight-fist it is today. There was always another room, another apartment. In fact throughout America many people moved their households every year. In September the vans appeared and the cars filled with cartons—all it seemed for the adventure of a different neighbourhood, for the expression of an alteration in desire or circumstance, or simply for restlessness.

I went back to Kentucky that first summer of decision in order to try to write stories. Yet I think there is more to my two landscapes than that. The wish to live in New York City came to me very early; in fact I can scarcely remember the absence of that dream. And I think now the wish was an early submerged desire about writing one day. My first actual visit to the city was by way of the Greyhound Bus with two other girls from my high school. We stayed in the middle of Times Square and it was June and much cooler than expected and thus our organdies and lace-trimmed cottons were not exactly drop-dead-beautiful in the lobby of the Taft Hotel. But we got a bit of drool because of our accents. Oh, oh, where you girls from?

Of course, New York City is not to be thought of as an island hospice congenial to that part of the day given to writing. It is for the rest of the day and for the night that the unsteady, unreasonable, unknowable city makes a strong appeal to some—to more in my youth than might be true now. It seemed to me a happy circumstance that America should have created a great world city, an intrusive settlement much like a foreign country. New York is not necessary to the national psyche; it is disputatious, in no way forthright or gallant. And generally unreliable. But it was the new world for many of us as well as for those from the old world.

I believe that a decision to struggle with the arts is likely to involve a break with something, the main leap often being away from the former self. At the very least one is saying to the family and old acquaintances: Well, I guess I haven't been thinking what you might imagine about these streets and faces, about the piano tuner or the minister's wife. I have never known a family to be entirely pleased by the first printed works of a child. If no personal offence is given, there is always the offence of subject matter. Why that scumbag alley and not a mention of the arboretum for which the town is admired all over the state? And experience, imagined or otherwise, infects the familiar atmosphere most uncomfortably.

In any case, I went back to Kentucky for a few summers after leaving Columbia. And there you are, up in the old bedroom, typing and typing, going through the fantastical calesthenic known as writing something. And outside the cardinals are roosting in the maples and the bluejay is quarrelling. No, you cannot write that the bluejay is quarrelling since you have read that the jay is in fact more peaceable than the dove. Information—there's always that to give pause to the ready image.

I began to write stories and gradually one was published and then another. What disappointments were contained in "gradually" I have forgotten, but can imagine from later knowledge. My first novel, *The Ghostly Lover*, reads like a first novel with its pounding autobiographical stresses in the thoughts of the young girl, Marian. In truth the family of the novel is not at all like my own—very much the opposite since my family was large and everyone was about all the time, thick as flies. I don't know why I chose a lonely girl whose parents were feckless, wandering and left her in the care of a grandmother. I think, reading over the book,

281

that this loose family, the boredom of the mother with her children because of an obsessive jealousy of her husband, was an angular representation of that strange state, marriage, the condition that roamed like a spectre over the young lives in my town at that time.

As a girl, I grew up believing, as most of us did, that hidden about somewhere was a he who would take care of me, a hand-me-down creed contrary to the observations of a baby in a crib. People, he or otherwise, so often don't like taking care if they can escape it. If you fell violently in love, the strain was educational but somehow failed to overwhelm the basic assumption that marriage was a triumph of some kind, and if not that, well, don't give it another thought, just do it. I notice that the women in *The Ghostly Lover* are very determined in pursuit of a he, even if the heroine turns aside.

I wrote my stories and my novel and did not get married in my early twenties as my friends did. I remember telling a young man, a faithful suitor from "down home": If my novel is published I will marry you. A wild offer brought on by anxiety. Of course I betrayed him and waved goodbye from the window of the old C&O train that went through the hills of West Virginia, stopped at Washington, and then on to New York.

Elizabeth Hardwick, New York, 1985